Pra...

"Truly dazzling." —KEN BRUEN, Barry and Sh... ...us award–winning author of *The Guards*

"Tons of emotion and suspense are packed into this fast-paced crime thriller....The reader makes off with the 'goods' in this read because it's a gem."
—FreshFiction

"Piccirilli (*The Midnight Road,* etc.) tells the gritty, violent and dark tale in an appealingly noirish narrative style, highly economical yet bracingly intimate."
—*Publishers Weekly*

"Before racing to its conclusion, the book has been a savage novel of crime and violence, a surprisingly tender love story, and an insightful examination of what family means. Whichever aspect appeals to you the most, *The Cold Spot* is a hell of a ride." —Mysterious Galaxy

"Truly a great ride for crime fans." —Bookgasm

"Great characters, cool dialogue, and all-around excellent storytelling. Every crime fan needs to add the name Tom Piccirilli to his must-read list." —Edgar- and Anthony-nominated author VICTOR GISCHLER

"If you like action-packed suspense with serious bite, Tom Piccirilli is your man." —JASON STARR, author of *The Follower*

"Tugged in by a stark, masterful setup, you'll stick around eagerly for the knifelike prose, sharply drawn characters, and driving plotline. Lean, brutal and completely arresting." —MEGAN ABBOTT, author of *Queenpin* and *The Song Is You*

"[Piccirilli] tells energetic, action-packed stories that cut deeper and probe questions about what it is to be human, to love, to change, and how the things that happen to us in our lives shape the person we ultimately become." —*Crimespree*

"*The Cold Spot* is a gripping and powerful novel from an author who makes fans out of almost everyone who reads his work. . . . And really, there's no better recommendation than simply: read this book. But be warned: once you hit that last page, you'll be dying to read 2009's *The Coldest Mile.*" —*Crime Scene* (Scotland)

"The gritty narration, graphic violence and pulp gravitas should make fans of Jim Thompson and Charlie Huston feel right at home." —*Kirkus Reviews*

"This gripping thriller will keep readers on the edge of their seats. Piccirilli has a knack for creating believable characters in interesting and provocative situations, and his uses of narrative and flashback are top-notch." —*Romantic Times*

"If you want to write a good thriller, master the art of the shock twist.... Piccirilli is one of those rare writers who knows his craft and is approaching the top of his game." —Bookgasm

"Tom Piccirilli's fiction is visceral and unflinching, yet deeply insightful." —F. PAUL WILSON, bestselling author of the Repairman Jack series

"Tom Piccirilli is a powerful, hard-hitting, fiercely original writer of suspense. I highly recommend him." —DAVID MORRELL, bestselling author of *Creepers* and *Scavenger*

"Piccirilli is the master of that strange, thrilling turf where horror, suspense, and crime share shadowy borders. Wherever he's headed, count me in." —DUANE SWIERCZYNSKI, author of *The Wheelman* and *The Blonde*

"Tom Piccirilli's work is full of wit and inventiveness— sharp as a sword, tart as apple vinegar." —JOE R. LANSDALE, Edgar Award–winning author of *The Bottoms*

"Piccirilli is a master of the hook.... A gripping read any suspense/thriller/mystery fan will adore." —*New Mystery Reader*

Also by Tom Piccirilli

A CHOIR OF ILL CHILDREN

NOVEMBER MOURNS

HEADSTONE CITY

THE DEAD LETTERS

THE MIDNIGHT ROAD

THE COLD SPOT

THE COLDEST MILE

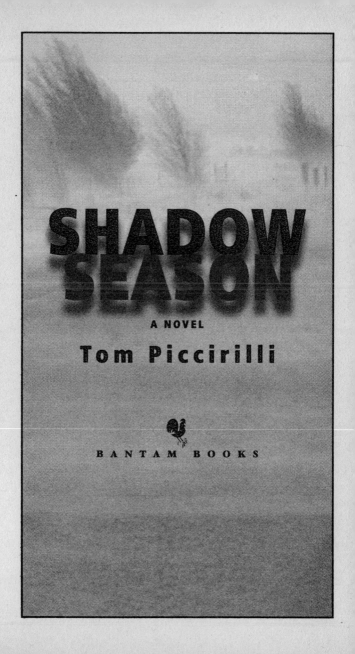

SHADOW SEASON

A NOVEL

Tom Piccirilli

BANTAM BOOKS

Shadow Season is a work of fiction. Names, characters, places, and incidents either are the product of the author's imagination or are used fictitiously. Any resemblance to actual persons, living or dead, events, or locales is entirely coincidental.

A Bantam Books Mass Market Original

Copyright © 2009 by Tom Piccirilli

Published in the United States by Bantam Books, an imprint of The Random House Publishing Group, a division of Random House, Inc., New York.

BANTAM BOOKS and the rooster colophon are registered trademarks of Random House, Inc.

ISBN: 978-0-553-59247-4

Cover design by Jae Song
Cover image © Ilona Wellman, Trevillion Images

Printed in the United States of America

www.bantamdell.com

2 4 6 8 9 7 5 3 1

For Michelle
who leads me from the dark

Many thanks to the folks who've helped in both large and small ways to shape this novel: Norm Partridge, Eddie Muller, James Rollins, Allan Guthrie, James Langolf, and my agent, David Hale Smith.

And uber-gratitude goes out to my editor, Caitlin Alexander, who helped to deepen and burnish these shadows.

Between the desire
And the spasm
Between the potency
And the existence
Between the essence
And the descent
Falls the Shadow

—T. S. ELIOT, "THE HOLLOW MEN"

One fine day in the middle of the night,
Two dead boys got up to fight.
Back to back they faced each other,
Drew their swords and shot each other.
One was blind and the other couldn't see,
So they chose a dummy for a referee.
A blind man went to see fair play,
A dumb man went to shout "hooray!"
A paralyzed donkey passing by
Kicked the blind man in the eye,
Knocked him through a nine inch wall
Into a dry ditch and drowned them all.
A deaf policeman heard the noise
And came to arrest the two dead boys.
If you don't believe this story's true,
Ask the blind man, he saw it too.

—ANONYMOUS, "THE TWO DEAD BOYS" (FOLK RHYME)

PART I
PUPIL

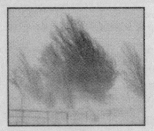

THERE'S THE SCENT OF BLOOD. FINN raises the back of his hand to block his nostrils, but it's already too late. The smell twines through him almost lovingly, caressing at first and then spiking deep. His head burns a slick, wet red. He says, "Ah..." The next word should be "shit," but he can't quite get it out. Memories surge forward into the center of his skull. A nimbus of rising color and movement tightens, clarifies, and takes form.

It's his wife Danielle on the morning of their twelfth anniversary, naked at the stove, glancing back over her freckled shoulder. She asks, "Pancakes or French toast?" Still moist from his shower he leans in, nuzzling her throat, nipping at the throbbing blue pulse, reaching around her waist to feel the taut smooth belly, and then draws her down to the kitchen floor. He likes the feeling of the cold Italian tile under his back.

The aroma runs down his throat. He coughs and there's another sound there, maybe a chuckle. The experience is strangely pleasant, almost familiar, but it still makes him a little panicky. The surgeons say it's impossible. His psychiatrist says it's unlikely, trying to give the benefit of the doubt as she worries a tissue between her hands. She's getting one-fifty an hour—from his perspective she owes him a fucking doubt or two, even if he does only visit her once every six or eight weeks.

They all admit that the olfactory sense is closely linked to memory, but they tell him that fresh blood has no scent because it hasn't had a chance to oxidize yet. And Finn is always talking about such small amounts. Sometimes only a couple of drops.

He knows it's true. He's been around blood. He's aware of the many ways it's likely to flow, spatter, splash. The way it drifts into cracks, the way it tastes, his own or someone else's. He's been covered in it, he's lost plenty.

Jesse Ellison has cut herself on a rough corner of the metal windowsill and she grunts demurely while trying to snap the lock shut. She's sixteen and clumsy, gangly by the sound of her awkward gait. She drags her feet in the halls, often late for class and bursting through the door a minute or two after Finn's begun his lesson plan.

Despite her lankiness she's got heft, muscle, a kind of earthiness. When she brushes against him—usually by accident but occasionally by confused teenage intention—he senses an innate strength. She plucks at his sleeve in an effort to help him along in the hallways, always trying to mother him.

Finn imagines she has large hands with long, dull fingers. The other girls laugh at her and call out with derision. She seems to handle their jibes with a maturity beyond most of her classmates.

When he pictures her, he sees the daughter of a domestic-dispute vic, one of the last cases he ever worked. Husband and wife radiologists, penthouse on Park Ave. Husband finds out the wife is bopping the doorman and the window cleaner, and does her with a drain cleaner cocktail.

While Finn asked routine questions, the teenage daughter wandered around a living room lined with black-and-white murals of her parents striking semi-nude provocative poses, her elbows knocking photos off the piano. The girl had an open face, empty caramel-colored eyes, and slack lips, and that's what Finn sees when he sees Jesse.

Icy air seeps in the window and wafts across his face. It's going to snow like a bitch tonight.

The sound of students and their families packing up SUVs, wishing each other Merry Christmas, and saying their good-byes floats up to the second floor. He recognizes several of the fathers' voices from various parent-teacher conferences. There's a certain flat annoyance in each of them.

They're working men trying to give their daughters a leg up on the world by sending them to a private institution. Putting in twenty or thirty hours overtime and weekends to afford the tuition, now forced to take a day off to pick up their kids and take them home again for Christmas vacation.

Their colorless speech proves they're part of the same brotherhood of pain and uncertain values, Saturday night bowlers who want their daughters to marry better men than themselves. They shout and honk to one another as they pull away.

Jesse finally manages to clamp down the lock. She hisses at the sight of her own wound. He hears her fidgeting, turning left and right, unsure of what to do next, how to stop the bleeding. A small maiden sound works up her throat.

Finn reaches out to touch the blackboard and steady himself. The rage strikes quickly with the scent, as it always does, threatening to overpower him. He makes a fist with his left hand and tightens it against the head of his cane. He's cracked a lot of them this way. His hands still retain power.

The dark comes to life again, replaying what the investigators called "the incident." He's trapped in the splinters of his own fracturing skull and feels the echoing stab of agony. It takes a second to get ahold of himself and remember where he is now, who he is now.

I am stone in the night, Finn thinks. I will not break.

"Have Nurse Martell look at that, Jesse," he tells her, his smile natural and easy, hiding nothing and hiding everything. He reaches into his back pocket and pulls out his handkerchief. "Use this. She's still in her office, isn't she?"

He knows she is. He hasn't heard her car drive off yet. Roz's car is a flatulent '58 Comet on its third turn of the odometer. There have been grease fires in the engine block, and it blows enough smoke that he can feel the oily residue on the breeze settling against his skin like a mist. When she stomps the pedal it backfires like a twelve-gauge, often making the younger girls giggle. Back in the city, it made the gangbangers dive to the curb.

Jesse says, "I think so." She plucks his handkerchief from him with a short, fierce action. "How did you know I hurt myself?" she asks with a quiver of a grin in her voice.

Like most people, she's moderately impressed by this sort of carnival trick. It's one of the reasons she has a crush on him. It's the kind of thing that raises him to just above pitiful and makes him almost cute. Sometimes the girls want to hug him, the way people like to coo at babies or pick up midgets.

He swings the cane up to tap at the stack of novels resting on the corner of his desk. "Don't forget to take the Kerouac, Robbins, and Vonnegut."

"Thanks for lending them to me, Mr. Finn."

"Sure."

"I'll be careful."

"I know."

"You always take such good care of your books. No cracks in the spine, not a single dog-ear anywhere. Some of the girls, during study hall, they're so nasty they spit between the pages. It's *uber-disgusting*. But your copies look brand-new."

Despite the fact that it's true, Jesse doesn't realize how ludicrous her own comment is. He's grateful for that. She shouldn't always have to worry about making a mistake around him, to be terrified of talking. There are some people who can't even start a sentence with *I* around him because they think they'll hurt his feelings.

Still, the rage bucks against his sternum, trying to get out, wanting to scream at the kid, I fucking can't see, what do I give a shit about books anymore?

A blind man taking good care of his library. If the comment is silly, the fact is absurd. He used to be a bibliophile. He used to be concerned with the look of words and the structure of sentences. When he was a rookie he'd write up his daily logs with a kind of lyrical zeal until his lieut came down on him for it. He used to frequent secondhand shops in the city and spook the neighborhood when his radio squealed. He used to be a lot of things.

Finn's left plenty behind but there's more he doesn't have the courage to give up. There's no reason to thumb through his favorite hardbacks anymore, even though the urge is still there. They sit on the shelf wasted. They are paper and he is stone.

Jesse's been borrowing novels from him all semester, one of the few students who actually does outside reading. Or even curriculum reading, for that matter. She's hitting that phase where novels that caused a stir in the fifties and sixties hold a great interest for her. "I can't stand how *repressive* the school library is," she says now. "You know someone erased the word 'fuck' from *Catcher in the Rye*? And they crossed out all the 'god's in 'god damn.' Isn't that illegal?"

"It is if it's the librarian doing it."

"I don't know who's doing it. My mother would throw a fit if she knew I was reading *Slaughterhouse-Five* and *Even Cowgirls Get the Blues* and *On the Road*."

She's right, Mrs. Ellison would, and without even knowing why. Simply because there are others who've told her that certain fiction shouldn't be read, especially by young girls in private schools. But Finn believes that parents who would send their daughters to the St. Valarian's Academy for Girls are already guilty of living by outdated notions of gentility. This school gives a lot but is ultimately for suckers.

He thinks, Why aren't you reading Judy Blume, kid? Or Jackie Collins? Why aren't you cyber-stalking some jock from across the river? Why do you give a damn about Billy Pilgrim and Sal Paradise and Sissy Hankshaw?

Let the parents throw their fits. He doesn't care. He's learned he can get away with a lot. People feel too ashamed to give him much grief.

"You don't narc on me and I won't on you," he tells her. "Deal, Jesse?"

"Deal, Mr. Finn."

"Solid."

She makes a grab for the novels and nearly drops them. She moves in close, her breath a mixture of fruity gum, mint toothpaste, and Duchess's breakfast of waffles and eggs Benedict. The syrup reeks. "It's going to snow tonight. Your coat, that one you wear when you go for your walks, I don't think it's going to be warm enough for you. I can run back to your cottage and get you something heavier, if you like."

"Thanks anyway, Jesse."

"I really think I should." Her voice is a little sharp, like a mom who's fed up.

"I'm okay."

"I mean, it's no problem. I don't mind. It'll only take me a few minutes, and I think I should—"

"That won't be necessary," he says, appreciative but annoyed by her careful attention. It would be so easy to allow himself to go with it, to become weak, the way he nearly was with Vi, the way the world wants him to be, so it can decimate him. "I'll be fine."

"You need a hat. You never wear a hat. Maybe Santa will bring you one."

She leaves the room, hesitating in the doorway, watching him for a moment longer before she turns and ambles off down the corridor. She won't visit the nurse. She'll knot his monogrammed handkerchief around her cut flesh and stare at his initials. Maybe she'll buy him a hat. She'll replay their puerile conversation over and again until it takes on a much greater meaning. He was once sixteen too, a bony boy with a bumbling step.

She understands they're two of a kind, in some way. Lonely outsiders, a pair among the handful left behind during winter vacation for lack of families or other reasons. Finn does a quick count. There are ten students and faculty members left on campus. Eleven if Vi has stayed, and he suspects she has.

Of course she has.

Roz's car starts up in the lot out front. It grumbles, falters, and gurgles. She's off with Duchess to pick up extra supplies for Christmas dinner before the snow starts.

The scent of the girl's blood lingers, keeping his head red and sticky.

He reaches into his desk for the bottle of cologne he keeps there. He dabs some on his index finger, covers his top lip, and breathes, and breathes. It doesn't drive away the vision of his dead wife Dani, naked and glaring, sticking the S&W .38 in his face and pulling the trigger.

ST. VALARIAN'S ACADEMY FOR GIRLS IS a small but prestigious school with a relatively meager staff. Four satellite cottages surround three buildings built a century and a half ago, protected by the historical society because a minor Civil War battle occurred on its front steps and Rutherford B. Hayes once slept here back when the school was a hotel. Whenever you told anybody that, you also had to explain that Hayes was the nineteenth president of the United States. They'd ask, Ah yeah, what did he do? And you had to explain, He got the last federal troops out of the South after Reconstruction, he ordered the Panama Canal built, and he reformed a corrupt and bankrupt Civil Service.

Everyone would go, Ah yeah, what's his name again?

An hour and a half north of Manhattan you were in the deep sticks, nearly as off the map as if you'd gotten lost in the Ozarks. When you said "town" you were talking about Three Rivers, which really wasn't much of a town at all. Just a main street five blocks long with a handful of stores that made most of their money off St. Val's. A couple of stoplights, hardly any road signs.

There are truck stops with bad food. There are train tracks but no station. Juke joints with country rockers blaring solid bass tracks and mean harmonizing so the strippers could hump the poles and get nasty enough to make a few bucks. Enough to feed their habits and feed their kids.

A small rural town like most others, except this one's on its way out. To the east is a closed sugar factory. To the north, an abandoned feed mill. A lot of stores are still open but more and more are closing. The nicer houses close to Main Street still look well kept, lawns trimmed, flower beds heavy with new growth in summer. The owners are retirees set with their pensions, with nowhere to go anyway.

Moving out from the center of town through neighborhoods you see cheaper properties going to hell. Huge Victorians that should've been converted years ago now boarded up. There are halfway houses for runaways, dopers, the mentally challenged, abused wives. Nursing homes where the elderly look near-enough dead on the porches that every time you pass by you've got to wonder, He still breathing?

Spiraling out from there you see the effects of inflation and recession more blatantly. Shacks are scattered into the hills as if they were tossed there by hurricanes. They lean, propped in odd directions, pine-board doors hanging from busted hinges, roofs and walls ready to collapse.

The old ways don't die, they persist through poverty, illness, depression, murder. Floods have washed the land into beautiful and strange patterns, boulders and uprooted trees stacked against the rim of the box valley. Cinder-block roadhouses still kick it up each night, more lively now than ever.

All of this Roz has described for him in great detail.

A lot of the land has been sold to developers who are waiting for the economic stimulation promised by the president. Most men of the holler have worked their lives away in the sugar factory and the feed mill. Many of them drifted down to the city or up to the Canadian border towns. Those left can only survive now by cooking and transporting meth.

There's one river nearby, ten minutes to the west, which overflows every couple of decades and takes a number of lives. The diners, bars, and hardware stores have newspaper clippings showing the devastation going back to the 1890s. Mud that reached the third-floor rain gutters, dead children stuck in treetops.

The story goes that three creek beds converged there, giving the area its name, but if you ask why the place isn't called Three Creeks instead you'll get no answer.

St. Val's is south of the holler, situated in its own valley. The land is lush and beautiful in the summer, set off just far enough to always be considered outside of town.

The only other guy currently on campus is Roddy Murphy, an off-the-boat Irishman from the north side of Galway. Chief custodian, electrician, snow-removal expert, groundskeeper, and all around fix-it dude with an attitude. As Finn collects his belongings from the classroom, he hears Murphy downstairs dragging equipment across the front walk in preparation for the blizzard.

Last year around his birthday Murphy got lonely for home and decided to bond with Finn a bit. They spent the night drinking Jameson in Murph's apartment and Finn learned that drunk Irishmen really do sing

"Kathleen." As Murphy outpaced Finn three to one he got louder and more physical, pounding on Finn's shoulder and sort of dancing around his living room.

Halfway through the night Murph admitted that he'd fooled around a bit with a couple of the young wans. He called himself a fookin' idjit and tried to sound abashed and contemplative. Finn got the distinct sense that Murphy was lying in order to impress him, maybe get Finn to confess his own sins. The next day, Murphy claimed not to remember most of the night. Maybe it was the truth, but it had left Finn feeling a little cagey ever since.

Carrying his overcoat, Finn makes his way along the empty corridors, the annoying tap of his cane the only sound. He hears it as if someone else is making the noise and finds himself becoming increasingly upset with that person. The silence of the building causes him some anxiety. He relies heavily on noise.

Judith's door is open. Before he can knock she says, "Hello, Finn. You really need to cut back on the cologne, dear."

Her lips are wet. He can tell by the soft snapping of suction when she parts them. She's on her feet near the window, where she twists a knob and lowers the volume on the Mahler CD playing. She smokes menthol 120s and the smell is barely present in the office. She's like a kid hiding her habit from her parents, sneaking a cigarette and blowing smoke out the window.

He knows she wants to talk. She damn near always wants to talk, always did want to talk, even before this thing with Vi.

"Judith. I'm glad I caught you before you left."

"No need to worry about that," she says, and he's convinced she's depressed, and not just because an empty campus makes everybody depressed.

"No? Why not?"

He shouldn't ask, but she wants to be asked. He's got to do his part. Sometimes you play the role and sometimes the role plays you.

Judith Perry is the dean of St. Val's, an administration wizard and a top-notch science teacher. In the Victorian era she would've been called a headmistress and been admired for her hard-edged dignity. The girls think she's overly rigid and demanding because she's repressed and miserable. Finn thinks they're not far off. She has the voice of an exacting, sharp woman that occasionally softens with plaintiveness. She takes tiny but solid steps. He has shaken her hand only once, during their initial meeting when she hired him three years ago.

Since he lost his sight, his mind craves details. If they can't be provided by his other senses, his brain fills them in. The surgeons told him this is normal. The shrinks tell him not to worry, this is normal. It doesn't fuckin' feel normal. When he sees Judith he sees his mother. It's both strange and calming. He has to stay especially focused because it's easy to go along with the fantasy, and he has to stop himself from calling her Mom.

Judith shares other traits and particulars with his mother. She's twice divorced, on the downside of a third marriage, and has an ungrateful adult child. She is probably bipolar. She's had several affairs that she believes to be secret but are common knowledge to anyone paying even a little attention. Judith believes herself to be fat

but she's only brawny. Touch her arm and you can feel
how physically powerful she is. You wouldn't want to roll
around in the mud with her, but you might throw down
in the sack.

That strength doesn't seem to mean anything to her.
She'd prefer to be dainty and delicate, a starved wisp
that men would fawn over. She uses too much perfume
and hair spray and bathing oils in an effort to be more
feminine. She doesn't know how to laugh. Her sense of
humor pretty much sucks ass. She's always on the edge
of a world-class sulk.

When they find themselves alone like this without
any need for going over reports, they speak honestly and
with some real depth.

People open up to him because they can see him and
he can't see them. It's like playing the peekaboo game
with a baby. If you can't watch them, you can't bear witness. You're not really there.

The snow begins to fall, ice crystals brushing
against the glass.

Judith tosses her cigarette out the window, flicking
it hard with her fingernail. After the thaw, Murphy and
his crew will be out there plucking bits of cotton filters
out of the bushes for days. He'll shout up to her, "Shite,
can't you smoke unfiltered Camels or get the hang of a
good pipe, now?"

She very carefully latches the window shut and
fights to keep from sighing. She only partially succeeds.
He knows she's pining for Murph. Or at least lusting
for him.

Finn sits in the comfortable leather visitor's chair

and extends the question. "What are you still doing here, Judith? Why don't you head home to your family?"

"And why would you want to wish that hell on me?"

He can't help but smile. "Troubles again?"

"Troubles, dependable and enduring."

"You'd better leave now or you'll get caught in the storm."

"A ready-made excuse, not that I need one." She shifts her stance, comes down hard on one heel. "There's no one to tell it to." She clears her throat. "I'm maudlin, I know, but bear with me."

"You're not thinking of staying here for the whole two weeks, are you?"

"Why not? It's supposed to be a vacation. If I go home, it'll be anything but relaxing. The tree's still not up. The presents are unwrapped, what few there are. My son has been out of work for the last eight months. I don't have the energy to argue with him, so I'm just as responsible, irresponsible really, as he is. My husband put twenty-five years into the fire department, retired, and still works in a volunteer capacity every holiday. He hasn't been home for Christmas or New Year's for the last four years, which is eighty percent of our marriage. He doesn't even have the ambition to cheat on me, which would do him a world of good and make him at least a bit happy, and that would be pleasant. No, I really see no reason why I should rush home."

Home is forty minutes away over the Connecticut border in a posh township. Her husband's name is Mike or Mark, but she never addresses him as such. Her son's name is Billy. Or maybe Bobby. Billy-Bob? She refuses to say his name either. Finn wonders what his psychiatrist would think about that. Is it simply detachment or de-humanization?

But he never thinks of his shrink by her name either, she's just his shrink. Maybe he'll broach the subject of replacing names with titles and what the psychological ramifications might be the next time he visits her. If he ever goes back.

"You could always invite the local orphans to your house," Finn says. "Give them the toys your kid won't play with."

"My goddamn kid is thirty-two."

"You could build snowmen, go to church, find the richest mean-hearted bastard in Connecticut and melt his icy exterior. So that everybody learns the true meaning of Christmas? So the angels all get their wings?"

"Fuck that," Judith says. She's naturally foul-mouthed and has a hard time holding it back around the kids. When she gets a chance to cut loose, she lets fly. "My kid also has prescriptions for three antidepressants. He's never held a steady job, never had a girlfriend, and spends all of his time online playing *World of Warcraft* with people in Senegal and Polynesia."

"Really?"

"Like I would lie about that?"

"I mean, Polynesians stay inside on the computer? When they could go outside and enjoy being in . . . Polynesia?"

"Apparently so."

"Christ." Finn sees lots of topless brown-skinned ladies in grass skirts dancing, covered in flowers, holding fresh jungle fruit. "Well, we could sit around and get drunk on spiked eggnog."

"The thought has crossed my mind repeatedly, believe me."

"I do."

"I know you do."

Judith lets out a hiccup of laughter, trying to sound quaint. What she really wants is to get bombed with Murphy and rip it up. Finn hopes she'll overcome her insecurities long enough to let it happen. He has to force his mind away from imagining it because when he does he sees his mother down in the custodian's apartment doing extremely un-Mom-like things. It makes his stomach churn.

She walks around behind him, staring at the side of his face as she does. He can feel the faint gust of her breath disturbing the air as she goes by. The skin on his cheek tightens. The earpiece on his sunglasses cools a couple of degrees.

Despite the entire floor being empty, she closes her door. This is what he's been waiting for. She only shuts the door when they talk about personal issues. The only personal issue left is Vi. He thought he didn't want to talk about Vi, but he probably does. Otherwise he wouldn't have come to Judith's office in the first place.

"Tell me how things have been with Violet Treato," she says.

"Status quo."

"And that status being?"

"She's staying the hell away from me."

That's not going to be forthright enough for Judith. She needs to expound and dig. She tsks and taps her lengthy fingernails lightly at the corner of her desk. It's not all an act. She smells of nervous sweat. The school

only has 250 students and the economics for small private institutions are growing worse all the time. She's
got a lot to deal with, and now this.

"It's a precarious situation."

"Yes," he admits.

What, like he's going to argue? He's got to take his
medicine again, and it's all his own fault. Still, he's got to
force himself not to wag his head, everything falling into
place step by step, the way it has for months. His fist
tightens on his cane and slowly exerts pressure, waiting
to hit the exact point when the stress will begin to snap
it. He's got to keep himself busy, has to play these sorts
of marginal games to constantly keep himself aware that
he hasn't vanished.

"I'm not overdramatizing, Finn."

"I know. I've done what I can."

"I'm worried."

"I know that too, Judith. I offered to resign."

"I don't want your resignation."

"Not yet anyway."

"That's right."

It always comes back to this. He can't help but repeat himself. "Well, when you need it, you'll have it."

"Don't play the martyr, you prick, you know whose
fault this is."

"I'm not playing and yes, I do."

That's left out there for a few seconds, the room
heavy with expectation. He fills it. "So, there's no
chance she's leaving for the holidays, I take it?"

"No. Her parents are spending the chilly months
traveling the Mediterranean."

For every working-stiff father putting in overtime,

there's a fat-cat blue blood sending his kid through St. Val's. "How very nice for them."

"I would've hoped the lure of the Aegean would have been too tempting to resist."

That's a setup for a nasty comment. She wants to slap him around some more. Finn actually braces himself in his seat. He assumes it will be something like, *But presumably you're the greater temptation, the more powerful lure.* A young girl's heart wants what it wants. And her body as well. Finn feels guilty over the fact that he doesn't feel as guilty as he should.

Judith says, "I want you to be careful around her."

"I am. I will."

"We can't afford another misstep."

What the hell does he have to say to that? He tries not to incline his head and can't quite do it. His chin drops toward his chest like a dog ready for a beating. He nods to cover. "I know."

"Her grades have been improving all semester."

"That's good to hear."

"Of course she's always been excellent in English."

"Yes."

"She's trying to show off for you. She's hoping to be the woman she thinks you want. Educated. Sophisticated."

"I realize that."

"Finn—"

"I know."

"You don't know shit."

The conversation is little more than a repeat of last week's. Judith is feeling him out, seeing if he'll suddenly be overcome by guilt and admit to greater or ongoing shenanigans. Finn doesn't blame her. Trust is in short supply all around.

She's going to mention Roz now. Only because she wants to hear again that some relationships under the worst kinds of strain still manage to work out. Also because she dislikes Roz, and she wants to remind him of that. Roz is only here because she and Finn were a package deal, and that fact has always annoyed Judith.

"What happens if Roz learns of this?"

"I tell Roz everything."

"She knows about the events with Vi?"

By implication he's already answered, but Judith always needs additional confirmation. She reminds him of DAs he once had to deal with, always worrying the same nugget of information.

He told Judith all of this three months ago when Vi first hit on him. Events. She makes it sound like the Olympics.

"Yes," he says.

"I'm glad."

"Are you?"

"I just said so. Yes."

He wants to ask why but lets it slide.

This isn't Peyton Place, but anytime you throw men and women together in an environment as lonely as St. Valarian's, in an area as rural and declining as Three Rivers, you're going to have to deal with all this movie-of-the-week shit. He knew it would happen, he just didn't know it would happen to him.

He realizes he can't pacify or help Judith, and that he should just keep out of her way for the next two weeks until classes start up again. He stands and expects her to say something about joining him at dinner, but she doesn't. He's relieved and lets it go at that.

"What are your plans for the break?" she asks.

"Roz and I will spend New Year's in the city. We're splurging on the Plaza for three nights. We've got reservations for Tavern on the Green."

"What's the occasion? Are you finally going to pop the question?"

Finn doesn't answer.

But Judith is waiting. She's not quite through with squeezing out as much drama as she can.

The truth is, Finn's terrified of even spending more alone time with Roz. And after all these years he doesn't know why. She's been good for him, as good as anyone could be. Maybe it's the city. Manhattan used to be the hub of his world. The action, the grind, the heat, and the juice. Now they'll just hang around a suite in the Plaza paying two grand a night so they can make love in a bigger, softer bed. The food will be better. The view will be amazing, for her. They'll take in a musical on Broadway. She'll think he'll be able to enjoy it. He won't. But he'll sit there and smile and applaud the way he's supposed to. The other patrons will be glad that he doesn't have a seeing-eye dog with him shedding on their best evening wear.

Finn once rousted a low-level syndicate mook out of the Plaza, wrestled him through the lobby, and threw him in the fountain out front. The guy hadn't been resisting arrest, Finn just wanted to embarrass the prick and really ruin his day. Finn knows that when he and Roz arrive at the hotel, he'll be thinking about that mook and others just like him, spending wads of dirty green on their girlfriends. Roz will want to toss a coin in the fountain, and he'll stand there in the sun while she asks him to make a wish. It's the kind of small romantic gesture that she never used to care for but has now taken on greater meaning. She needs something more from him, and he simply can't give it.

But he's still got to try. That's all this vacation signifies for him. A last ditch effort. Another act of will. To see if he can sit there in a hansom cab while the driver points out picturesque areas in Central Park, and Finn listens to the endless clip-clopping of hooves and smells the horse shit, and children laugh all around them and Roz tightens her hold on his arm, and he grins politely and swallows his screams.

Judith says, "Finn?"

"Let's just say that after hearing your inspiring tales of wedded bliss, I will seriously consider it."

"How are you otherwise?" she asks.

"Fine."

"And how are the nightmares?"

It's what she calls his memory surges that occur when he smells blood. She's a scientist at heart, practical in the extreme when it comes to others. She's done the research, spent hours online looking up info and reading it to him in his office, trying to make him see reason. She thinks he's hallucinating or having waking dreams.

Judith's got texts that practically verify it. She constantly snaps her finger against the pages while rereading selected paragraphs aloud. She walks on thin ice. Considering the fact that her kid plays online games with the Senegalians and her husband prefers watching empty warehouses to her company, he figures she shouldn't feel quite so fucking comfortable hanging around all night long, reading Finn printouts about how crazy he's supposed to be.

He tightens his grip on his cane and says, "I'm handling it."

FINN MOVES DOWN THE ENORMOUS STAIRWAY forgoing the banister, brushing his index and middle fingers against the wall. He's hardwired into the history of the school and can feel the layers of dust and stain beneath his hand, all the trapped ghosts still twitching there.

His fingertips tingle with the touch of smooth ancient oak. It's like reaching back a century. Step by step he descends, and even after all these years he can't shake the sensation that he's moving down into the earth itself. Into his own grave.

At the bottom he stands on the unevenly textured slate floor. He sometimes stumbles here, but everyone does. Girls are always taking headers and banging their knees, backpacks flying. He must always keep aware of subtle shifts and deviations. In the ground, in direction, in people.

Duchess has left a tray of baked cookies out on a table in the lobby. He smells that they're still fresh. Chocolate chips with macadamia nuts. His mouth waters.

He sees Duchess stirring pots with a big wooden spoon or a ladle. This is his subconscious image of what a cook is, and it's a revelation to learn how insipid his deep-rooted notions can be. Duchess is the house-mother and head of the kitchen staff. She lives in an apartment off the west wing of the student suites, across the hall from Roz. She's a sixty-year-old black woman raised in the South Bronx who uses equal amounts of street wit, intimidation, and incredible cuisine to keep everybody in line. She's big, wide, has some serious hips, and is always bumping into him and excusing herself. It's sort of sexy but everything is sort of sexy to him now. A brush of fingers against his wrist can get him hard.

Her voice comes down from above him, which means she's over six feet tall, at least in her shoes. Her laughter resonates from deep in her belly and slams like a sonic boom. It sometimes rocks him back a step. When she and Roz go on their little shopping excursions, he feels twice as lonely.

Hey now, check this out.

Someone is sneaking up behind him.

It's a joke. It's a gigglefest for the girls. It's a game meant to drive him into action.

This is another parlor trick. People think they're being silent as ninjas because they can't hear anything above their own breathing and heartbeats. He doesn't mind playing the game anymore. He has little else to do besides put on a show anyway.

He squares his shoulders and whips the cane around to snap lightly against flesh.

"Ow!"

Now comes the laughter, a pair of insolent titters.

Neither is Vi's.

"Hey, Mr. Finn, party in the dorm tonight!" It's Sally. "Starts at dark and goes until dawn!"

"Why should tonight be any different?" he asks.

"You stopping by?" It's Suzy. "You gonna rock out with us? It's going to be a blast, you know it will. You mind picking up a keg for us?"

They're both named Smyth even though they're unrelated. They're two of the more serious JDs of the school, always getting caught with pot or sneaking out to ride the back hills with boys from town. In the city it would be considered normal, but out here in the sticks he worries. It's just so fucking boring in the valley. Of course they're going to get into trouble. He tries to think of them as independent and willful, but Judith tells him there's been at least one abortion apiece and a couple of brushes with cocaine. A couple of shoplifting raps, one liquor store smash-and-grab where they hooked a couple bottles of Wild Turkey. He's put kids like these in rehab. He's put kids like these in jail.

"We can give you the cash," Sally says. "Please, oh please, Mr. Finn." She throws in just enough of an exaggerated whine for him to realize they're not serious, this time. "Come on, it'll be a gas. You can tell us what it was like when you were young, drinking mead down by the Nile, watching baby Moses float by in his wicker basket."

"Those were good times," Finn tells her. "Waving to the pharaoh's barge. Watching the pyramids go up. All the slave girls waving the palm fronds. Still, why don't you just spike the punch like all the other delinquents do?"

"Mr. Finn's no square, he knows our action."

"He's hep to the world. He doesn't see but he sees."

"That's why we like you, Mr. Finn."

"Yeah, you hear everything but you don't judge and you never rat."

"Not so far as you know anyway," Finn says.

He wonders when the fifties lingo started to come back into style. A few of the girls use it now and it keeps throwing him off, like he's listening to a Hot Rod drive-in flick.

"We know all right," Sally contends, and puts an arm halfway around him, tapping the small of his back gently.

"We trust you."

They huddle closely together and too near to his face. They have no true concept of personal space. They force him into almost nestling with them. Finn wears expensive black shades, more because they remind him of his father than anything else. When the girls speak to him, he can feel their breath fogging his lenses.

"Do me a favor, you two," he says.

"You ask and we answer the call. Don't we always answer the call?"

"You do."

"Then ask."

"Don't break curfew for at least a few days until after this storm passes and we dig ourselves out, okay? It's supposed to be a bad one."

"Us, break curfew?" Suzy tries to sound offended. "You can't be serious, dad, we're not those kind of janes."

"Like you said, I know your action."

"Yes, you do."

"So promise me."

Sally, about two inches from his chin, "Only for you, Mr. Finn. Righteous?"

"Sure."

"You want to walk with us?"

He shakes his head. "I'm heading home for a while. I'll meet you for dinner."

"Right on."

They move gracefully but without lifting their feet high enough. Their heels scuff the slate as they sort of skip-shuffle to the front doors of the building, called the Main House. He assumes they're holding hands. His brain is fiery. No one ever told him what kind of details he'd hunger for.

When he sees Sally Smyth, he sees a girl he once stood beside at the concession stand at Jones Beach when he was fifteen. It was a murderous summer, and he'd just gained another ten pounds of muscle, filling out pretty good by then, and the girl was a touch sunburned already, wearing a bikini with a T-shirt wrapped around her hips, copper hair in a ponytail, sunscreen a little too thick on her forehead and chin, but cute as hell. She was buying a soft-ice-cream cone covered with colorful sprinkles. The wafer cone had already softened and was dripping vanilla. She turned too quickly and accidentally tapped him with the tip of the vanilla swirl directly in the center of his chest. She smiled and apologized. He grinned and began to flirt, and within seconds a loud-mouthed guy arrayed in tattoos rushed up and threatened to kick Finn's ass. The beau glowered at Finn, flexing wildly and making his tribal ink ripple and flutter. As the girl drew her boyfriend off, Finn stood there with his chest sticky, staring after her, surrounded by indifferent people shouldering past.

When he sees Suzy Smyth, he sees the same girl.

It's Vi he has to worry about.

Violet Treato is the princess of body brushes. She's just shy of eighteen. She has a refined sense of flirtation and seems to genuinely want him. He's never had the best impulse control, and in the dark she's almost impossible to resist.

A week into the fall semester he returned to his cottage and found her drinking his Glenfiddich. She could hold her liquor but was still pretty far gone. She brought her lips to his and tore open her own blouse, pressed her moderate tits to his chest and mumbled about his cock. She threw his cane aside and urged his hands between her legs. She'd already dispensed with the panties. Her voice coursed through him. She was wet and shaved. The freshness of her skin and the tremendous warmth of her cunt nearly threw him over the edge.

He stopped himself and stopped her. He spoke in muted tones for over an hour and gave her a lot of coffee. When he asked if she understood his position she said, "Yes, of course, Finn, but you have to understand mine too. I'm not a little girl. I care for you. I want you. I won't write our names inside hearts all over my notebooks. I won't even bother you. I'll prove myself to you though. You can't force me to quit trying that. We're going to be together. I believe that, and I believe in you."

It was the kind of speech you wait your whole life to hear, and it scared the piss out of him. Five minutes after Vi left Judith walked into his cottage without knocking.

She saw the bottle of Glenfiddich out, the cups of coffee, maybe a blouse button on the floor. Finn later found two on the throw rug.

She'd clocked Vi going out. He'd forgotten that bored, unhappy people were always inspecting everything. He had to start locking his door.

Finn puts on his coat and steps outside. The snow is coming down roughly now, still hard crystal. He hears Murphy in the distance, scraping off one of the walkways with a shovel. Within an hour Murphy will have the snowblower out, clearing paths between the academy buildings and the cottages. Later on he'll drive his truck with the plow out front across the main parking lot. If the blizzard is as bad as they're saying, none of his hard work will matter much. Judith will go out and offer him hot chocolate at least two or three times, but she won't chat with him at all. She'll just hand him the styrofoam cup and retreat back to her office, and return to her vigil.

Instead of heading home, Finn walks toward the cemetery, feeling the urge to push himself. It's about a quarter mile behind his cottage, down a dirt path that follows the naturally twisting grades of the area.

This is the last chance Finn will have to get out and walk for a while before the storm comes down in full. He needs to move. If he doesn't move, he's afraid of what might happen.

He's got to test himself constantly. It's too damn easy to grow complacent and docile, to stay within readily defined boundaries. Others always want to grab him, lead him, aid him, lock him down, hold his hand. He's always this close to becoming a cripple.

On the job he'd met two blind shut-ins. One hadn't been out of his apartment for forty years, completely cared for by his wife. When the old lady died, the blind geriatric left her on the bed for three weeks, bloated and black with flies, because he was paralyzed with the fear of what might happen to him afterward. He lived on watered-down cans of soup and dropped twenty pounds until the stink alerted the neighbors and Finn showed up.

The other was a seventeen-year-old kid who'd been homeschooled all his life. He'd never been outside his apartment unless his mother was latched around his throat, and then only to the small garden in back of the building. Even when one of the windows got blown out by a stray gunshot from the street, the mother lied and said it was a golf ball. Like people golf in the East Village alleys every day. The kid was happy and well cared for and smiled like a doofus, intentionally kept stupid, with no idea of what he was missing out there. When Finn left, the mother was having metal shutters put in.

As he got used to counting off steps to his classroom, to the dining hall, to Roz's quarters, his front step, Finn realized that a couple hundred square yards could become his entire world. The safe embrace of it is too appealing to him. He thinks of that petrified old man and it gets him moving. He wanders, gets lost, sometimes calls out for help, fighting to keep the terror from his voice. It's better than the alternative.

The snow drives against his face and he feels it building up on his glasses. What a bad joke that he has to clean them off.

He slows his pace, unsure of why. Something is distracting the hell out of him. He focuses past the warble of the wind through the trees. The snow lands on the back of his neck, but he's already gone cold.

Finn's always been a man who trusted his instincts, but now he relies on them almost entirely. He has to. He's a slave to his remaining senses. It makes him want to scream. It makes him want to scream right now.

The graveyard is one of those half-hidden places. It's pitted, choked with weeds, and filled with crumbling tombstones and uncleared rock.

He takes another step, then another. He swings his cane. He's close to the first grave. By running his fingers in the grooves of the stones, he's memorized the names on many of the markers. He knows their distance from the path.

This is how he can still be a man, standing on his own.

This here, this is just a chunk of rock. Another dozen steps down the aisle and he reaches out with his cane and strikes a statue. It's a kneeling angel, with her wings partially unfolded. Her hands are clasped together in prayer. She's missing her index fingers.

He walks on. A part of him expects the next tombstone to ring like a bell when he hits it. He opens his mouth to say something but has no idea what. Who is he calling to? Who does he want to respond? He wonders where the hell Roz is. He thinks of Vi but he's always thinking of Vi. His shrink tries not to sound judgmental, but his shrink is really fucking bad at hiding her feelings.

This stone. This is Abbie Waylon, beloved mother, struck down by a jealous neighbor, 1812–1847.

"Hello again, Abbie Waylon," he says. He wonders

about the neighbor, what prompted him or her to lash
out and murder Abbie. He thinks about those tight-ass
Puritans. Abbie might've flashed an ankle, forgotten her
big hat one day. Maybe she failed to blush at the per-
ceived right moment. What did her neighbor covet? He
imagines Abbie's kids visiting the grave, standing where
he now stands. Side by side, three or four of them in a
row, dressed in yellow on Easter, and laying flowers
across the muddy earth.

An animal's ugly mewls are nearly lost in the wind.

Finn turns toward the sound and drops his shoulders. The muscles in his back and legs contract. He angles the cane in front of him and assumes a defensive
stance. He carries a four-inch blade in his back pocket.
His shrink actually suggested he carry pepper spray,
telling him that it was important for him to assert his independence, feed his need for security, and take a hand
in his own self-preservation. She didn't know he was already carrying the blade. Pepper spray never saved anybody.

A pained whimper, something crawling through the
thickening veil of snow collecting on the ground.

It's not a goddamn dog or a fox or a deer.

"What?" he says. "Hey?"

He starts wondering what the hell the girls have gotten up to now.

Praying to Christ it's not Vi down there, drunk and
slinking up on him.

"Hello?" he calls.

Blustering wind tugs at him like insistent childish
hands.

Finn breaks from the trail and heads deeper into the

cemetery. The mewling becomes a brief moan that merges with the lamenting gusts. Something might be dying. When he tries to imagine it he sees only himself, as he used to be. The man he was periodically whimpers in his dreams, wanting to return to life.

The noise leads him past clawing maple branches. He reaches out to steady himself against the tree, bumbles over a root, and feels another gravestone fixed painfully against his calf.

Sliding his palm over the frozen face of it, he dips a finger, clears out snow, and feels the chiseled name.

KELTON MOON, AGED 2 MONTHS, GENTLE CHILD, MAY THE LIGHT OF OUR SAVIOR GUIDE YOU INTO ETERNITY. 1863, YELLOW FEVER VICTIM.

The dead give him his bearing.

He knows exactly where he is now.

The need to speak rises within him, but he's afraid his own voice will answer. He moves again and his toe touches what he knows must be a body.

Christ. Finn bends, goes to one knee, places both hands on the figure. It's a girl. The wind shifts and blows ice against his lips.

She's bleeding and the scent fills him. It fires color into his skull, and makes him tremble. His head tilts back and he says, "Ah . . ." He can't help it and grins like a doofus.

He falls to his knees as the past embraces, fondles, and murders him.

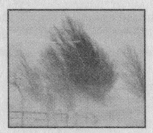

FIRST TIME HE EVER SAW DANIELLE, Finn's shooting hoops with Ray in the gymnasium, up eighteen to sixteen. Both of them are sophomores taking criminal justice and English lit courses, killing time while waiting to be called up for the next NYPD Academy class.

Dani walks in from the football field side by side with some no-neck bruiser who's getting a lot of local press because he's the grandson of a pro. Everybody's wondering what he can do on the field, and so far it isn't much.

Finn continues dribbling but doesn't drive forward, just watches her over Ray's left shoulder as she steps onto the far end of the court. She's wearing tight shorts and a bright yellow tee, her sports bra perfectly outlined in sweat. Whoa mama. Her blond hair is tied back in a ponytail with a red ribbon, and it bobs with her deep breaths. She's sipping from a plastic bottle and passing it back and forth with the bruiser. She's been running around the field while no-neck does extra drills with the coach.

Ray tries swatting the ball out of Finn's hand and Finn lets it go. Ray passes the ball twice between his legs before rushing past, giving it a little left-handed toss off the backboard and watching as it ticks into the basket.

Ray returns, notices the look on Finn's face, and loops around.

He looks and says, "Hey now—"

"Yeah."

"I like the ponytail."

"Oh yeah."

"Not every girl can make it work."

"Yeah."

"Makes you think, hair up like that, all it might take is some good conversation, a half a bottle of good wine, a vegetarian dinner nicely seasoned, snowy mountain backdrop through a cabin window, and she yanks the ribbon like a rip cord, the wild mane comes down, the real woman shows through."

He hates when Ray is thinking his thoughts. "Sure."

"She shows a pitiful lack of taste in men though."

"Life is for learning."

"The fuck does that mean?"

The bruiser is the same as every guy. He enjoys showing Dani off, but doesn't like other men staring. He stops and gives a death glare. Ray smiles, amiable to the max, throwing his usual charm. Finn can't take his eyes off Dani.

She's not beautiful exactly, but she's incredibly cute, has that thing that touches him deeply which he can't name. Maybe it has to do with confidence and fortitude and sensuality, all of that or maybe none of it, he's still not sure. All he knows is very few women he's met so far have the thing that makes him wake all the way up. She's got it, and it eases out from her and it reaches into him.

She makes brief eye contact with Finn, sort of nods his way. The ponytail bobs. That gets to him too. Her calves are sharply defined. She's a runner, a sprinter, captain of the track team. Her breasts are large for such a petite frame. It starts him thinking what it would be like to take her to bed after the bottle of good wine and the veggie dinner. He appreciates the curve of her jaw, the length and smoothness of her neck.

There's a lot of distance between them, maybe sixty feet, but Finn says in a normal tone of voice, "Hi."

Her lips move and she answers, or possibly answers, too quietly for him to hear.

The no-neck slowly marches toward Finn, his eyes burning, juiced up on adrenaline. The coach isn't working him hard enough.

Dani, in a voice as flat and commanding as if she's berating a dog, says, "Howie, no! No!"

Howie's been shifted to three different positions this season, the team trying to find a spot that will fit his meager skills. He can't block, can't catch, and can barely run. But his grandfather used to come down and rally the team and the fans, sign autographs and take pictures with the locals. It's out of respect for the sick old man that they keep trying with no-neck. He's in shape but way too massive on top, his legs like sticks beneath his bulk.

Howie pulls off his gear and his shirt as he approaches, and Finn can see the hard nodules on both arms where steroids have been shot directly into the muscle tissue. The university's been cutting this guy a lot of slack and turning a blind eye for the use of his name.

Time hangs there, the way it's supposed to for big moments like this. Finn keeps staring at Dani, and gives her his best smile. She doesn't smile back, firms her lips and frowns like he must be crazy. He's used to the look, has been living with it all his life. But still, she cocks her head a little like she's curious to see what's about to play out.

Ray, who always lets Finn take point in a fight even if he's the one who starts it, chuckles beneath his breath and retreats a few steps so Finn's out front.

Finn hasn't been in a brawl for over six months, since he was put on probation last semester for smacking around a bouncer in a local club who was smacking around a drunk kid upchucking on the floor. Punching out a lightweight for vomiting in a bar like The Tenderloin was just ludicrous and cruel. Finn got into it pretty good with the punk bouncer and the asshole bat-wielding bartender, until all three of them were thrown into County.

But he's kept up with the boxing and had just started an introductory martial-arts class. Ray keeps asking him, Why do you want to punish yourself like that? On the streets all you need is your piece. You think you're going to karate-chop a crack dealer carrying an assault rifle?

Finn can tell that it won't be easy to stop this no-neck. Howie's got too much going on in his head and careening through his veins. Finn completely understands since he has a loud head too, and occasionally his blood ignites.

Ray says, "You need some help?"

"Nope."

"You sure?"

"Not exactly one hundred percent," Finn admits.

"High nineties?"

"Maybe a little less."

Howie's got his whole life written in his face as he stomps forward. He's angry but nearly expressionless. Beneath it all there's a grim kind of sorrow. You can see that the pressure he's under to be a star player is stealing the soul out of him. It's not hard to believe that he loves his grandfather and hates the man too, for forcing Howie into this life.

A black vein bucks at his temple. He's got crow's-feet etched around his eyes and something like a burn scar flares over his right brow. As he rubs it with the heel of his hand it looks like Howie's trying to force something out of his head. Or into it.

He glares at the center of Finn's chest and continues making his way toward him. Howie has a hitch in his stride, probably because he's taking needles in the buttocks too. Howie wants to share his pain.

"Heya," Finn says.

Raising his fist, Howie seems to suddenly forget what's set him in motion. His eyes are an intense blue and they flicker with confusion.

Then he remembers. "I don't like the way you're staring at my girl."

"No?"

"No."

"Okay."

"Okay?"

"Sure, how would you prefer I stare at her?"

The question puzzles the no-neck. He seems to

seriously consider it for a second and then wags his head like he's got an earache.

Finn wonders if Danielle has been set up with the guy to help him feel and act more like an ace. He turns and glances in her direction, sees she's moving toward them too. Gracefully and with a beautifully controlled exertion, like she's about to break into a run and launch herself into a routine on the mats. Finn is having a little trouble keeping his focus. He can feel his imagination starting to tug him away.

"Howie, stop!"

Dani still doesn't know that a girl yelling "Stop" is pretty much the same as a girl yelling "Kill his ass." A screaming woman inspires men toward greater stupidity, no matter what she's screaming. Finn can feel himself getting dumber, listening to the sound of her voice.

The same is happening to Howie, who's pretty dumb to begin with. The 'roids are ripping through his system and maybe withering his testicles. Whatever's going on, it's not helping him achieve the alpha state.

The coach must've really given him hell out there on the field, perhaps even in front of Dani, which would humiliate and piss anybody off. Finn feels a strange camaraderie with the no-neck and suddenly wants to just sit down with him, have an iced coffee. Dani arrives and the four of them are huddled at about center court.

"You sure you don't want some help?" Ray whispers.

"Not yet."

"Okay, well, do some of that Bruce Lee stuff on him."

"I've only had two classes."

"Just don't kick. Kicking's for sissies."

"You are such an asshole."

"You love me anyway."

"Not always."

Howie doesn't seem to be aware that anyone is talking. He's concentrating on Finn's mouth like a deaf man trying to read lips. Finn figures his next words will carry a lot of weight, and he tries to come up with something for the ages. Asking about the withered testicles doesn't seem to be the way to go.

For a second Danielle doesn't know what to do, and again makes the worst choice. She tugs on the bruiser's arm. He tightens his biceps and the large knots where he's taken the needle stand out like walnuts.

There's still time to avoid any real confrontation, but Finn makes a mistake too and allows his gaze to linger too long on Dani. There's a trinity of freckles at her shoulder and a dusting of dried salt. He breathes deeply as if taking her in.

Howie actually growls, the animal sound coming from deep in his chest and far back in the most ancient strands of his DNA.

He lumbers forward on his thin legs and Finn skips back a step, preparing himself. The no-neck swings his enormous right arm and Finn draws his chin in about an inch. The massive fist passes by his nose and Finn realizes with some shock that if the blow had connected it probably would've broken his neck. There's almost no anger in the air, nothing yet has happened that's irredeemable.

Finn fires two sharp jabs into Howie's nose. The bruiser's head snaps back twice but he makes no sound and his expression doesn't change in the slightest. Finn imagines that Howie hears the cheers of hopeful crowds, screams, wails, women holding up their babies in the bleachers, but all the applause is for his grandfather. Howie is given fixed looks of disappointment and pity.

Once again Finn's chest fills with a kind of sympathy and remorse. Howie lunges, tucks his chin in, and barrels along. His hands are open now and he grabs hold of Finn's left wrist, tries to twist and shatter it. Finn right hooks Howie to the temple as Danielle scoots in agitation and follows the fight around the scuffed gym floor. Her breasts jiggle, the meat of her thighs is tight but also bounces nicely.

Unable to get his wrist free, Finn tries a few other maneuvers. He hammers the no-neck on the point of his jaw. Stomps his instep. Nothing fazes Howie. The bruiser puffs and his spittle-flecked lips vibrate, but that's it. He hasn't made any sound of pain, hasn't backed up a step, hasn't said another word.

So much of Howie moves into Finn that for a moment he hates himself. He sees himself the way the failed football hero would. Intense, deep-set eyes flashing with intelligence and ego. Dark curly hair with a thin streak of premature white that high-school girls hated but college girls seem to dig. A grin that appears when it shouldn't, like now. Someone who fights because he likes it and not because he has to. Who searches for trouble and when he finds it has a difficult time denying it.

Howie glances at Danielle and sees what Finn sees, a total lack of real feeling for him. She's come to a decision to cut him loose, not because of this fight or because he can't win games on the field, but because he's allowed himself to be pressed into the service of others. His willingness to turn himself into a terrified hulk in order to satisfy people who abuse him and fans who aren't his own.

Ray moves to her, places his fingers lightly on her arm in a kind of charitable gesture, and says, "Hey there, I'm Ray. Don't let this upset you at all, okay? It's going to be fine. Trust me, I'm never wrong about these things." Finn watches Ray's hand stray to those freckles on Dani's shoulder. It makes him hiss.

Finn can picture the kind of cop Ray will be, handling the families of victims murdered on the streets, thinking about widows and their dead husbands' insurance policies, walking up and going, "Hey there," and flashing the teeth.

But Ray putting his hands on Dani only inspires Howie to real animosity, and he growls again, much louder this time, and allows the sound to grow and evolve into a roar. He's still got hold of Finn's wrist and tightens his grip until Finn grunts and, fueled by sudden panic that his arm might soon snap, manages to tear himself loose and stumble away. Howie's not so slow anymore, his cloudy eyes are beginning to clear. Finn feels himself coming into focus as if crosshairs are lining up on his forehead.

You've got to wonder what any of it means. Maybe there will be revelations and understanding at the end, but probably not. You don't always get the answers you need.

Finn never used to think in a fight, but the last few, especially while he was duking it out with the bouncer and the prick bartender swinging the Louisville slugger, he found his mind drifting, like it is now.

This shouldn't be happening. He wants to ask questions but he doesn't know what they might be. The no-neck shrugs and now he really has no neck, the points of his shoulders up around his ears.

What the hell, Finn hooks Howie to the temple again.

The bruiser doesn't feel it. His head is like an outcropping of rock that has existed since before the dawn of man. Finn tries once more. The fury of Howie won't let him feel anything. The fury of Howie is connected to 10 million years of sons disappointing their fathers. Finn is a part of it. Ray is a part of it.

Finn can't help but look over at Dani. He catches her eye and feels the deep tickle under his heart. His dreams unravel and he thinks about asking her to a dance. What dance? Finn doesn't dance, why does he suddenly want to dance?

Danielle's face becomes the face of all the girls he's ever known. His current squeeze who keeps talking about her ex-boyfriend. His prom date, his first lay, the girl he cared enough for to try his hand at poetry. The ones he learned to love and the ones he learned to hate. The girl seated diagonally from Finn in his creative writing class who has whore's eyes and wants to write children's stories about talking teddy bears.

Finn moves in again and Howie feints with a slow left, then loops a heavy right across his chest and into Finn's gut. It's got a lot of rage to it but there's also plenty of self-pity, which weakens the jolt. Howie's face is as bland as dust but inside he's crying and has been for a long time.

The basketball is somehow between them, bouncing about an inch off the floor. Howie kicks it straight into Finn's nuts.

It's a seriously cheap shot and Finn buckles. He wonders if he has enough breath to tell Ray, Now, Jesus Christ, I need help now!

But he sees that Ray is speaking pleasantly to Danielle, smiling and nodding while she glances distractedly back and forth between Ray and the fight. She's got her hands tightened into fists and is holding them up against her magnificent chest. Howie's got his hands around Finn's throat and is lifting him slowly off the floor. Finn's vision is starting to turn black with yellow spots at the edges.

The two martial-arts classes have concentrated on sweeping the legs, tripping your opponent, learning how to fall properly. Finn's not sure any of it will work for him here, but he angles a kick upward into Howie's skinny knee, trying to blow it out.

"Hey now," Ray calls, "what'd I say about kicking, huh?"

As Finn gurgles and tries to snap his heel against the no-neck's knee again, Howie suddenly screws his face up and turns his head. He lowers Finn carefully and releases him, taking a step back. He rubs at the burn mark over his eye as Finn coughs and sucks air, his mouth full of blood from biting his tongue.

Aware that they're a part of the same brotherhood of pain, Finn reaches out but Howie is stumbling for the locker-room door. He trips over the mats and almost

takes a header, weaving blindly with his eyes still shut
and watching whatever visions or memories are playing
out in his head. He shoulders the wall and follows it to
the locker room, where the dark doorway swallows him.

Finn never sees him again.

With some difficulty, Ray draws himself away from
Dani, looks over at Finn, and says, "If you plan on being
my partner, you've got to be sharper than that. My life's
going to be in your hands. You think you're instilling any
trust here?"

A few seconds go by where anything can happen.

Finn might not be able to catch his breath, his windpipe could be crushed. Danielle might rush away, call for
security, go date the QB instead. A low-flying plane,
heard in the distance, could bank sharply, break into a
nosedive, and crash through the roof. Left behind,
Howie's fury might dissolve the foundation of the
school and send everyone spiraling.

All seems imminently possible. A breeze from the
still-open gym door washes inside and flaps the ends of
the ribbon in Dani's hair.

She steps toward Finn and Ray's whole body jerks.
His hand rises as if he might yank her back to him.

Finn's belly tightens. All the stupid poetry he's ever
written sings in his ear.

She presses a palm to the side of his face and says,
"Are you hurt?"

He has a strange premonition then, in the moment
that they first touch. A silent voice speaks very clearly,
telling Finn that he will be a fine cop who will bring a
small standard of justice to his scrap of the world. He
and Danielle will have a home on Long Island down by

the water, where he'll learn how to fish. They'll have a dog named Portnoy. A cat she calls Blue and he calls Boo. They'll raise two children, Adrian and Madison. He'll put his twenty in and make a difference. His career and life will have some meaning. They'll move down South to North Carolina and find a place on the coast, have some room for when the grandchildren visit. He'll die ancient and beloved, a ring of glowing, wet faces around his bed.

He grins at her while blood leaks off his chin. The sweet agony of infatuation blazes through his brain as he says, "I'm Finn, the love of your life."

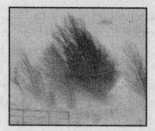

"...YOUR LIFE..."

Finn hears his own voice whispering.

He finds that he wants to answer. Without realizing it, he's been on the move, a thickening layer of snow beginning to coat him.

In his arms is about a hundred pounds of deadweight. Long, ice-encrusted hair whips into his face and stings his nose and cheeks.

He knows better than to handle someone who might be badly hurt, but he's got to get her out of the storm. There's a warm wet spot on his chest from where blood has dribbled from the back of her head. She has a possible concussion and maybe even hypothermia; her breathing is a touch ragged. Sticks are snagged in her clothing as if she's run through the deep woods.

The trail is quickly being covered over and he's having a hard time following it. There's no way to stay focused. He's weaving and only knows he's gone off track when he feels the slight incline as he totters up onto the snow-thickened scrub. Soon he won't be able to tell the difference.

He has no cell phone. Everyone in his world is within a hundred yards of him at almost all times. Nobody ever needs to get ahold of him that desperately, and he worries about how easily he might become dependent on it. Calling Judith or Duchess in the middle of the night just to hear the sound of their voices. Or if he gets turned around on the paths, suddenly snapping the phone to his ear and asking Murph, Heya, I think I'm lost, can you come find me? Murph answering, What the shite, man? You're twelve feet away, I could piss and hit your shoes.

But in Three Rivers cell phones are pretty much a moot point anyway because there are no relay towers. Some of the girls climb up onto the dorm roof and shout, I've got two bars! One! Two! I've got none! One! Duchess chases after them with ladles, rapping the backs of their legs. It's what he sees.

Now he's bringing another young girl to his cottage. One he's got his hands on, pressing the palm of his hand to her sternum to check her heartbeat. The shadow of serious trouble that already surrounds him abruptly grows and deepens. Maybe he causes these things to happen somehow. The fuck is wrong with him.

She stirs in his arms. "Daddy?"

Finn wonders how he should answer. He wants to comfort her. Waking up in a storm being carried in the arms of a blind man whacking his cane around, it's bound to spook a kid. But saying, Yes, Daddy's right here, angel, just isn't going to work.

He hefts her a little higher so he can speak quietly in her ear. "You'll be all right."

Struggling weakly, she shifts and the blood leaks down across the back of his left hand, warming his knuckles in the cold. "Heya, man," she says, "what are you doing with me?"

"I'm carrying you."

"Oh."

"You're hurt."

"Am I?"

"I think so. You hit your head."

"I remember. Wasn't me who thumped it." She brushes snow from herself, then swats at his chest, neck, face. She takes off his glasses. They're thick with ice and she clears them, then awkwardly replaces them on his nose.

She grunts softly like she's mulling over the scene, deciding on what to say next.

"Where's your dog, blind man?"

"I don't have one."

"I thought all you folk had dogs."

"Not me," he says.

"How do you get around, then?"

"I walk."

"Yeah, man, but do you know where you're going or do you just mostly hope for the best?"

"A little of both."

"Your ears are blood red."

"I don't have a hat."

Her breath is hot against his chin. "Well, that is a foolish thing."

"So people keep telling me."

"You got metal in your head."

It stops him. "How do you know that?"

"Where you taking me?"

There's an abrasiveness to her words, and he finds it

refreshing. It's better than listening to all that hep-cat juvie talk. It's not a Southern accent exactly but it's close enough that he sees her as the Tennessee belle who moved up the block from him when he was fourteen. A teen beauty queen who was always talking about riding the floats in the Apple Cider Pageant or Blueberry Day Parade.

He imagines her there in his arms, staring up at his face, blue-eyed with a spatter of freckles across her cheeks, a darker beauty mark at the corner of her eye. Dirty blond hair always loose and wild. The Blueberry Queen.

Finn starts forward again and says, "How about if we put this conversation on hold until we're out of the storm?"

"Time's low."

"What?"

He feels her shrug. "I'm not afraid of a little snow. You?" The hard wind tears her words from him so that it sounds like she's being pulled away, even though she's here in his arms. "There's plenty worse to fear in this holler. Aren't you aware?"

"Let's get to my place and I'll call someone to help," he tells her.

"God no, you want to die?"

"What?"

"Don't call no one."

He frowns and feels the ice crystals trapped in the furrows of his forehead. "Tell me why."

"We got to settle accounts."

"Who does?"

A grunt rumbles in her chest. It's the sound of a very old and bitter woman. "Don't everybody?"

"Listen—"

"You listen to me, man."

The dread and determination are distinct in her voice. He's heard resolve like this before, and knows the truth of it immediately.

"Explain what you mean," he says.

"I mean you need to listen so no big wrongs come this way. That might not mean much to you but it's of considerable stake to me." It hurts her to speak, the words softening as she tries to concentrate beyond the pain. "They say you blind folk got good ears. You hearing me good, blind man?"

"Yes. Can you walk?"

"If you put me on my feet and lend me a shoulder, I'll see about it."

He eases her down carefully. "What's your name?"

"Harley Moon."

"Moon?"

She clucks her tongue. "I said it."

"Like on the tombstones?"

"That graveyard is full of my people. Most holes around here are."

Sometimes when he's sitting on the back porch of his cottage and the breeze is right, he can hear someone walking there among the wrecked gravestones. He's called out before but never gets a response. "You visit them much?"

"This is what you want to talk about, man?"

"Just asking."

"They got no real need of me, nor me of them. What

are you doing prowling around back there with my late kin?"

"I live nearby."

"I know that. But it doesn't answer the question."

He hears the wind chimes clatter on the porch of his cottage. They're bamboo with Asian symbols carved into them. They strike together with a dull clacking. Not particularly musical but they're distinct from the ringing metal chimes hanging near the front doors of the three academy buildings. Roz hung them all in place shortly after she and Finn arrived at St. Val's. It was a good idea, but Finn can't help feeling a mild resentment toward Roz for it. Anytime anyone does something helpful it pisses him off.

"You listening to me, blind man?"

"What?"

"I said—"

"Can you make it to the school?"

"No, not there."

"Why not?"

"Not there, please."

There's a hint of fear in her voice. Somebody thumped her. There are worse things than a little snow. She should be looked after. He thinks Roz might be back by now. "We have a nurse. She can help you."

"Can't go there to the Hotel, I said."

He's heard the holler folk still referring to the academy as the Hotel. It hasn't been a hotel in forty years, but small-town memories are long and stubborn. "Tell me why."

"It's not safe. They'll be coming sooner or later."

"Who?"

"You ask a lot of simpleton questions."

"I'm starting to get that feeling."

There's a slight popping sound as she snaps her mouth shut. He sees the Tennessee beauty queen with her lips smoothed, grinning at him, flirting the way she did but always dancing away. He'd ask her what a Blueberry Day Parade was all about, and she'd answer, Blueberries, a'course.

The wooden chimes are louder. The trail leads to the walkway in front of his cottage, already cleared once by Murphy. Finn stumbles a bit as his feet touch cement.

Harley grabs hold of his arm and tries to steady him. "This your place?"

"Yes."

"Right here within view of every hotel window? Don't you worry that they stare at you at night?"

"Who?"

A shrug of thin shoulders inside an oversized jacket. "Anybody."

"Come inside. Let me call someone."

She follows Finn inside. Considering the situation with Vi, he should be more careful. Here he is inviting another underage girl inside his place, but what the hell else is he supposed to do? He goes for the phone but Harley grips his wrist. Her hand is extremely rough for such a small girl, and she sort of slaps him across the knuckles. It's an assertive and humiliating gesture.

Instead, he gets a towel, bandages, and hydrogen peroxide from the bathroom. She snaps the towel from him and wipes down his face before she does her own. She dries her hair with quick, violent motions. He holds the bandages and peroxide out but she ignores him and eventually he puts them down on the kitchen table.

"This is a lonely place, what you got here," she says.

"Why do you say that?"

"There aren't no pictures on the walls. Should have some, for visitors at least."

He's never thought of it before. She's right. He imagines how empty a house without pictures on the walls looks. Roz has never said anything about it. He thinks of Ray's apartment in the city. Long wood floors, lots of nice furniture, the best stereo and home-theater equipment available, but no photos, paintings, or prints. The burning white walls leading up to a vaulted ceiling like a glacier.

This little girl makes him wonder.

"What do you do there, at the Hotel?" she asks.

Like he might say elevator operator or bellhop. "I'm a teacher."

"What do you teach?"

"Literature."

"What they call modern? Or what they say is classical?"

"Both."

"So that's why you got so many books around," Harley says. "Dad likes Westerns. Someone reads these ones to you?"

"They're mine, from when I could see."

"Yeah, I can see the scar on your head now, since your hair's wet. How do you teach somebody words when you can't read them yourself?"

"I have an assistant who helps me. She reads me my students' essays so I can grade them."

"So what happened to you?"

It's a question almost terrifying in its simplicity. It's the one that gets all the wheels turning forward and backward. It makes him wag his head. That's his only possible response.

She steps to the fridge and he can hear her uncorking the half-full bottle of Zinfandel and swigging directly from it.

Wonderful. A drunk underage girl covered with bruises in his place. He might as well hold his wrists out and just wait here for the snap of the cuffs.

She burps without covering her mouth, with no embarrassment. "You got a girlfriend?"

"Yes."

"She the nurse?"

It's not exactly a secret that he and Roz are an item, but there's something about the way Harley Moon says it that makes him think that someone told her this in confidence. "How do you know that?"

"So she's not just your partner."

"My partner?"

"I know some things. I been around. I heard some chatter."

"Whose chatter?"

"The worst kind. The kind I wasn't supposed to hear. But I got big ears. It's the only way to keep my family out of any real bad trouble, as much discomfort as they can keep out of, and them who want to stay out. I look out for my little brothers and sisters, 'cause the bigger ones are touched. But sometimes folks see my ears are twitching, and then I'm in the path of misery myself."

He thinks, Christ, how this girl talks in romantic tragic terms. This dying town has taught them their own kind of merciless poetry. "I don't know what you're saying."

"Yes, you do. Things aren't good for you, blind man. You got an ill will thinking on you."

"An ill will? What do you mean?"

"Make it right."

"Make what right?"

He feels very stupid. Has he ever asked this many questions? Even when he woke up in the dark in his hospital bed? He holds his palms up to the girl trying to get her to slow down and make some sense.

"I'm trying to help. I want to do some good. So pay what you owe. Do it fast. Do it now."

Finn listens to her drink down the rest of the wine and thinks about exactly how many academy rules and criminal laws he's currently breaking. He hopes the storm's bad enough that Judith isn't watching his door. Or Violet. The shit you have to worry about, every second of the day.

He repeats himself. "What do you mean by that? And how do you know about the metal plate in my head?"

Harley Moon doesn't answer him. She floats around the room for a minute, hitting one spot and then another. Finn gets the distinct feeling she's just looking at him from different angles. Now here, now here. Checking out his scars, the blank gaze. Her footsteps soften. There's a willful, strained sound at the back of her throat, as if she's urging him to make the right choice.

"Harley?"

A breath of cold air sweeps against his throat and then there's only warmth and silence. The implacable, impenetrable darkness seems to almost thin for an instant. Now here, now here. The girl is gone.

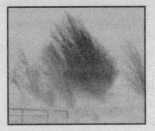

A HALF HOUR LATER, ROZ WALKS in, stamps snow from her boots, and asks, "What's happened?"

Only one second inside the room and she's already aware. Again Finn thinks that he somehow gives off signals, generates a field that alerts the sensitive to his predicaments.

He ventures a lie, never the smartest move when you're talking to someone who's already on to you. "Nothing."

"Don't give me that, Finn." There's no real heat in her voice at all. "Was that Treato kid in here again?"

"No."

"Thank Christ for that. All the wine's gone. Who are these bandages for? Are you all right?"

Roz is sniffing the air. For what? Cookies? Spermicide? Unoxidized blood?

She moves in on him too fast, the way he hates. She blitzes forward until she's only a half inch from his nose, so intense and demanding that he rears his chin back. Fuck. He forgets how quickly she reverts to the woman she used to be, the one working all the action.

"Was it Vi?"

"I told you, it wasn't Vi."

"Jesus, another one?"

"Nothing like that. A holler girl. Twelve or thirteen. She was hurt. I found her unconscious in the graveyard."

"God damn it, Finn—"

"You listening? She was hurt."

"What were you doing back there? You know you shouldn't go walking on your own with a storm breaking."

As they often do, they talk at cross-purposes. Five years they've been together, and they've never been able to get through a conversation without heading off on some kind of fucked-up tangent. "Forget that, Roz. Her name is Harley Moon."

"What's that?" Her breath squeezes from her. "Moon?"

He relates everything that Harley said to him. What she told him and what she implied. He knows he's not doing a good job of showing how concerned he is because Roz is tsking now. It's a trait she's picked up from Judith, and it really crawls up his ass. He's just not getting his point across.

"What was she doing out there?"

"I don't know."

"Who hit her?"

"I told you, I don't know."

She tosses the empty wine bottle in the trash. "Well, she couldn't have been too bad off if she left on her own. Did she make a play for you?"

"Not every teenage girl has a crush on me."

"That's a precarious position to take, Finn. Okay, I'll rephrase the question. Did you touch her?"

"I carried her inside."

"Did you touch her?"

He knows he deserves this, but Jesus Christ.

"No. This girl was hurt and scared."

The answer actually seems to calm Roz a bit. "But she didn't say why."

"No."

"Maybe she was running away from some aggressive boy."

"Maybe."

"Or she didn't want to catch a beating from her father. You know how these holler families are."

"Yeah. But she didn't want me to call the cops, and she didn't want to come to the school to get in from out of the blizzard or get her head looked at."

The tsking again, hard and flat. "They don't trust the police any more than city street kids do, and they don't trust outsiders like us, no matter how long we live in their backyard."

"I know, you're right," he says, and closes his lips on any further response. "She calls this place the Hotel."

"They all do. They always have."

"They've got long memories."

"Everyone does."

Maybe she's talking about him, or herself. Either way it's true.

"She knew about us," he says. "That we're together."

"So what? We've been up here in the sticks for three years. We're sort of an open secret."

"Even to the townspeople?"

"Sure, I suppose. Why not? They don't care enough one way or the other."

"Not like we move in the same social circles. I've never said more than two sentences to any of them."

"You've never said more than two sentences to just about anybody, Finn."

Roz reaches out and runs a hand through his hair, brushing his curls back, covering his scars again. She rests her palm on the side of his face and rubs, like she's trying to scour lipstick smears away. She's telling him something in that touch but he has no idea what. He knows it'll come to him, later, when he least expects it, in the night or in the middle of class. Something will click and it'll all come together, and he'll think, That's what it meant.

He should let it go, but he can't. The girl has stirred the cop in him, gotten him buzzing. "Harley said someone's thinking bad thoughts about us."

"Bad thoughts? About us?"

"An ill will, she said."

"What's that even mean?"

"I'm not sure."

"Does it even matter? They're all fucking nuts out here. Crystal meth has taken over this valley in a big bad way. Could she have been using?"

"I suppose, but it didn't seem like it to me."

"You would know?"

"Probably."

"You can't tell who's cooking or distributing. Whole families are involved now. The children act as couriers. They bathe the babies in one washtub and cook in another. They're raised in the life, it's normal and natural to them."

"Sure."

Finn tops it as the worst street drug to come into vogue the last couple decades. Fuckers are making it in their bathtubs, burning out their eyes with gas fumes, selling corrosive poison because they're screwing up the proportions of acetone, methanol, and lye. Some of the cookers use paint thinner. It's getting harder to get pseudoephedrine and iodine nowadays, so these part-time chemists who never finished high school are experimenting with anything that looks like it might have a similar chemical composition. Finn once made a bust on a lab where the teen idiots thought the red phosphorus they needed came off the heads of matches. They'd scraped thousands, not realizing that the phosphorus is on the striker pad. You could only guess at how many people they'd poisoned because they'd gone to the wrong website for instructions.

Still, it still feels odd that it happens here in the hills, the farmhouses, the backwoods. When Finn was a kid this was always his father's idea of heaven. They'd vacation up around this way a couple times a year. His old man would talk about retirement and how he planned to live out his days fishing, hunting, playing the harmonica, whittling. Finn's mother would say, You'll slice your fingers off and I'll be stuck cutting your steak for you for the rest of my life.

Roz opens the fridge and gets out a full bottle of Chardonnay, uncorks it, and pours two glasses. She sits beside him on the couch, pressing the cold wine lightly against his forearm. He takes the glass and sips from it, wishing he had a double shot of Jameson instead.

She places her hand on his leg and her fingers slide toward his inner thigh, coaxing. Sometimes this means she's worried about him, sometimes it's a subtle demand for sex. The first time she ever touched him like this was in a grease trap all-night diner, where she spoke in a husky, lust-laden voice and implored him to stop Ray.

She'll never age for him. She'll always be twenty-five, wearing the white nurse's uniform that he first saw her in.

She always tells him when she dyes her hair, reading the colors off the boxes and saying each name with a kind of glee—*Light Golden Chestnut, Creamy Caramel Twist, Almond Rocca, Chocolate Cherry*—they make him hungry. But his image of her will never change. She remains a brunette with natural red highlights that shimmer like copper when she throws her head back. Her hair will always be cropped short. Even when his hands are working through cascades of it falling past her shoulders, he can see only the boyish haircut, parted on the left and feathered across her forehead.

Her smile is knowing and slightly coy. Her laughter discriminating but thick, and she usually raises the back of her hand to stifle the sound. Eyes expressive and full of interest. Lips glossy as if she used balm, but later he found out this is entirely natural.

He remembers how, as she checked Ray's bandages and fed him ice chips, gentle but tough as she explained how he might lose the foot, Finn thought she'd be the perfect girl for Ray.

Roz likes to talk in bed. Not the fun, dirty stuff, just whatever's on her mind while he's trying to get his groove.

Somehow the opening maneuvers of their lovemaking cause her to consider the great questions of her life.

He'll be working away, doing his thing, seeking out her nipples with his tongue, pressing back her knees, slotting himself in, and in the middle of it she'll suddenly ask something like, Do you think it's wrong that I haven't spoken to my father the last fifteen years?

It gets distracting. He loses his place a lot. He wonders what it would be like if he started talking that way, riding her to the edge and then blurting out, Roz, honey, I'm going to kill Ray someday.

As uncomfortable and angry as Roz gets with the idea of Vi coming on to him, she's also titillated. Jealousy causes a spike in her desire for him. Whenever she sees the girls helping him out in any way, Roz moves in and gets a touch territorial.

"How'd the shopping excursion go?" he asks.

He's clearly shifting topics as Roz's hand grows more insistent on his thigh, but he needs a chance to focus. The throb of a headache is starting up beneath his scars, which always makes him think that the metal plate there is dinged, dented, turning to rust.

"A good time. I always have a good time with Duchess, even if we're doing nothing. She's a storyteller, has hundreds of relatives, and every one of them has taught her a grand and moral lesson. They all have such wonderful names. Her father is Justice James the Third. Her sister is Sweet Forgiveness. She mentioned a cousin called Truth and I'm still not sure if he's real or just a metaphor."

He's a metaphor, Finn thinks, they all are.

"At least this town has gone out of the way to dress up for the holidays," she says. "They've got lights strung up on the lampposts and hanging over Main Street, and there's a huge tree in front of the courthouse with hundreds of candy canes and decorations. They don't want to act like the place is shutting down store by store. They're trying to keep their spirits up."

"I bet the guys who've lost their jobs at the mill and factory think it's all a big waste of time and money."

"And it is, but it's important too, right? You know that. You've got to play the game, keep up the mask, the false front, otherwise what's the point? You give in and run." She finishes her glass and pours another. "They seem to have a thing against Santa, though. They've got Jesus and Rudolph all over the place, the chipmunks, the wise men, the Virgin Mary, but no Santa. I'm serious. Doesn't that strike you as strange?"

"Yes," he admits.

"I'm serious."

"You said that. I agree, it's kind of strange."

She's always spotting some kind of weird subversion or sedition up here because she's so bored. Like they've got a cult in the sticks to stamp out St. Nick. Back in the city, she clipped articles about dirty cops and mob informants and a corrupt mayor. She knew firsthand that conspiracies existed, and it shook her faith in the world, got her searching beneath appearances. The scrapbook is under the bed. Finn picks it up sometimes just because he likes to feel the weight in his hands.

"Maybe it's a backlash," she suggests. "This isn't exactly the heartland but it might as well be. They might hate Catholics here as much as they hate anybody else, so good-bye St. Nick."

"Sounds reasonable to me," Finn says, thinking,

Santa's a Catholic front man? But what, Rudolph's a WASP?

This is one of the reasons why he likes Roz so much. She always comes at the world from a different perspective, sees things he never expects no matter how much time they've got behind them.

Her fingers return to his leg, massaging, assertive and determined. She leans in and kisses him with a mouthful of wine, which she allows to run down her chin to splash his shirt. She likes doing things like this, leaving signs behind her, making a mess, so that later when he's cleaning up he'll think of her.

He says, "Hey now, that bottle was eight bucks, don't waste it."

It brings a throaty chuckle out of her that works into him until he's hard and needy. This is Finn at his best and worst, and she knows it.

Wrapped in each other's arms, still kissing, she lets him lead her to the bedroom even though he's got to brush his back against the bare walls to get there. He still can't fully concentrate. He's assailed by the idea of not having any pictures or paintings and wants to ask if it bothers her. Three years of these cold, impersonal rooms, but she never said anything about it. Finn begins to speak but her lips tighten on his and she swallows his words down her throat.

They fall backward onto the bed. Roz enjoys undressing him. She's adept and softly scratches at his chest and neck as she eases off his shirt. She kisses his belly button, catches skin between her teeth. She presses her fingers against his toned stomach, then quickly undoes his belt. She unzips him, and works his pants off. He's thankful that she offers so many caresses and nips. Sometimes, especially when he's excited, he can forget the contours of his own body. He needs his skin to be on fire.

She digs her nails into his ribs. He likes it and says so. She laughs in his face. She scratches harder.

In a moment, Roz is naked. She feeds Finn her breasts and he suckles them for a long while. Again the throaty chuckle escapes her as he eases his erection forward into her hand.

Pumping gently she brings him to full hardness. She spits in her hand and jerks him faster as he juts on his knees. She leans up and kisses him passionately and slides his cock across her belly. He relishes the feel of her flesh.

The things that can drive you out of your head. He holds her legs open and licks her calves and fits himself at the edge of her cunt and waits.

She laughs again and bucks forward and he's inside her.

"Say my name," she tells him.

When it's like this, she wants to hear Rose, not Roz. It's her real name, but she gave it up a long time ago. But she comes back to it in bed.

"Rose."

"Again."

"Rose."

"Yes, that's it."

"You're Rose, a beautiful rose."

First time they met, she said, I'm Rose but everyone calls me Roz.

He asked, Why?

Why what?

Why do they call you Roz if it's not your name?

She answered, I suppose because I let them.

Finn fills her tightly and her juices are already flowing thickly, dappling his pubic hair. It's a smell he enjoys as he plunges and keeps his pace slow and even, going deep so she knows every thrust has a real meaning, a true purpose, whatever it might be.

Everyone needs affirmation. Roz moans and the sound is laced with a sweet, self-indulgent giggle. Sweat streams across his face. The wind chimes are clacking together out front, the solid thunking nearly in perfect sync with his action. He decides he's got to get some prints up. Renoir, Van Gogh. The snow pounds against the bedroom window, urging him on, a force of will to add to his own.

It's telling him, Come on, come on. The hum of the wind is impatient, almost angry. He can feel its attention on him.

This is a natural reaction for him, treating the sounds of inanimate objects as if they were people. His psychiatrist says it's normal for someone in his *situation, under these circumstances,* to personify *things*—stressing the word "things" in such a way that there's almost a sexual connotation. My thing. Your thing. Let's discuss this thing. She tells him that the brain is deprived and needs to be fed. He's an imaginative man, she says. She's right. He kicks into high gear.

Finn gets in too close and bumps his forehead against Roz's. They both say "ow." She whimpers, "Don't close your eyes."

He thought they were open but realizes now they're not. "I won't."

"Look at me," she groans.

"I will. I am."

"You have such beautiful eyes."

Women have always loved his eyes, and he never appreciated it. They're brown, not blue like most of the girls he knew went for, but they're flecked with gold and somehow that always got to women.

Roz licks his eyelashes. It invigorates and repulses him.

His cock continues to heat inside her as he quickens his tempo, and the quick burn of orgasm is already nearing. He locks hands on her hips and pulls her toward him so violently that she's instantly seated on top of him. Snow snaps against the glass like it wants him to turn and look for a photo op. Hey, over here, over here. He worries about Harley. He wants to know why she asked, Do you want to die?

Won't Ray be surprised when the blind guy shows up ready to kill or die in the middle of—

The honest rake of Roz's nails recommits him. She grunts and stiffens as he slams forward. Like always he's thankful that he can get her off first. She cums hard and immediately orgasms a second time. He holds himself deeply inside her and leans down until his nose brushes her and says, "You're lovely, Rose." Her pussy tightens to such an extreme that he lets out a yelp.

Roz pants, and when he's nearly there she says, "Did you know Duchess's granddaughter was denied entrance to St. Val's?"

God fuck it.

Fighting to retain his rhythm, Finn flubs cresting on the wave of climax. Roz zigs to his zag and misses meeting his thrust. He hisses in frustration, and now he's thinking about what that scene between Duchess and Judith must've been like.

With the lightest touch to the small of his back Roz calms him and gets him back on track so he can finish. He locks up and grunts and spills himself inside of her.

Finn drops forward and turns on his side, pulling her to him so he doesn't slip free. His expression must be ludicrous and she whispers, "Sorry."

"Jesus Christ, Roz!"

"I know. I'm sorry. I'm sorry."

"God damn, honey!"

"Let's just—I mean—"

They relax like that for a while and lightly stroke each other. The tips of their tongues toy together. He lies back with a few bad thoughts starting to squirm loose. The storm is knocking at the window. It wants him to turn and look. Over here, over here.

Roz is about to say more, she's at the point that she wants to discuss *things,* but Finn feigns sleep, wondering if she's visited Ray in prison lately.

Some of these things he can speak of, some he never will. He keeps them under wraps because he needs them there, constantly being fed into the furnace. It's what warms him, it's what keeps the engine going. He is planning to kill a man and he thinks that, even though his shrink only hears about twenty percent of what he says, she might catch wise to that. It doesn't much matter.

What else could she say except that it was normal, it was understandable, let's return to that, let's revisit that, let's explore that, your time is up. Roz senses the truth. She understands. She knows he's waiting and she's decided to wait alongside him. She has her own mad fantasies, although she's never shared them. She probably dreams of murder too, or at least great pain. Some of it is her own, some of it is Finn's, some of it is reserved for others. He's tried to cut her free but she never leaves. She's afraid to go it on her own. She's always needed to stick to a rough man. She's as confused about love as everybody else. Lately, though, he's noticed a change in her. She's both drawing away and asserting herself. It's a good thing, probably. He suspects she's going to kick free soon. Maybe she's found herself a new rough man. Maybe it's because of this whole Violet situation, maybe it's just the right thing to do. Five years stuck with a blind asshole is forever. He's got a very small and petty reason to live, but it's his and he holds to it selfishly. It's not time for him to move yet, but when it is, he will spring and strike. His story has it all. Friendship, partnership, mob wars, deception, betrayal, and Finn just doesn't feel much. Another man would look for answers. But Finn knows there is no answer. Standing beside him are his many ghosts, all his mistakes and lost loves, the dead and the nearly dead and the missing. Finn tilts his chin. The past is cloudy but he feels like he can almost see the future unfolding before him. In the darkness he's aware and his hands are trembling so badly with the need to do something that they nearly hum. Your time is up.

WHATEVER DUCHESS IS COOKING, SHE'S GOING heavy on the molasses and lemon. Finn moves to their table in the dining hall, which used to be a restaurant known as the Carriage House back in the hotel days. It stirs his imagination, thinking of late-nineteenth-century travelers stopping at the inn. Captains of industry up from the city heading into New England spending the night, talking politics of the day. It's not difficult for him to hear coach wheels spinning loosely on bent axles. It's the kind of thing that makes him drift.

He arcs his chin toward Roz. He's about to ask where everybody is, but he doesn't get a chance. She tells him, "Damn it, I forgot something. Back in a few minutes."

"Forgot what?"

"Back at the store."

"At the store? Which store?"

"The market."

"You mean you're going back to town?"

"Yes. Back in a jiff."

A jiff? The fuck's a jiff? "You can't, it's a whiteout, isn't it?" Just walking over from his cottage has left them both breathing heavily.

"It's not that bad, really, and this is important."

"What is?"

"I need to get something, make sure of something."

"Need what?" He moves to grasp her and she dodges him, always so fast on her feet. The girl always in the center of the action. He tries again and misses again. "Make sure of what?"

"Back soon!"

"Wait a second," he calls. "Roz? Rose!"

But she's gone.

He thinks, This got something to do with the lack of Santas?

A jiff? She's never said "jiff" in her whole damn life.

Before he can sit, Duchess touches him on the elbow. He knows her hand. She smells of ham and honey. There are subtler scents too. He coasts for a moment on the aroma of brown sugar and chocolate.

She's got him by a couple of inches. Her voice comes down from above. She says, "Hold on, let me dry your hair before you catch your death from pneumonia," and pulls out what must be a dish towel, hopefully a clean one. She begins to roughly rub his head with it. He thinks of Harley doing the same thing to him. His neck cracks twice while Duchess snaps him back and forth. "Don't you think you ought to wear a hat if you go out in the middle of a blizzard?"

Again with the hat.

"I only have two and I don't like them," he says, which is true. They're both wool caps with a poof ball on top. His old man used to wear a homburg on special occasions, dressed to the nines. Finn feels a slight tug of nostalgia wishing you could get away with that sort of thing nowadays.

"Yeah, those I've seen on you were terrible. Made you look like a special child standing on a corner waiting for the short bus."

"So why didn't you tell me?"

"Figured you already knew and were just asserting yourself."

"Who the hell asserts themselves with stupid-looking hats?"

She clucks. "Not for me to question how you empower your own self."

"I wasn't empowering myself with a wool hat."

"No," she says, "not with that poofy ball on top. Not that way. But you should've told me sooner. It's Christmas, I would've bought you something different, something you'd like. You a fedora man?"

Finn thinks about it. "I don't think so."

"Nuh, I'm not sure I like 'em either. Not since Harlem, about '73 or 4. Men knew how to wear a fedora back then. It was all in the tilt. So I'll consider it some. You think I want to trudge all over creation, up to your office and out to your little house just to spoon-feed you chicken broth? Clean your dirty balled-up tissues? Carry you to the bathroom when you got the runs?"

"I can't imagine you would, no," he says, although she's already done it for him three years running. He catches the flu. He hates hats. He likes broth.

"It's fine for you and Roz, of course. I don't mind ministrating to you two. But Judith, she's another one trying to empower herself in stupid ways."

"Say what now?"

"Oh, you heard me. You damn well heard me"

Even while her hands are on him, combing his wavy hair down with her fingers, he sees her stirring pots. He can't get close enough to look inside and check what she's cooking. He wants to see just what the hell would need so much goddamn stirring. He doesn't know where the image of a black cook comes from, some old Technicolor film probably, or a commercial from the seventies, but it's so ingrained that he can't shake it.

Duchess takes his wrist and pulls him down to his chair. She sits beside him and says, "And instead she's left hurt even worse than before, and sitting in a pool of her own tears. Or vomit. She's taken to drinking Irish whiskey. You know how many times I've had to clean her up lately?"

Not the sort of thing they should be discussing out in the open, but she's past the point of trying to mask her indignation. There's a real bitterness there. Her rage speaks to his rage.

"Duchess—"

"Isn't that my way?" she asks. "Don't I always give my best?"

"You do."

"You think I'm selfish because I have expectations?"

"No."

"Everyone else does. And none of them, not one can say I left them freezing their fool heads off—"

"Hey now—"

"—or lying with their face half in the toilet, with their bloomers around their knees. Nobody can say that."

"Nobody would want to either."

"They sure as hell wouldn't! That's exactly what I'm talking about!"

A painful lament has wedged itself in her voice, a sound he's never heard from her before. She's right there in front of him, solid and unmoving, but he still sees her with a big ladle, running around from pan to pan.

The idea of Duchess, a cornerstone of the academy, unhappy here makes him worried in a way he hasn't felt in a lot of years. He imagines her reaching out and shaking the pillars down around their heads.

"I heard about your granddaughter being turned down at St. Val's," he says. "I'm sorry."

"They told her it was her grades."

"And you don't believe that's the reason."

"I think it's simpler to keep a black teenage girl who has a baby from attending the academy, even if she deserves to get in, than it is for the admissions board to face up to the grief they'll get from the rich white-bread snobs who think the stink of the streets will rub off on them. She's an A student. So how can it be her grades?"

There are already eight black students at St. Val's, eight Asians, and a pair of sisters from Mexico City who speak in richly textured accents that remind him of East Harlem. So Finn doesn't think that racism is quite the dress of the day that Duchess is making it out to be. The country-club set might stick up their noses and pass white-bread snooty comments, but they do that everywhere, to everybody. And the blue-collar parents might bitch and piss a little if their property values are directly affected, but he doesn't think they give a shit if their daughters sit side by side with a black girl.

He knows the game, senses it at work all the time,

it's always there, but doesn't feel it at St. Val's any more than anywhere else.

"How'd she do on her entrance exams?"

Duchess lets loose a breath she's been holding in for days. It warms his face. "She didn't do too well on them, I admit. But she learned from her mistakes, studied extra hard, and was hoping to retake them. But she'll have to wait until next year. Not next semester, but next year."

"That's standard, Duchess."

"Maybe so, maybe not—"

"It is, trust me."

"—and she'd be an asset to this academy. She's got plenty to offer."

"I believe you."

"Her extracurricular activities list is three times as long as your pecker."

"Hey now!"

"And none of this French club or cheerleading shit, like some of these girls. My baby was out there truly helping people. She's assisted in homeless shelters, rehab clinics, worked with abused women and the mentally challenged. Crack babies. She's made a difference in the world. That girl has a heart inside her that drives her to comfort others less fortunate. And she takes care of her own child all the while."

"What's her name?" he asks, seeing Duchess really slapping those big wooden spoons around now, banging enormous skillets and pans like drums, steam rising and kinking her hair even more. Her face drips with sweat. Her lips are contorted. She looks up and spots Finn standing there watching her, and she glowers at him, vicious, unyielding.

"My granddaughter is Ruby. She's sixteen. Her own baby is Gem, and she'll be one at the end of January."

It gets Finn smiling, but his smile doesn't lift Duchess's mood. He figures that she's not only upset because Ruby was denied entrance to St. Val's, but also because Duchess wants her own family close by. It gets lonely here. Duchess, like Judith, like all of them maybe, has reached a turning point.

"They're in the Bronx?" he asks.

"With my daughter, Lady. Did I ever tell you how I wound up here?"

She's given him two different versions, and they bear no resemblance to each other. He's decided they're both lies. Anyone worth a damn has secrets.

He says, "No."

"Yes, I have. Two or three times, in fact. Isn't that right?"

"My memory's not what it used to be."

"Like hell. I'm guessing it's only gotten better. Anyway, you want to hear the truth? The real truth?"

"No," Finn says, which is the truth.

It doesn't stop her. She's got a need to confess. It's his own fault. He's drawing the venom from her, like sucking at a snakebite.

He wonders, Where the fuck is everybody? What did Roz forget at the store that was so important? He puts out a hand because he wants to pat Duchess's shoulder, make contact, calm her a touch if he can. Show some support. But she shifts aside so he can't reach her, the big spoons held up like knives, ready to thrust into his chest.

"It's not much of a story. Judith's son, he was in rehab a few years back, down in the Bronx Psychiatric Center, and I was cooking for those people. She liked the food and thought I'd make a fine addition to the school. There it is. Sounds so . . . so *coincidental* it would almost be funny, forgetting about all the drug addicts and how I used to hand out methadone like a side dish with most meals."

"What the hell was her kid doing down in a Bronx psych hospital?"

"I'm supposed to know that? I don't know that. You want to know that, you go ask her. Can I go on?"

"Sure."

"Well, thank you. Now I'm here, a great-grandmother who's nowhere near her babies. That hurts, that hurts in a way I just can't explain, you understand?"

"Yes, I—"

"Stop interrupting. You don't have kids so maybe you can't see your way. My point being, I worked hard in my life, harder than most. Taking care of my parents, my man, my child, and each one of them giving up on life in their own ways. Every one of them trying to throw their lives down the sewer. But I held strong."

She's right. It's not much of a story. A common drama, an average tragedy just like everyone's. When you boiled it down to the highlights you realized that you were where you were because you took a left turn instead of a right. Because you ran a stop sign. Because you went back for your wallet. Your father didn't come home. Your mother burned the milk. You stayed over too long. Told the white lie. Fudged the report. Skimmed off the top. Read between the lines. Didn't pay the ticket. Couldn't take the shot.

"You should be proud," he says. It's bullshit, and he knows how trite it sounds even before the words are off his lips.

"I am proud, but I'm also angry because my baby girl Ruby has worked hard all her life, and I don't want her to have to go my route. I don't want her to have to run into someone on a mental hospital food line who takes a chance on her to get somewhere. She deserves to make it on her own."

"But even so, what you're really angry about is that you couldn't pull any strings."

"Hell yes," Duchess admits. She swings her arms and the sugary scent rolls out from beneath the heavy odor of sweat. "Ought to be good for something, putting my time in like this. Asked Judith if she could make an exception and she made an ugly face like I'd just farted in church."

"She wouldn't mind church-farting nearly as much. St. Val's is all she has. She wants all of us to play by every rule."

"Except herself. I wonder what school regulation says she's supposed to drink on the job and get her head stuck in the shitter with her nasty old-lady bloomers down her ankles?"

"We're always the exceptions to our own rules."

He doesn't have to tell her that. She knows it, maybe better than him, and for a second he wonders if she's going to say so. She gulps a deep breath and lets it swirl around inside her, and then lets it out a brooding exhalation that flips his front curls.

The doors open and several chattering girls enter. Duchess stands, pushes her chair in, turns to the kitchen, and gets ready to start serving dinner.

"Why aren't you home with your babies, Duchess?" he asks.

"My children can take care of themselves. It's these intelligent ones here who did so well on their entrance exams that would be licking tree bark without me."

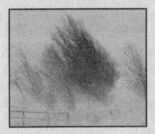

MURPHY SITS AND SAYS, "I'M PARCHED! *Slainte!*"

That means he's raising his eggnog for a Christmas cheers. Distracted, Finn fumbles for his glass and nearly tips it.

Murph's hand knocks Finn's aside, like swatting a child reaching for matches. It's something the Irishman knows he should never do, but he does it a lot anyway, the prick. Finn swats back and grabs his glass.

"Och, you bastard," Murph says. "No need to be so lively. I just didn't want to see you ruin your lovely meal of lamb."

"And I haven't," Finn tells him.

"You need some mint jelly on it now."

"No, I really don't."

This has to do with them being the two alpha males on campus. There's a curious sort of tension between them even when the rest of the faculty and staff are at the school. The big dogs always have to bark at each other. It reminds Finn of the kind of shit that used to go down between him and Ray.

"Heathen, you're no connoisseur," Murph says. "You just don't know how to eat."

"So Duchess keeps telling me."

"A fine woman there, cooks like me ma, with genuine skill and love. You can taste it in each bite."

Tonight there's honey-baked ham and lamb, and Finn's never tasted it cooked better in his life. There's a lot of laughter in the dining hall, assigned to the five or six tables being used. Even with only a handful of students left on campus, they've broken into their little cliques and subsets.

The emptiness of the large room causes a little snap in the distance that isn't quite an echo. Finn turns his chin to it, sensitive to the noise. It sounds like somebody back there clapping his hands.

Judith is still in her office. She's always late because she wants everyone seated before she arrives. It allows her to control who she sits with, who she impresses herself on. That's a minor but important bit of her sovereignty. Usually she'll sit across from Murphy, on an angle so she doesn't have to look into his eyes but will still be part of the conversation. Judith feels so powerless over her emotions that these small affectations of authority take on a much greater meaning.

Finn understands completely. Egos are delicate. Inconsequential achievements are sometimes the only ones you get.

Murph has a bad shoulder that clicks when he turns his head. He's looking around now, taking notice of the girls, listening in, just like Finn is. Snatches of conversation tumble through the air.

Jesse Ellison is discussing Vonnegut a little too loudly with Lea Grant and Caitlin Jones, probably hoping Finn will hear. Knowing that he will. Suzy and Sally Smyth are quietly snorting with obscene laughter.

Maybe they really have spiked the eggnog, or managed to talk Murphy into doing it for them. Jesse gets nothing out of the other girls and starts invoking Violet's name, trying to involve her, but Vi says little in response. Finn tries not to dwell on Vi but his thoughts have been so jumpy lately that he's almost glad to have her to focus him for the moment.

Violet Treato isn't listening to Jesse but responds with appropriate noises of interest to keep Jesse chattering. Vi's presence is strong enough that it keeps drawing Finn in, making him shift his eyes. It's the one time he's glad for the shades. He thinks, In a lifetime of mistakes, she's only about halfway up the list, but she might be the one to finally bring me down. He still can't shake the feeling he got from touching her. His fingers tremble slightly as if they can still sense her wetness and heat.

Murphy leans in. He smells of shaving lather and whiskey. He's been working nonstop maintaining the walkways in the storm. To keep himself warm he's knocked back a pint or two from his flask. A significant breach of regulations, but what isn't around here? Murph's vitality is always apparent, he's forever on the move. Even drunk in his apartment, he flutters about grabbing different CDs, listening to one or two songs on each, then tossing them aside and finding others. His musical knowledge is impressive. He tries to educate Finn but Finn doesn't like music as much as others might think. He finds it cloying and overpowering. He prefers to hear what's around him, the adornments of background noise.

"Has any more trouble found you lately?" Murph asks.

He says it with just enough wry amusement to make it seem that he knows about Harley Moon in Finn's house. It snaps Finn's chin up and makes him wonder if Murph had seen him out there stumbling around in the snow, holding an unconscious girl in his arms, and let him just continue pitching about.

Finn does one of his blind-guy tricks, takes off his glasses and stares hard, studying Murph.

"And what's that look for?" Murphy asks, a bit shaken. Finn's glad and digs on the feeling of being top dog again, if only for the moment.

"What look?"

"You angry that I've had a wee nip of Jay?"

"Not at all."

"You say that but there's a bit of the lash in your tongue."

"Just don't share with the young wans."

"I'd never."

"No?"

"Hell, they can get their own."

The girls have discussed Murphy and called him everything from cute to hot to sexified and sweet ass and douche bag. They like his Irish accent. Everyone likes his Irish accent. The accent alone is probably what's driven Judith halfway out of her head with desire for him.

When Finn sees Murphy he sees Ray. It makes him a little anxious and sometimes confuses him, but he can't shake it. Slim hips but assertive frame, lips always tilted in a grin, hair black and curling down across the feverish eyes. The whores working the Upper East Side used to call Ray a sweet ass too. Murph has the same compelling self-confidence that Ray had. A graceful strength and the strength of grace.

Murph's neck clicks. He's looking out the window. "In Galway it's the rain that never ceases. It's endless and seeps into everything. The earth, the rock, even the people. Only the dead care for it. The dead and me ma, but she hated anything lively."

Finn's heard Murph curse his mother during drunken midnight bouts. The austere woman drove his father to suicide, he claimed, by her relentless mean-spirited need to crush all learning and humor beneath her heel in the name of pragmatism. She found music, literature, sports, fine food, and good clothes to be a waste of money and time, and in direct violation of God's will.

Mean as a dyke nun surrounded by altar boys, Murph has said, and she'd chase after him with a hurling stick made of ash if he ever missed a Sunday at church. The priests would watch him walking funny down the streets of the city, knowing he was nothing but a mass of bruises and welts. They'd clap him on the back with a hard hand and say, Your mother is a fine, loving, devoted, and high-minded woman.

At first Murph would only nod. When he was older, setting his sights on getting the hell out of Ireland, he'd respond, She murdered my da with the help of you and your like.

"What do you mean the dead care for it?" Finn asks.

"In Galway, we accompany our dead, and our dead travel with us. The funeral procession, we follow behind it, walking through the old city. But the dead are warm in their coffins, they can finally enjoy the weather. Me,

I'm still not wrung out. In Galway it's the rain, and here it's the snow. You can feel it just the same, all the time, even in the middle of summer. The snow well hidden, but always in attendance." He lets loose with a self-effacing laugh and says, "Shite. And the wind of Galway. It hangs inside the ancient rock, and when you hit the face of an alleyway, the wind tears through you like a harridan swooping down. More than one tinker's blown into the river. On days with no breeze, it's waiting. I would come out of my flat and know it was there, calling my name."

"Christ," Finn says, "are you Irish Catholics always like this, or is it only when you get near the sweet baby Jesus' birthday?"

"Always. It's in the blood, and we can't run from it, try as we might. It's our lot in life, that wind and rain and stone. It'll always be with me, I carry it wherever I am."

"You're a fucking laugh riot, Murph."

"That I can be."

Finn knows a little something about carrying your history with you, but Murph's eating his meal now and seems to be done with this track of conversation. He grunts and croons with enjoyment as he chews and swallows. He's hell with the condiments and spices. Finn likes to listen to Murph digging in with such verve. It reminds him of the way he used to eat Dani's meals.

Murphy knocks back a large glass of milk and says, "Where's Judith? She's missing out on this fine meal, and I'll wager she likes mint jelly."

"Twenty says not."

"You're on. I can use the cash."

Again with the jelly. Finn understands that he and

Murphy have nothing really interesting to say to each other. But still, there's a need to shove and tug at the texture of their personalities. He sees Ray grinning at him, looking around at the girls, easing back in his seat, gracefully.

Finn's worried about Harley Moon. He's concerned that Vi is giving him sidelong glances, perhaps growing to hate him as time goes by. He's alarmed that Roz still isn't back and wonders what was so important she had to head into the blizzard again. He wishes he could sneak a couple of swigs from Murph's flask.

"I'd best get back to the shoveling."

"How bad is it out?"

"Growing worse by the very minute. Don't be wandering off back to your cottage. Have someone walk you, I don't need your carcass thawing out come April and ruining my hard-fought landscape."

Finn raises his glass. *"Slainte!"*

"There's a good lad. It's like you were born a son of Michael Collins or Saint Patty himself."

As Murphy stands and turns, Finn sees Ray standing and turning, dressed in his blues, stepping away from his locker. Taped to the inside of the locker door is a letter from a nine-year-old boy written in pencil on a sheet of loose-leaf paper. The kid's scrawl is enormous and angled to the left. In the note he thanks Ray for saving his and his mother's lives during a bodega holdup. Ray broke regs again and marched inside and popped the perp in the chest while Finn called for backup.

Murphy zips up his coat and makes a decision to single Vi Treato out and tell her how lovely she looks with her cheeks glowing such a wild rosy red. Vi says thank you. Murph owns the room as he saunters off.

Suzy Smyth, still too boisterous and loud, comments on Murphy's packed drawers and several of the other girls giggle softly, aware of Finn.

Before Finn takes two bites of the lamb, Judith sidles up to the table. She asks the girls if they like the lamb and they all respond favorably. She sits across from Finn in Murph's seat, knowing it's Murph's seat, still feeling his heat. Finn tries not to think about her underwear. Her *bloomers,* as Duchess put it. Christ, he tries not to think about her so bent out of shape that she needs to drink herself into an oblivion that ends with her passed out on a bathroom floor with her face in the toilet. A discussion starts up around him over something he doesn't give a shit about.

The snowblower growls distantly.

Murphy isn't just a talker, he likes to listen. He asks Finn a lot of questions about his years as a cop. Once, while they were both listening to the cruel strains of some Irish punk band, Murph passed the Jameson and whispered, So open your heart and tell me...do you miss it, brother?

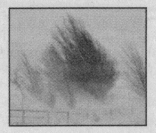

BEING A COP, IT'S GETTING YOUR guts kicked out by twin midgets who live inside your deepest place. You've got your good little fucker and your bad little fucker, both of them taking turns working your soft center.

It's using your action, your gamble, your itch, and your edge every minute of the day. You press down your hate and your cool and let it seep into your thoughts and fists. You hate your gun and you love it. You understand why so many of the fraternal order go out of the game by eating their own pieces. Being a cop, it's everything you've ever heard it was, and it's nothing like that at all.

Your third week on patrol you catch the squeal to a liquor-store holdup.

The owner's been winged and two armed punks are on the run through the neighborhood. Your partner's an old roughneck on the slide, just drawing checks. He's got nineteen of his twenty in and mostly wants to sit back and roust prostitutes, maybe break up the occasional backroom mahjong game because the Chinese humble themselves and slip a little cash.

Serpico's been off the grid for thirty-plus years so you don't rock the boat, but you don't take a cut either. Not that it's offered.

As you reach for the siren and turn the corner ahead the punks go running right in front of the patrol car and you're on the move. The chase is over before it starts. You stamp the gas and are ripping up behind them when they both turn on a dime and fire, unloading full clips into the windshield.

You and the old man duck down together and try to hide under the dashboard. You say fuck and your partner says ahgoddamnittohell and you both fumble for the radio, getting in each other's way so nobody makes the call.

After the shooting's over, you both sit up, look around. The punks are gone, people are milling about like nothing's happened.

Your experienced partner who's supposed to teach you the ropes has taken one in the left side of his chest. A little hole there right over his heart, spritzing a looping arc of blood that paints the inside of the smashed windshield in slithering strands of red.

He doesn't seem to notice, says something about the paperwork you'll both have to fill out. You jam your finger in the hole and feel the pulsing muscle beneath.

You think, Holy motherfucking shit right here.

You work the radio with your free hand, trying to remember the code numbers, the proper phrasing, your own name. It's not officer down, he's sitting up, and now he's talking about his Chinese girlfriend, the things she can do with a bottle of soy sauce. You really don't want to hear about that, it may even be a tad more disgusting than your index finger jammed down into his aorta.

When the ambulance gets there, the paramedic tells you to keep your finger where it is as they load the old man in. As you climb up into the back you think, Keep it there for how much longer? You're starting to cramp. The ambulance passes a Chinese restaurant and you know you'll never eat that shit again. In the emergency room they finally take over and give you your finger back and let you return to the station.

In the locker room, Ray sees you're covered in your partner's blood but you don't have a scratch on you.

Shaking his head, the grin not a grin at all, he says, I don't like how this is shaping up for the guys who team with you.

Nine months later you're reassigned together.

He says, I'm ever shot in the heart, you keep your hands out of my guts, right?

You think, Right on, solid, hell yeah.

Being a cop, it's climbing a tree in Chelsea and getting a kite out of a branch, the kind of family-values shit you see on pamphlets printed up by the Church of Jesus Christ of Latter-day Saints. The smiling officer handing out life lessons, the kid with rosy apple cheeks giving the thumbs-up, a nubby-tailed puppy at his feet, and Jesus with his arms around everybody.

But on the way down you tear the seat of your pants so you've got half your ass hanging in the wind, and the kid and his mother grab the kite and turn away without even saying thank you.

It's wanting to rush up after them and rap them in the backs of their heads with your nightstick. The rage is there, trying to take over. Down the block, the kid starts flying his kite again and it dive-bombs onto 23rd Street and gets run over by a cab. The kid doesn't even seem to care, but the mother is pissed at wasting eleven bucks. Ray sees the look on your face and tries for some quip, but you don't hear him, your temples are surging. Your left butt cheek is bleeding.

It's watching as a father takes his own newborn son hostage and climbs up to the hospital roof, waving a scalpel and threatening to stab the kid or cut his own throat.

You've been on the job less than eighteen months. You look around at the hardware, the rows of sharp-shooters perched on buildings across the street, the ne-gotiator sounding weak and nervous. The father takes a running start and stops at the ledge. He's laughing, in-sane, sobbing, because his wife had a heart attack ten minutes after delivery. You try to feel for him. You try to think what it would be like if it was Dani on the table.

The veins in your throat twist. The kid is wailing, but sleepily. You've been sent up to the roof to guard the stairway and told not to engage the father. It's not a bad word to use in these circumstances, "engage." Your lives will be as entwined from here on out as if you had gotten married.

You lack the clarity of vision that Ray has. He sees everything in black and white, makes his choices in-stantly, and sticks with them. He wants to rush the fa-ther and shoot him in the head.

You're the one who has to say things like, But what about the baby?

It makes you sound whiny as hell, and Ray gives you the look.

He starts to walk up behind the father, who's doing a jig out on the ledge, howling like a dog now. Ray takes aim knowing damn well that no one can possibly find him at fault in this. They'll give him a medal. He'll have his picture in the paper for weeks and be crowned a hero. This is the way to a gold shield before you're thirty. So long as the baby doesn't go over the edge too.

Your mind is a blitzkrieg full of theatrics. There's no calm, there's only the action. You see yourself rushing forward, diving, and catching the infant. You can almost hear the cheers, see the kid coming up to you in twenty-five years to say thank you, trailed by his wife and two children.

Ray is trying to be silent, hunched and moving in a reptilian creep and crawl. He might as well be banging a kettledrum but it just doesn't matter. The father is yelling so loudly he's deaf to everything else.

You think of a dead woman in the hospital morgue two levels underground, her breasts full of curdled milk. You think what a fucking waste all of this is.

Ray isn't even going to try to get close. He's maybe forty feet away and gets into a proper shooting stance. You can tell he's eager and rushing the situation because he doesn't want some sharpshooter to get the credit. The negotiator's plaintive voice sounds like nothing but sniveling up here. They should only know.

You make a tentative grab for Ray's shoulder, but he shrugs loose and gives you the look again. This time with real heat. You say, Wait, wait. And he says, No. You watch events unfolding along a prescribed line and understand exactly what's going to happen next. You think, There's no way Ray can make the shot. If he pulls the trigger, the kid is dead. Ray is one of the worst shooters on the force, consistently in the lowest bracket.

He's either going to miss the father and scare him off the ledge or he'll put one right into the baby.

Maybe it's the truth. You move like it is. You see a chance to do something here, whether it's right or wrong, and you act.

The adrenaline darts into your heart. The rage is in full bloom. It's been waiting for you to catch up.

You kick Ray in the ass and knock him down.

You holster your weapon and walk across the roof toward the father. The negotiator sees you and starts to squawk and squeak. There's a chain of command you're not following and that's going to piss off a lot of people.

For an instant you wonder if the sharpshooters will sight on you. You feel as if you're in the crosshairs already but you always feel that way, so it's something of a relief to know it might actually be happening.

A glance back and Ray's still on the ground, giving you the look, but it's a different kind of look now. What the fuck.

Hell, right there the whole day's been worth it.

Being a cop, dealing with the two little mooks drawing switchblades inside your gut, it's like being constantly torn in half.

The father's holding his child out in his arms like Abraham making an offer to heaven. You lift your hands up in a kind of *Come on, man, don't do this* sort of gesture. You hear yourself as if from a distance. The voice is accommodating but not soothing, it sounds like you're appealing to an older brother who you're on the outs with.

The voice is chattering, jumping from topic to topic. It covers grief, envy, fatherhood, second marriages, Little League coaching. You're annoyed with the

Shadow Season   **99**

voice and tell it to stop, but it doesn't. The father also tells it to stop, and it doesn't. The negotiator below tells it to stop, and it still goes on.

The baby is crying. The father is crying. The mother is dead. Ray's on his feet, watching. The edge is near and coming closer. The father rubs his wet face on the blanket wrapped around the newborn and sniffs deeply, smelling his child. He must be smelling his wife too because his eyes fill with an even more profound despair. You inch closer. He inches closer. The baby hums for breath.

The end is here and you know it. This moment will seal your fate in ways you'll wish you could have avoided, all the while knowing it was impossible to do anything else.

You hold your hands out to take the baby, and the instant you touch the blanket the father's face ignites with madness and he screams. He was dead the second he hit the roof, the only question was whether he would take the kid with him.

He's going to try.

The edge is only eighteen inches thick. You fumble and try to grab the child, but there's no point. The guy's holding the baby like a football now, tucked under his armpit, and he's flailing. He's got his hands on you and grabs your shirt. His fist tightens on the material. You're being tugged off your feet. The sky is very blue and there seems to be as much below you as above you.

You've got half a second to think about your obituary. Once you're dead you'll be a hero cop. The headlines will be kind. The pretty newscasters will pull sad faces. They're usually courteous to the dead.

But in the locker room, in internal memoranda, they're going to flay you for being so fucking dumb. They're going to be lecturing rookies about you for the next decade. You're going to be an object lesson on what not to do.

You shift your center of gravity, still trying to grab the kid. It's the right thing to do if you can't do anything else. You think, At least I can hold the baby on the way down. It's not exactly comforting but it's something.

Then there's blood in your eyes.

The father, with only half a head, cocks his chin and his brains slew out to the left and pour over his ear in a gush.

He tries to speak, perhaps say a name. His own or his wife's or the child's, if the kid has one yet. But then his tongue just unfurls and hangs there as dead as he is.

You snatch the kid free.

The guy rocks back on his feet and topples over, venting explosively as he hits the concrete. The negotiator's slacks will never be the same.

Ray stands there looking at you, still holding his gun out in front of him like he might pull the trigger again. The two of you face each other. He chuckles like he can't believe this shit. He gives you the full-wattage charm. You think about how easily Ray's shot could've taken off your head instead. Right after you thank him for saving your life, you want to break his jaw.

He signals the all clear. You carry the kid downstairs and then you catch hell from your sarge, your lieut, the captain, and the commissioner. After all the yelling they let you slide, because they have to.

There's a million photographs and miles of video

of the scene. You and Ray are heroes. You get commendations. You both get medals. The orphaned newborn gets picked up by an elderly spinster aunt from Brooklyn who has no idea what to do with a baby. In all the photo ops she wears a dazed expression like she wants to throw up.

Dani is standing beside you, one arm around your waist, smiling perfectly for the cameras so that you feel, second by second, torn by pride and humiliation. The mayor constantly leans over to her and dips his lips close to her ear, sometimes whispering, sometimes speaking loudly enough for you to hear. He slobbers empty declarations of esteem. The mayor's tongue is a wet, hungry leech seeking Danielle's fresh blood. Your breathing hitches, sweat breaks out, and your face pales.

The mayor is saying, He's got a bright future ahead of him. The leech almost reaches her, and you imagine it slithering inside her ear canal.

And Dani answering, He's more driven than anyone I've ever met.

Everyone switches places on the stage a few times. The crime-beat paparazzi shout names to get you to look this way, this way, over here, over here. You wind up between Dani and Ray. It's a strange feeling, like you're coming between lovers. You wonder about drive, whether you really have any or not.

You scan the crowd but can't find any faces you recognize. Later on, Ray fades off the stage but you know he's still somewhere in the room. You don't have to see Ray to know he's there. You've never had to see Ray, will never have to see Ray, to know he's forever there.

Reporters ask why you took such a risk and you can

think of nothing to say. You stumble over your words, coming out with something tepid and clichéd like, It's my job to protect the innocent. It stuns the room into silence until your lieut cuts in front and starts talking. He's good, articulate. He enjoys the spotlight.

The reporters eat it up. All of them invariably edit your few comments to make you sound much sharper.

But Ray taunts you with that line for the next ten years, throwing it out every so often, sometimes letting eighteen months go by, sometimes hitting you with it three times in a week.

But always jabbing you at the worst times.

Kneeling beside some meth mama who's starved her baby. Cuffing a teenager for knifing her own brother for reasons you can guess at. During a hostage situation when you're out front with fifty other cops listening to a couple of meltdowns popping the patrons inside.

It's my job to protect the innocent.

They let you slide, but Ray doesn't. Ray holds that kick in the ass against you right up until the end.

Now, all this time later, you rarely feel the need to unburden yourself, at least through conversation. But on occasion, as Murphy shows greater interest through the deepening nights, and the Jameson is going down smooth, you find yourself rambling on about being a cop. You haven't cried since you were a child, but sometimes your voice will catch as you talk about what it was like to carry a badge. Murphy listens intently, chuckles, and goes, Oh, but that's a mighty cracking story.

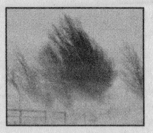

FINN RETREATS TO HIS OFFICE, FEELING edgy. His instincts are prodding him along, driving him toward a bad mood. He feels the way he did in the city, always expecting the worst and enjoying the feel of an oncoming heartache. He can't shake what Harley Moon said to him.

God no, you want to die?

There's a gentle knock at the door. His first thought is, Maybe here it is, maybe this is what's finally going to shove me off the roof.

"Mr. Finn?"

It's Vi.

He's been expecting, dreading, and dreaming of this moment. The one where they're alone together, and he can confront the weakness inside. So he can test himself against it once more.

His voice is hard, unwavering. It doesn't match his guts. "You shouldn't be here, Violet."

Since the beginning of the semester he's had to willfully exclude and shun Vi. For his own good, hers, and the academy's. She can't help him mark essays anymore, can't sit and discuss Baudelaire or Twain. He can't act as an advisor, a counselor, or a friend. He can hardly even act as her teacher. And it's his fault.

"I think we should talk," she says.

"We've already talked, Vi. We've done enough talking. Everything that had to be said has been said. Now you need to go."

If he had any real balls, he'd step up and start addressing her as Miss Treato. Put some of that blue-blooded snoot into it, the kind of thing she's probably used to getting from her other teachers. He had a college professor who could make "Mis-tah Finn" sound like a boot heel scraping shit loose on brick.

He wouldn't have to be mean, just remote. Brusque, short-tempered, inaccessible. His stomach knots. He turns his face aside because the force of her stare is enough to make him blush. He thinks, What if Ray could see me now. What if Dani could see me now.

You never know what's going to do it to you. What gets under your skin and burrows in deep. What it is that sets you on fire. Who climbs under your defenses and whines in the night, what you suddenly need in bed. Finn's seen honest men become ax murderers because of a burned roast. He's seen millionaires licking the floors of crack dens. He's arrested more than one priest, and he was nearly strangled by a stocky nun. He's seen college kids suicide over an A minus. He was once introduced to a politician's wife who turned out to be a high-priced call girl in her spare time. It was an open secret. Nobody brought her in. Finn was pretty sure his lieut had partaken. Nobody's in control.

Vi makes his skin heat up. He feels rooted and established. The world is already too far from him. He can't find it within himself to push it even farther away.

The air grows unsteady. She moves closer. Finn draws his chin back to his chest. She takes another step, and her heels whisper across the tile. He thinks the things that all men think, imagining scenarios that can never be.

The girl wants to be a woman. The girl is becoming a woman for him. It's a powerful narcotic. Her breath touches his throat and it stings his skin.

"Finn, you don't have to worry," she tells him, dropping the "Mister." She's trying to sound a little more like Roz. "I won't cause you any troubles. I don't want you to lose your job. I'm here to help you. That's all I want to do. Really. I hope you'll trust me."

His face is as impassive as he can make it. "This isn't help, Vi, and it's not what you want. Not what you should want."

"But I—"

"You need to go."

"Can't we just talk for a little while? We were friends, weren't we?"

"No."

"No?"

"No."

"We weren't friends?"

"No, I'm your teacher and that's all I am."

"There's nothing wrong with saying we were friends. Nothing."

"Please don't come back unless it's during my office hours."

He sounds like a prick. He sounds like every prick

he's ever met that he wanted to smack in the chops. It makes him nearly as disgusted with himself as his frenetic thoughts painting pictures that fill the dark and start to arouse him. He's as bad as the burnt-roast murderer. He can't control himself for a fucking minute. He's failing this test big-time boffo.

"I understand, Mr. Finn," she says, the "Mister" back in place. But there's an amused lilt in her voice, as if this is foreplay. Maybe she thinks it is. "I really do. But look, what happened that day, it was—it was—"

Idiotic? Asinine? Disgusting? Insane?

"—it was no big deal."

She's so young that she actually believes what she says is true. He tells her, "It was, and you need to realize that."

"It meant a lot to me, but I know I was wrong. I shouldn't have pushed. It was *impetuous* of me."

Impetuous. Good word. He's taught her well, at least.

"Vi—"

"But you didn't do anything wrong. It was me, and I just want to apologize to you for it."

What do you say to that?

Jesus fucking Christ. Finn shakes his head. "Violet—" He can speak her name but nothing follows. How ineffectual. He tries again. He's this close to talking real to her, and wonders if he should go all the way.

"You should've gone on vacation with your parents and seen some of the world. You shouldn't have stayed behind. There's nothing here for you. This is just a pit stop to help you grab the keys to the kingdom. There's so much ahead of you. Start focusing on that."

It's the kind of thing a really old guy might say. A grandfather, some arthritic uncle, somebody so disconnected from the situation that everybody else just nods when he speaks. Nods and immediately dismisses his wrinkled ass.

"I don't need to think about it," she says. "I already know what's ahead of me. My parents have told me all about it. I'm being primed to marry a rich doctor. They know a boy. His name is Mark Reynolds. His father is in business with my father. His parents are currently in Greece traveling with mine. He's there too. I've met him only twice. We fucked both times. It was good but not very good. We didn't talk much before or after. We lounged around on the beach. We drank a lot. We visited the temples of Athens. My mother asked if I fucked him. It was important to her that I didn't annoy him and play hard to get. That's the way she thinks. It's the way my father thinks as well. Maybe everybody thinks that way, I don't know. They want to double up on the family fortunes. Mark's already got his kids' names picked out. His kids, not ours. Eleanor and Kenneth. That's what's ahead of me. But I'm my own person. I'm going to choose to do something different and be someone else." She pauses, catches her breath, wets her lips. "You know what he did with the condoms? He knotted them and threw them down behind the backboard. He left them there for the maid."

It's a lot to share and, in a way, Finn is flattered.

She knows how to say "fuck" the way a man likes.

"I have the courage and strength to go my own way." Vi sounds determined and very young. "You taught me that, whether you realize it or not."

What Finn realizes is that he's never taught her any such thing. He's just been on hand while she's matured and learned it all on her own. Perhaps, in some small regard, the literature he's given the class has helped. But when your mother wants to know if you're fucking the boys in Greece, he finds it hard to accept that Flannery O'Connor or Albert Camus is facilitating maturity. He feels more inadequate than ever.

"Tell me the truth about one thing," she says.

"All right," Finn says, and he knows that whatever he does next, he's never going to tell her the truth.

"Do you love Nurse Martell?"

"Yes," he says.

"I don't believe you."

"You don't have to. Violet, it's time for you to go." There's nothing to do but repeat himself. "I don't want you to come back here during vacation. And you're to stick to regular office hours during the semester. You're not to show up at my cottage anymore. If you do, there's every chance you'll be expelled and I'll be asked to leave or forced to resign."

"Or put in jail," she says, and the worldly edge to her voice takes him low in the belly. He likes it too much.

"Yes."

"You like my voice, don't you?"

Before he can stop himself he answers, "Yes."

"You still want me, don't you?"

She reaches out and touches the scars at his hairline. She draws aside a curl so she can get a better view. Danielle would brush his hair away to stare into his eyes. Vi's fingers are strong. She's on the swim team and the gymnastics team.

Her warm touch is enough to make him shut his eyes and shut his mouth and dream. It's a holdover from before the incident. The darkness beneath his eyelids is different from the darkness when his eyes are open.

"Stop it," he hisses. He stands and backs away a step.

She follows, reaching so she can still trace the scars, stretching on her toes to keep in contact with him. She moves up against his chest. He's backed to the window. He wonders if he should jump.

"I can soothe you," she tells him.

"No, you can't."

"I can do things."

"But you shouldn't."

"I can make you feel good."

"I said stop it."

"I promise, you won't ever be sorry. I can take away your pain."

"No, believe me, you can't."

"I want you."

"It's not going to happen."

"If only you'd let me—"

"That's enough, Violet."

It's more than enough, and still not enough. He imagines her with the kid in Greece, staring into the boy's face as they finish making love, the kid knotting his condom. Her mother talking to his mother about what the wedding should be like, which universities Eleanor and Kenneth will attend.

"Don't be frightened, Finn."

He knows twenty moves to get her away from him, but they'll all hurt.

This can only play out one way. With calls from Mr.

Treato's attorneys. Charges being filed, headlines lev-
eled all over again. Is he still a short eyes if he can't see?
He imagines how it might go for a blind ex-cop child-
raper in prison. It would pay to back off. It would really
and truly pay to back way the fuck off. Finn thinks about
that as Vi's fingers probe and trace his scars, tapping
here and there to feel the metal plate nailed down over
the hole in his skull. Her fingers fit into the deepest
grooves. His scalp tightens and slithers with cold sweat.

Being a blind teacher in an all-girls school during
winter vacation with a student pressing her hand to your
knitted bones, it's a lot like being a cop. There are two
small fuckers inside his gut going at it, and one is really
getting sliced up.

With a swift rustle of cloth she turns away. Already
he misses her touch.

"There's someone out there," Vi says.

PART II
LENS

FINN MOVES TO THE WINDOW AS if he can see out.

"Who?" he asks.

"I don't know," Vi says. "Some girl. A town girl in the snow."

"What's she doing?"

"Just standing there."

"That's all?"

"Yes. She's pretty far away, like she doesn't know where to go. Whether she should come to the school or not. You know the holler folk still call this place the Hotel? She's got to be freezing. The storm's getting worse. And the sun is going down. I can barely see her." Vi turns and looks into his face. The smell of her toothpaste is strong on the swells and billows of her breath.

He tries to keep expressionless but he thinks it's Harley Moon out there. Harley's been wandering around out there for hours, afraid to come near.

"You know her, don't you," Vi says. It's not a question.

"No."

A stray thought hits him. Is Harley another of Murphy's young wans? Is that why she was worried and didn't want Finn calling anybody? Was she protecting him? Is

Murph the one with such ill will? Finn can almost believe it.

He cracks the window. Snow heaves into his face. It
feels good, the cold sting against his flushed skin, the
grainy blast scouring Vi's touch away.

"Is she talking to Murphy?" he asks.

"No. I don't see him. Why would she be talking to
him?"

"Does she look hurt?"

"No, I don't think so. I mean, she's not staggering or
anything like that. Why did you ask? Who hurt her?"

As he leans on the sill, Vi encircles his waist with an
arm and gives a little tug, pulling him toward her. There's
jealousy and demand in the action. This has got to stop.

But before Finn can shrug free she lets him go. Her
timing is perfect. She dances along the rim of his every
boundary. Her knowledge of men exceeds that of most
women twice her age. He wonders who there was before
the boy in Greece. He wonders exactly what the hell he's
going to have to do to get clear of her.

"Who is she?" Vi asks.

"Just a holler girl."

"Are you fucking her?"

He stands a little straighter. The hinges of his jaw
tighten. He's glad the resentment is thick in her voice. It
makes her almost ugly, and he needs that. Her harsh
tone centers him. Heavy snowflakes rise against the
back of his neck. His lips cool. She shifts her weight.

Finn moves with the speed of a snake, grips Vi's
wrist, and holds it tightly, just rough enough so that she
gasps in shock but not pain.

It's not lust this time that makes him reach. He sets his mouth and takes off his shades. He glares at her.

"Don't ever speak that way to me," he says, no heat at all, hard and dangerous. This isn't a teacher's voice.

She flinches. She's not taking his handicap for granted anymore. She doesn't want to mother him now. He's not the cutie-pie blind guy she can run rough-shod over. His eyes have always been intense, and they still are.

He releases her, puts the shades back on, and moves to his coat. "Lead me outside to her."

"What? Why?"

"It might be important."

"Why is that important?"

"I'm not sure."

"You're not sure? You can talk to me, you know. You can rely on me. What's going on?"

It's a good question, and one he can't answer. Something about the way Harley Moon spoke, that dramatic cadence of misfortune, it started an engine inside him that won't turn off. He's got to know why she's here, who she was talking about, and how she knew about the metal plate in his skull. Only a few folks know. His pals, his confidants. Roz, Judith, Murph, Duchess, some of the other teachers, and why would any of them be discussing him with a holler gal?

But Vi, like every woman, hates to be ignored, and wants his attention. "Please tell me," she says.

"Violet, stop asking questions."

"Well, then answer a few of them." She sounds like an assistant DA hammering away at him.

"Let's just go."

"She's gone. I don't see her anymore."

"Did she head into the Carriage House?"

Vi shrugs demurely, her blouse softly sliding across her breasts and shoulders. "I don't know."

"Or the Gate House?"

"I don't know. I don't think so. She was there one second and the next she was gone. How am I supposed to know where she got to? You sound worried, Finn. You sound sick with panic, and that frightens me."

"There's nothing to be frightened of."

"You're lying. You don't trust me at all."

He faces the window once more, breathes against the glass, and hears a drop of condensation slip free. The wind murmurs. The chimes on the three school buildings jangle and clang. He needs to know what Harley Moon meant when she said that she was in the path of misery herself. Another kid has gotten under his skin. The pulse in his throat throbs against his collar.

Of course he's handled everything wrong, and it's going to cost. He's upset Vi. She's taking harried breaths, arms wrapped around herself, lightly rubbing her elbows. His time here at St. Valarian's is quickly coming to an end. He slumps into his desk chair and lets the snow keep blowing inside and across him.

"I would never hurt you," Vi tells him as she shuts the window. With a perfect amount of tenderness she runs a hand through his hair again. "Not like your wife."

Then she leaves him there alone in the dark.

Finn sits there worrying and wanting to touch her again. He shifts his growing fear from one part of his mind to another while waiting for Roz to return. For an instant he's consumed with bloody daydreams. A shudder works through him. Christ, will it ever end? The storm is growing worse inside and out. He reaches over and touches the windowpane. With the wind chill it's got to be barely above zero outside. His skull is loud with someone shouting. Maybe it's himself, maybe not.

The words become less distinct but take on a greater meaning. He's thinking, Roz, where are you? What have I done to you?

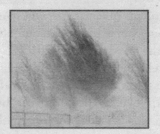

THE INTERNET NEVER FORGETS, AND IT'S not much on forgiving either. When Finn was a kid, if you wanted information, you had to scope microfiche for hours, unspooling rolls and working them through machines that brought up old newspaper print in reverse negative. Now all you needed to do was type a name into Google—it didn't even have to be spelled correctly, the Web would fix it for you, offer alternatives—and you had somebody's life history at your fingertips. You didn't have to dig because the bodies weren't buried that deep.

He'd made the newspapers a lot there at the end. First with Ray and Carlyle, then with Dani. His face on page 5, page 3, page 1. Sometimes the hero, often the fool. A lot of mixed messages in black-and-white.

IAD was up his ass nearly as much as Ray's. The photos generally had him looking stoic and slightly insincere out in front of One Police Plaza or the courthouse building. Ray could work a crowd, always smiling, doing the Nixon double Victory sign.

Later on, a couple of photographers sneaked into the hospital and managed to nab a few pictures of Finn with his head shaved, the Frankenstein scars crosshatching his noggin. Roz saved the clippings until he was off the critical list, then read them to him one after the other. After she was done she asked, Do you want me to save these?

History had as tight a hold on her as it did on him, which was probably how they wound up together in the first place.

So Vi had been looking him up on the Net. The events of his life weren't common knowledge in the sticks. He should have expected it, that one of the girls would eventually care enough to tumble to his story. Still, it felt invasive. Vi working her fingers through his hair, through his life, knowing about Danielle. Christ.

His past wants him more than he wants it.

Finn puts on his coat and feels too warm inside it, takes it off again. He folds it over his arm and carries it, steps out his office door into the corridor. He wonders if Vi is still nearby, down at the other end of the hall, watching him. It's easy to become paranoid, always feeling eyes on you. He struggles against the sensation but it washes over him.

A snap of his cane on the floor and the echo claps up the corridor. If someone was standing there, the report would be different, like a whitecap breaking over an obstruction. The technical term is "facial vision," where the blind develop a sensitivity to sound waves in the bones of their faces.

But Finn feels it everywhere. In his shoulders, his hands, playing across his ribs. It's another topic that makes his shrink feel like she's earning her pay by saying, Let's revisit that.

Vi is gone.

For a moment he experiences vertigo and has to

reach out and grab the wall. It's not dizziness, it's something like an intense momentary depression. It feels like he's falling down a sinkhole. It hits him from time to time. It has less to do with anxiety than it does with isolation, an awful sensory deprivation within the darkness. The black is infinite and his very identity sometimes buckles beneath the weight of it.

Finn loses himself for an instant.

He holds on to the wall.

The wall gives his hand shape. The shape of his hand gives his arm substance. The arm helps to delineate the torso. The neck grows from it. He feels the definition of his face and head again. And residing within his skull is his brain, and within that his mind, and within that himself.

Finn breathes deeply, the experience waning and finally passing.

The roof creaks and clacks in the wind as if children are running along it. The occasional howls and whistles form a tune he recognizes but can't name. He listens, allowing the song to fill his chest. In the city the concrete held the wind back and waited for you to come around the corner before it smashed your face in.

Roz is out in the snow and so is Harley. He imagines them struggling against the storm on a direct course for each other. He wonders, What is the girl saying, explaining, implying? And does it really matter in the end?

He hears a heavy noise down below.

He's heard that sound many times before.

It's the sound of a body falling.

"Hello?" he calls.

Someone has collapsed. He takes the stairs almost

casually, left hand on the thick wooden banister, right gripping the cane tightly. The thumping of the storm is in sync with his heartbeat. The history of the building moves into and through him. Thousands of people have walked these corridors. Dozens have died in these rooms. Ghosts heave about no differently than anyone else.

Finn hits the ground floor and stands on the uneven slate. The lingering scent of Duchess's cookies makes his stomach groan. He hardly touched his dinner.

"Somebody here?" Then more urgently, with a growl, "Answer me."

Instinct makes him walk at an angle, his left arm up, like he's stepping across a boxing ring. He drops his chin a little, swings the cane a bit harder than he needs to. The body language is aggressive because it has to be.

He takes a left, heading toward Murphy's apartment. This wing of the Main House once contained the private quarters of hotel employees. Except for Murph's apartment, the rooms are now used for storage of extra furniture and custodial equipment. Floor waxers, paint, tools, whatever Murphy and his staff need to keep St. Val's running. The groundskeeper sheds are outside the west door toward the back of the building. Murph can slip in and out without disturbing any of the classes.

Finn heads to Murphy's apartment. The door is hardly ever locked, but it is right now. He knocks hard enough that the hinges squeak. There's no response.

He tries again. "Murph, let me in."

There's a body on the floor somewhere. He sees Harley Moon gripping a hatchet, standing over Murph's twisted body, his chest in pieces. He sees Murph holding a silk necktie between his hands, standing over the girl's blackened face, her tongue protruding. He sees Roz in there, cheating on him, lying half on the bed and half on the floor in some weird kama sutra position with Murph on top of her. Finn presses a hand to the door.

All right, he'll chalk this one up to his imagination. He's got to do that on occasion. Maybe it was shifting snow on the roof. A tree branch dropping against a shutter.

Finn puts on his coat, makes his way out the back door, and heads toward the dorm, which in the hotel days was called the Gate House. The snow's coming down much harder now. There's a not-so-recently-cleared track of walkway that he finds, stumbling as he proceeds. His ankles are covered but the trail is a straight line, and he sweeps the cane, feeling the much higher banks on either side.

In his rookie year, there were days in the city when he'd have to use his nightstick to prod half-frozen homeless out of the alleys and try to get them into shelters or onto heating grates someplace. Sometimes he'd knock a half inch of ice off a corpse's face, a dead dog stuck like tacky tape to its side. He was never the first one there. The shoes would always be gone, pockets turned out, liquor bottle empty. He'd sweep the park and follow the smell of burning trash to a garbage can under a stone bridge by the skating rink, a family of four huddled around it. A couple of ashen-eyed kids looking at him like he was either Santa Claus or the devil. He'd hand over a few bucks and some healthy munchies that Dani had loaded his pockets with—granola, raisins, sunflower seeds—the parents parceling out handfuls of trail mix like Christmas dinner. The parents would either be out-of-work assholes or on-the-run drug peddlers or just illegal immigrants who'd come over at a bad time, when even the sweatshops were at max capacity. Finn would either lecture or lend an ear or call INS. He'd get home that night and Dani would ask, How did the battle against evil go today?

A wild gust rocks him. He tightens his grip on his cane. The sun's gone down. His eyes sting from the freezing snow and he throws a hand up to protect them. Even though they're useless now, he still cares for them. He uses saline drops, does exercises to keep the muscles from atrophying. He fights to keep his gaze from straying. They're still his eyes, and that gives them a kind of purpose.

Finn resumes his course and passes beneath the arch where the chimes designating the Gate House hang. They're tangled together, ringing with garbled notes. He hasn't been to church in years, but there are always bells.

It doesn't matter at all, except that for some reason it does. He waves the cane and raps the chimes lightly. It doesn't free them. He smacks harder, working the cane up and down, trying to unknot the snarled strings. He only makes it worse. The disharmony plays on and on for him. He's goddamn useless. The rage tears through him and he lets out a strangled yelp of frustration.

He shoulders the front door of the dorm and gets inside.

The wind is so strong that the piano in the lobby thrums a low, brutal note. There's anger in it. Harmful intent. He imagines the piano rearing up and scampering along, looking for somebody to bite. He turns toward it as if to say something, to talk to the piano, tell it to relax, shut the fuck up. He thinks of his shrink again.

Her voice flat and lifeless as she tells him *it's normal, perfectly natural,* her breath growing heavy as she almost pants out *in this situation,* smacking her lips, swallowing repeatedly, her oral fixation so apparent, *under these circumstances to personify things.* He wonders if she has a power fetish for the handicapped. He imagines her stroking the stumps of amputated limbs, her eyes dark and alive, insane with need.

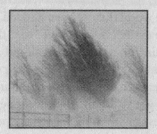

STARTING UP THE STAIRS, FINN HEARS two voices on the landing above him. Lea Grant and Caitlin Jones are having a whispered discussion. He hears the words "fear," "dissuade," "damaged spinal column." The phrases "realm of discourse" and "haunting lyricism of the damned."

He tries to figure out exactly which topic of conversation might include all of that or even any portion thereof, but he draws a blank. He appreciates their unpredictability in certain areas. They're his two best students and neither one could give a shit about literature or the English language or anything else so far as he knows. They've had their lives mapped out for them since before they were born, and the next goal won't be achieved until about age twenty when they, like Vi, get married to wealthy blue bloods on the fast track to a power base in a life of high finance or politics.

Finn suspects that, also like Vi, they have an even greater recklessness and coarseness about them than they're willing to show anyone except each other. He notes signs of it every so often. How they hold themselves and compose themselves, with a haughty air that isn't really affected so much as it's a kind of general disgust for the world they've been handed. He can imagine them very easily taking a hint from the politician's wife and starting up a part-time call-girl ring ten years down the road, just to fully embrace their own wildness.

He overhears snatches of them talking about their lives, and he's got to admit, their weariness and lack of any real interest in anything, especially people, tend to spook the shit out of him. In another life he would've considered them sociopaths without any criminal outlet. Now he just thinks they're two immensely sad, hyperintelligent kids about to be sent up to a fucked society of their parents' making. They have no real friends outside each other. They understand each other too well to suffer interference from anyone else. A friendship that close forfeits a hell of a lot. He knows.

Easing up a few more stairs, he smells the liquor on their breath. The good stuff, high-octane bourbon. Sounds like they're drinking from styrofoam cups. He might be in eyeshot now, but he doesn't expect them to stop talking just because he's there.

In their sphere, Finn exists to hand out perfect test scores and nothing more. Sometimes that fills him with a kind of vague sorrow. But when you get down to it, he accepts his role, and it's almost refreshing not to be taken that seriously. It's just a goddamn English class, after all.

Lea says, "They want me to visit him, in his little room."

"And you must, there's no other recourse," Caitlin tells her. "You have to act as expected and be the proper younger sister."

"But he *waves* it at me."

"Are we still talking about his prosthetic?"

"... plastic and metal ... they have others, much better ones it seems, that resemble a real human hand, but he prefers the hook. More specifically two hooks that snap together. He puts on little shows. Picking up a cigarette and lighting it. Playing solitaire, flipping the cards over with great verve. Snap, snap, snap. My parents would applaud but they don't like to display their hands anymore. They keep them in their pockets now, mostly."

"As I recall Michael had great verve in most things. On the hockey rink, for instance. Bashing players up against the glass."

"He did like to bash a few heads."

"And was quite good at it. On the football field too."

"Constantly clotheslining other players when the refs weren't looking. Aggressive tendencies."

"Nearly broke Toddy's neck two seasons ago."

"A couple of cracked vertebrae and he's set for life. My father paid handsomely."

"And Toddy never looked up very much anyway, as I recall, or raised his arms above the shoulder."

It's like they're rehearsing for a Russian play. Their monotone could drive Finn insane in the long term, if he had to live with it. He's suddenly grateful that these two almost never say a word in class.

Lea Grant is weighty in her demeanor and her physicality. She has the kind of dense importance of a brace pole holding up a ceiling. In her papers she generally uses at least two words that Finn is unfamiliar with and must look up later. He sends Roz to the dictionary and she says, This girl, she needs a good smack in the teeth.

When Finn sees Lea he sees Carlyle's mistress.

Sleepy eyes, thick ringlets working over both shoulders, only a faint trace of pink lipstick. Zaftig but a power walker, with muscular thighs that could crack a walnut. Carlyle ran a triborough syndicate that was hardwired with some top-ranking politicians and a bunch of cops. Whenever the DA managed to drag him into court, a lot of people would start to sweat and a half-dozen bodies would turn up in the East River.

Finn and Ray were both subpoenaed and had to take the stand because they'd busted one of Carlyle's runners. Finn found threatening notes in his locker. Maybe only one in every twenty brothers in blue was on the take, but it still added up. Once someone left him a photocopied picture of Dani with red ink poured over it like blood spatter. It was her college yearbook photo. Some fucker had done a little homework. Finn taped the photo up on the wall of the locker room and unloaded three rounds into it. It was a mixed metaphor but he figured the message would get through.

Caitlin Jones appears to him as a runaway Finn found in the Port Authority, twenty minutes off the bus and already bait for a chickenhawk who'd moved in for the kill. He was sweet-talking the girl and promising her a job in modeling, said he owned a luxury suite in Trump Tower. He had his hands all over her, this pale waif with dishwater-blond hair and bee-stung lips, huge blue eyes that tipped the balance of her face. The hawk had a two-hundred-dollar haircut, Hollywood hipster black duds, and a choirboy's smile.

Finn frightened the shit out of the girl by tossing her into the lockbox at the precinct for three hours. He showed her the file on the hawk, the photos of some of the girls he'd worked over. After that she called her mother, who owned a hair salon in Muskogee, Oklahoma, and begged Mama to wire her the fare back home.

The hawk was released without so much as a fine. Later that night, after Finn had changed out of his blues, he found the punk on the prowl in the Port Authority again. Finn fucked the choirboy smile up for all time in the men's room, washed the blood off his hands, found two porcelain crowns on the floor, and crushed them under his heel. He said nothing the entire time.

When he got home that night, Dani massaged the tension from his back while his fists soaked in ice water, and said, Whatever you did, I know you did it for the right reason, and that you made the right choice.

"Mr. Finn, you going to come up and say hello or stand there beneath us indefinitely?" Lea asks.

Caitlin says, "Perhaps by standing below us on the stairs he's commenting on and rebelling against some kind of social status or caste system?"

"Is he critiquing, staring at us on high and finding us lacking, as if situated in an ivory tower?"

"Or is it an observance of—"

Finn just can't listen to it. "It's not an observation, critique, comment, or rebellion, ladies," he says, moving up the stairs again. He sounds angry, even to himself. "It's a digression."

"From what, Mr. Finn?" Lea asks. "Life in general or particular circumstances?"

"From the present. I was reminiscing."

"Fill us in."

"No."

"Mr. Finn has enjoyed his times at bashing as well," Caitlin adds. "See it in his build, the set of his shoulders?"

"Brawny. Aggressive. I think you're right."

"Who do you plan to bash tonight, Mr. Finn?"

He sweeps up past them and can hear music above on the third floor. "Why aren't you girls at the party?"

"A party without male guests, excepting those of the faculty, isn't so much a *fete* as it is a klatch, Mr. Finn."

He wants to say, Well, pardon the fuck-all out of me, then.

But he decides that, when you get down to it, they're right. He can't blame any of the students for their resentment at being placed in an all-girls school in a half-dead town. In another year or three they'll be on some Ivy League campus where they'll get more of a challenge out of the world, some high-end demanding classes and the kind of social interaction that will give them the smack in the teeth they need. He has hopes for these two, even while they mock him.

"Say hello to Vi for us," Lea tells him.

It nearly puts a hitch in his stride, but Finn manages to ignore her teasing. At least they don't giggle. He appreciates that.

Finn continues up the stairway to the fourth floor, where Roz has a small apartment down the hall from Duchess.

He knocks on her door but there's no response. It's the original oak door, updated with a new lock, the old keyhole sealed with some kind of putty that's hardened into rock, but which is also cracked and powdering. He scrapes his pinkie nail across it and enjoys the graininess of the sealant, the divot at its center. Textures take up a large amount of his attention. He's constantly surprised by what small consistencies, grains, and compositions his fingers, on their own, seem to find so amazing and impressive.

The knob resists him. He leans forward and nearly presses his forehead to the door. He strains to hear anything inside the room, in effect trying to will himself inside. The resonant bass from the party below gets his foot tapping. His shoulders wag like he wants to dance. He tries the door again, asks, "Roz? Roz?"

Finn can't help feeling that there's someone on the other side of the door, exactly at eye level, mimicking his every move and listening, just as intently as he is, for any stray sound from the enemy.

THE PARTY'S KICKING UP IN THE communal suite on the third floor. It's a TV room slash lounge area slash kitchen where the students are allowed to have a hot plate and a microwave. There's a foyer with expensive futons where the girls can lie around and study. As if it ever happens.

Out of sight, he moves into the foyer, slumps against a cushion, and hears Jimmy Stewart arguing with Mr. Potter in the other room beneath the blaring music. The songs are rock versions of Christmas classics, the same ones he listened to when he was their age. It bridges the gap a little, makes him feel a touch less obsolete.

The girls are chattering. He concentrates so he can separate the voices. Only three of them. Jesse Ellison and the Smyths. When talking among themselves the girls sound so much different than when they're speaking in class, or even out of class in the company of adults. It's surprising the extent to which the characteristics of their voices vary.

He listens, breathing them in. The fruity soaps, acne creams, veggie body washes, the hair spray, perfumes, hints of cherry lipstick, powders. They fill him.

Jimmy Stewart is cut off in midsentence. The music continues. With the kind of glee reserved for tattletales, Jesse says, "Cable's out."

Finn's a secret sharer in their experiences. They welcome the chance to pass notes back and forth during class, sneak around the room, slip out the door, whisper while holding cupped hands to one another's ears, roll their eyes, make faces. They act out and he pretends not to notice, like they're all performing on a stage for someone in the audience, some cat seated in seventh row center. There's no need to blow their action. Kids need a chance to pull some kind of shit on the teacher, and he's an easy mark. Everybody's got a right to be as much of an outlaw as they want to be, so long as they don't cry foul if they get nabbed for it.

It's a comforting thought and puts a lot of his life into perspective, especially right now as he sneaks a chance to overhear them. There's a lot of air freshener and incense, but he can still smell the cheap whiskey on their breath and the sweet stink of a couple of joints. He vaguely wonders why Caitlin and Lea don't share the good stuff. He listens to their puerile conversations, their poor grammar, their self-absorbed dialogue. Somehow it makes him a little happier.

As Finn enters, there's some wild scrambling and then a communal sigh of relief. They were worried it might be Judith or Duchess. But Finn is only a minor inconvenience.

Suzy Smyth says, "It's okay, it's just Big Daddy-o."

"He's not here to break up the shindig," Sally adds, "he's just a boy who's come a bit late to the dance, right, Mr. Finn?"

"Hopefully my invite is still good."

"For you, right up to the midnight hour."

"Ladies, let me give you a life lesson early on. Always go the extra few bucks for single malt. And post a sentry."

The three of them explode into laughter. Jesse Ellison's is way over the top. Maybe she's a little lit or high, maybe she's trying to sound more earthy and present. When he used to get drunk as a teen he tried to sound like his old man, and she's probably going for her mother.

She knows he hates loud music and lowers the stereo. She gets in close. She's taken care of the cut on her hand. He can't smell it much anymore. The past wavers nearby, like it might break through at any second. It's just waiting for a drop of blood.

"Take your coat off, Mr. Finn. Would you like a drink?" She presses a styrofoam cup at his chest, but he doesn't take it. He figures that no matter how much trouble he's in, he can always get into more. He leaves his coat on.

"Thanks anyway, Jesse."

"It's only eggnog."

"But you're drinking beer. One of the microbrews."

"Jeez, Mr. Finn . . ."

"And you've tasted some Four Roses. It's hell. It was hell when I drank it as a kid. Don't make the same mistake."

"Jeez, Mr. Finn!"

Suzy says, "It's all we could get."

"And here I thought I was supposed to bring the keg. You girls have been stockpiling."

Jesse leans in so unsteadily that she nearly loses her balance. She's got to put her hand out and brace herself against his stomach to keep from falling over. He sniffs again. She can't really be that drunk so soon, can she? No, just klutzy. "It was me," she whispers. "I got a couple of six-packs."

"I told you, I won't narc on anybody."

"That's why we love you. There's some munchies too. Would you like some chips or pretzels? I think there's some cheese curls over there too...yeah, we've got a bag. Duchess made onion dip this afternoon."

His stomach growls but he figures he can hold out for a fresh ham sandwich. "No thanks, Jesse."

"I started *Slaughterhouse-Five*."

"When? I only gave it to you this morning."

"It's brilliant. The way Vonnegut weaves his own introduction into the novel itself. And casts himself as a character in the book? He only shows up a couple of times but it's great when he does. It gives the whole book the feel of a memoir. He even says most of it happened. The real parts, you know, not the alien stuff and the time slippage."

She's grinning, and her breath is a touch rapid. The little gusts of heat break against the hollow of Finn's throat. It tickles, makes him reach up and scratch. She's the only student who cares about anything he says and he almost feels sorry for her because she does.

"Do you know where Nurse Martell is?" he asks.

"No, I haven't seen her all day."

It makes him frown, something he never did as a cop but does a lot now.

Sally Smyth is talking about her college boyfriend

back home, whose name is Reginald. Finn thinks about the weight of all your forefathers coming down to burden and humiliate you with a name like Reginald. Sally is angry with the kid because he wants to change majors from engineering to architecture. Jesse asks what's so wrong with that and Sally barks, "You know how many architects can swing a house off Central Park South?" Finn has no idea, he figured they were all pretty much in the same tax bracket. Jesse turns and offers some murmured condolences as if somebody's dead.

"Sally?" he asks. "Have you seen Nurse Martell?"

"I don't think so."

"Suzy?"

"I'm not sure. No. Not for a while."

"How long's a while?"

"I don't know. Didn't she have dinner with us?"

"No."

"I don't know, I guess I didn't notice. You got the heebie-jeebies, Dad? She's got to be around, right?"

Sally asks, "Where the hell are Caitlin and Lea?"

"Doing their own thing tonight," Suzy says in a sharp, not so confiding whisper. Finn is privy even to their implied secrets.

He turns to go. She tells him, "Mr. Finn, come on, you're not leaving us here all stag are you?"

"Big Daddy-o wouldn't do that to his janes. That's not his action."

"Way not the cut of his jib."

"Sorry, girls," he says. "It's just not a Christmas party if Jimmy Stewart isn't saving Bedford Falls from evil Mr. Potter."

"Not our fault the stupid cable went out."

"You should all own a personal copy of the DVD."

"How square!"

"Failing that, there's no excuse for not having *Santa Claus Conquers the Martians* either."

"You're nuts, Mr. Finn."

"Way out there."

"You don't know the half of it," he admits.

Murphy steps into the suite and says, "A party, is it? Will you take in anyone off the street or is it by invitation only?"

"It depends," Suzy says. "Do you have a character reference?"

"Dozens," Murph tells her. "And not one would give me a passing grade."

"Then you're our kind of people," Sally says. "Load up."

"You've hearts as large as a heavenly choir of angels, every one of you."

"Not so much some of us."

"Then you truly are my people. Eggnog, is it?"

"Look around, Santa may have left a few presents early."

"Bless his bloated heart."

Someone hands Murph a cup. There's a pregnant pause in the room, a sure indication that some kind of sign language is going down—the girls giving Murph the hidden hard liquor. Murph accepting it graciously, no doubt with a cunning smile.

The girls respond accordingly, with some overindulgent giggles and a few flirtatious tsks. Murphy really works the brogue. Finn figures that with every sip of liquor Murph is consciously or unconsciously telling his ma that he hopes she burns in hell.

The girls waft off, back on the subject of Sally's engineer.

Murph asks, "And are you enjoying yourself, Finn?"

"Certainly."

Murph snorts. "Nothing certain about it, though this is a cheerful crowd. A trio of lasses has a way of brightening a room, even when the world outside is being battered. The sky is splitting and heaving, and you'd never know for their smiles."

It's the truth. The surrounding warmth of the living makes Finn almost feel like he belongs among them.

"Have you seen Roz?" he asks.

"No. Nor Duchess nor Judith, although there's two other wans on the stairs who seem to be a dash out of sorts. Odd girls, those. They live off in another room, as me ma might say." Murph takes a sip and shudders violently enough that his teeth clack together. "Gah, dreadful. Wealthy wans like these ought to have better taste." He huffs like he's warming his hands.

"I'm worried," Finn says.

"About?"

"Roz."

"And why's that?"

"She left to go do something."

"She left campus? When?"

"A couple hours ago."

"To do what?"

"She said she was going to the store."

"Which store?"

"I don't know."

"For what reason, now?"

"I have no idea."

"That is worrying. But don't let it eat at you. She drove off into the storm?"

"Yes, I think so."

"You only think so. Perhaps she's back already. Does she have a mobile?"

"A what?"

"A cellular phone."

"No. Did you see her car in the lot?"

Murph thinks about it, snapping his tongue off his front teeth. "To be honest, Finn, I've no idea. I didn't take notice. Doesn't mean it's not there, though. I'd give good odds that she's returned."

"If not, she might be stuck. How bad's the accumulation?"

"Four inches or so, and piling on. It's fierce and dark out there now."

"Her car can't handle much more than that on unplowed roads."

Murph goes on. "I'll do a bit more clearing of the parking lots and take a look-see. Hopefully the county workers will help out with some further salting and sanding on the main roads. She's a good girl, she knows her way about in this weather." He tries to hand a cup of whiskey to Finn, and Murph's hands are so cold that Finn flinches. Murph lets out a chuckle. "I'm halfway to frozen still. A few warming drinks should help me on that front, it's my belief. You'll not have any?"

"No thanks."

"I'm sure your Rosie's fine, perhaps having a bite

with Duchess. Wrapping presents with Judith, it's a woman's way."

"If not?"

"I said I'd take a look about."

"Thanks, Murph."

"Don't be a tosser."

Finn wants to ask Murphy if he was in his apartment earlier, and if so what it was that fell, who it was that had fallen, and why he didn't let Finn in when he knocked. He wants to know if Murph's been screwing around with Harley Moon. If he hurt her. If maybe he's having an affair with Roz. He called her Rosie. Almost nobody knows that her name is Rose, that she likes to be called that in bed. The questions writhe within him and prod him toward anger. His back muscles contract and he suddenly wants to slap the shit out of Murphy.

The girls are still chattering together on the other side of the suite. Maybe twenty feet off, but the generational tide has strong enough currents that he and Murph are being drawn away. Sally is talking about her boyfriend again. Jesse wants to know more. Their voices lower, their laughter explodes. Finn constantly has to remind himself how young they all are, how much they don't know, how much they'll never know, and how much more they know that he never will.

Murphy looks over, looks back, his neck clicking loudly. He says, "Breaks my heart, they do. All of life is perched before them, innit? They've the entire road left ahead. So many firsts that'll cause them such suffering, and give them so much joy. Pity the lads that will have their hearts snatched."

Murphy has told a lot of stories, but so far Finn

hasn't heard the big one about what's brought him to America and St. Val's. What he expects out of life from this point on, what he might be saving his money for, if he's got any. Finn wonders if, despite all the bullshit soap opera, Murph isn't simply biding his time until Judith splits from her husband, just so he can move in on her, get married, and then nab half of everything that belongs to her.

It's a heavy step to take, asking an Irishman about his personal life. Murphy's told him intimate details about his past, but always on his own terms. The few times Finn ever questioned him, Murph completely withdrew, his voice emotionless, saying, Shite, I've nothing to say on that.

Finn reaches out and gently grabs Murph's arm. "Do you know Harley Moon?"

"Is this a song title you're asking about? It's nothing by The Cramps."

"No, a town girl."

"Do I know a town girl? I know many, but none by the name of Harley. You've quite the grip on you. Strong hands those are."

"A teenager. She was on campus this afternoon."

"I saw no one on campus except the students and their families leaving for their holiday. You sound a mite irritated, Finn."

"I'm not."

"You mind letting me loose now or is it your plan that we dance?"

Finn doesn't let go. The noise around them, the presence of the girls, the smell of whiskey, the constant presence of Judith hidden somewhere in the wings, the fact that Roz is still gone, it all works to keep him on edge.

Four inches, the Comet can bulldog through that, but just barely. If she's not back soon—what, he'll drag Murph by the ear and force him to go scout for her? Suddenly it feels imperative that he knows more about Murphy.

He asks, "What's brought you here?"

"To the party? Drink, of course."

"To the school. To America."

Murph grunts like he's just taken a jab to the kidneys. He snaps his arm free. "I've nothing to say about—"

"How about if you just answer the fucking question?"

It takes him a while to respond.

"I had notions," Murphy says.

It means more than it sounds like, but Finn doesn't know why. He can tell by the way the word hangs there, full of meaning and substance.

"Notions?"

"I wanted to rise above my station. I wanted more than I should've settled for on Galway Bay. There, we're rooted in our shite history and accept our lot. The priests and nuns teach us not to exceed ourselves. I didn't want to be like me ma, who spent her mornings and afternoons in church, keeping her evenings free and brisk by spitting venom about. Or like my da, who enjoyed a book while feeding the swans, and seemed a happy man right to the day he jumped from the bridge with rocks in his pockets. I decided I wanted to go to Miami and live in the sun with the rich Americans."

Finn thinks he can read something between the lines, some serious troubles that kept Murphy on the move.

He's surprised when Murph continues. "Somehow I wound up in Phoenix, and then went on to St. Louis, and now I'm here balls-deep in snow. Still haven't been to Florida. But that's what comes of notions."

"And what did you want to do?"

"First thought, eh? To rob a bank."

"What stopped you?"

A knowing chuckle soaked with whiskey sweeps up into Finn's face. Easy to imagine Murph there with a devil's grin, his upper lip with just a hint of curl to it, eyes wired into a thousand-yard stare aimed at the girls. "Och, and who said anything did?"

BEFORE FINN HAS A CHANCE TO decide whether Murph is just fucking with him or not, Judith walks in. He can feel the way she cools everyone in the room. The girls are immediately a bit worried, wondering what they might get a lecture for, thinking maybe Finn and Murph won't cover for them.

They have to edit their conversations now. They have to consider the way they move, how loud they laugh, how their breath smells. Sally and Suzy Smyth are backed up to the opposite wall, near the window. He can feel their tension.

Murphy licks his lips heavily, drawing at the last of his drink. No different than any guy sucking on the last pull of his glass before having to turn and face the wife, the girlfriend, the woman he never called last Saturday.

He whispers, "Bollocks."

Finn abruptly thinks that the body he might have heard falling in Murphy's apartment was probably Judith rolling off the bed.

Murph asks, "Judith *a cara,* can I get you a cup of refreshing eggnog?"

"I'd love it if you would, Roddy," she tells him, and Finn is surprised that she says it with an almost friendly air, like a newly married couple talking. Murph walks off but is stopped by Jesse, who's recently read *Dubliners* and wants to know if Murph was raised in similar circumstances to Joyce and his characters. Murph goes on a minitirade on how Joyce is both the pride and the gobshite of Ireland, the fooker.

Mint and menthol stream from Judith's mouth. She's been chain-smoking the last couple of hours. He sees his mother smoking, something she never did in life, striking a pose and competently easing the filter between her lips, attempting movie-star glamour.

Drawn forward, he moves to Judith, moves closer to his mother.

She says, "You're staring at me."

"Am I?"

"Don't give me that."

"Have you seen Roz?"

"Not for the last few hours."

"She went to the store and I don't think she's back yet."

"She hasn't phoned?"

"I don't have a cell."

"Did you check your cottage?"

"Why would she be there?"

"I have no idea."

No, he hadn't checked. But Roz wouldn't make her way through the blizzard to his place without stopping off here first.

Judith works her lips. "It's dark out and it's coming down, but it's nothing to get worried about."

He hears the implicit *yet* in her voice.

"Finn?"

"What?"

"Did you hear me?"

"Of course I heard you."

"She's fine. Don't overreact."

He thinks, She's one to talk?

"You're still staring at me."

"You sorry you didn't get out of here when you could have?"

"Hell no. At least we've got a tree here. And liquor apparently. I can smell it, and everybody's acting just cagey enough. Am I going to have to check under the cushions for bottles?"

"You can let it ride, nobody's overindulging."

"You say that like it makes everything all right. And what happens when their parents find out?"

"Parents never find out, they know only what they want to know."

Finn's telling this to his mother, who never wanted to know much about his nights out.

"You worry me sometimes, Finn."

"I realize that, it's a gift. Did you call home?"

"You're actually more paternal toward me than you are to the children. And no. And no one called me either."

"I'm sorry."

"Oh shit, don't be. In my family, that means we're merely maintaining the status quo." She's giving him a little smack on the snout by using the term "status quo." He used it himself this morning when describing Vi staying the hell away from him, even if she really isn't. It's Judith's way of telling him to back the fuck off. "Balance is all-important."

His psychiatrist has told him this too, word for word, and he wonders if Judith's seeing a shrink as well. He can just guess at the contortions she undergoes and the verbal games that she plays, trying to keep one step ahead of revealing anything crucial or meaningful. It's how Finn does it too.

She turns and asks anyone within earshot, "Why in the world isn't Jimmy Stewart on the television?"

"Cable's out," Suzy Smyth tells her.

"Surely someone owns a copy on DVD?"

"How square! Can't we get satellite yet, Mrs. Perry? Please?"

Judith says, "Perhaps your father would be good enough to donate us a dish."

"I'll ask."

"You're such a dear."

"He'd probably expect you to pass me in physics though. That's just the way he is, to be honest."

"Undoubtedly he has expectations of me, but does he have any for you?"

"I'll ask."

Judith leans into Finn, and now he can smell that the mint and menthol are covering a hint of Jameson. More evidence she's spent some time with Murph today. On some level he hopes it's true.

She says, "I've seen that damn movie nearly every year of my long and mostly adventure-free life. But somehow it's simply not Christmas until I've vomited after that final speech about George Bailey being the wealthiest man in town."

"The richest man," he says. He shouldn't correct others in conversation, but he can't help it. He does it so often in class, trying to stay sharp, impeccable, exemplary. "I think it's a metaphor for love and family."

"I know, Finn, that's the saccharine shit that unsettles my stomach."

"I need to find Roz."

"Of course you do," Judith says. Murph hasn't returned with the eggnog. He must've already skipped out the door. The petulance is as thick in her voice as it is in her mind. "Off you go. Bitter nights are meant for lovers, aren't they?"

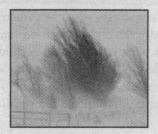

IT'S A QUESTION THAT BEGS AN answer. Finn actually gives it some thought, trying to find a response that doesn't come off as trite. Nothing comes to mind. He knows the draw of self-destruction.

He realizes Judith is walking the line. She's in a lot of pain and puts herself in the path for more and more. It's an addiction in its own right. Part of the ritual is digging into your own wound. He fights for the proper consolation, but by the time something comes Judith has wafted away and is conversing with the girls about Christ knows what.

The undercurrents flowing around Finn lap and break against his body. He rocks and sways on his feet. He imagines himself dancing with Roz, holding her close while the rhythm of the music moves them around the room. It impresses the others as he spins and dips her, the beat becoming their pulse, and the pulse knotting them even more firmly together.

Where the fuck is she? It's the one time he wishes that she carried a cell phone.

Finn's hands are fists. He loosens his grip on the cane. He checks to make sure he hasn't cracked it. It happens from time to time, this show of physical strength, and not always when he's frustrated or angry. It's as if his body cries out for his attention, trying to impress him with what it can still do. A child acting out in front of a neglectful parent. Notice me. See me. *See me.* Over here, over here.

With his open left hand he reaches out, willing Roz to take it.

Sometimes it feels like he'll never be able to hold any influence over the world again. And sometimes it feels like all he has to do is tilt his head or snap his fingers and whatever he wants or dreams will happen. It's a bad place to be, thinking like this. He feels himself starting to drift, and drops his hand. The question hammers at him again.

Where is she?

Finn heads for the door, brushes his shoulder against the jamb, slips out of the study room and into the corridor on the fly like he's in a hurry to catch someone.

The windows at the end of the hall rattle. They're mournful and at least as alive as he is. They're telling him, This way, please, please come to us. This loneliness is something he's well acquainted with. He moves to them. The personification of cold glass seems perfectly natural, its voice needy and human.

These windows want him more than anyone in the school. His footsteps are loud as he speeds toward them. The panes play a soft and adoring contrapuntal to the piano's brutal catcalls still resonating within his chest.

There's a breath of air against the back of his neck. His body reacts faster than his mind as he snaps away from a set of lips too close to his ear.

The dodge nearly sends Finn down. His heels slide. Murphy and his men keep the floors well waxed.

Harley Moon says, "Man, your house isn't settled."

This is how it happens with the burnout psych cases.

The folks mumbling to themselves walking down Fifth Avenue, holding deep conversations with their lost children, dead parents, their homeroom teachers, drill instructors, all the saints and martyrs, and other imaginary pals.

For an instant Finn wonders who it is that Harley Moon represents, what amalgam of his regrets and mistakes. His first lay, his high-school sweetheart, Danielle, Ray's hot broads, the fury of Howie, the girls in the morgue who never should have been there. The dead and the missing that rise from his subconscious and offer curious pursuits to keep him alive for another day.

Finn shakes his head. He feels himself quite plainly dividing. The Finn being formed at this instant, who'll never be the same from this moment on, and the Finn made up of everything that's gone on before. He's in transition, second to second. Maybe he always has been. Maybe everyone is.

Harley asks, "You listening to me, blind man?"

It would be childish for him to say, Would it be too much to ask you to call me Mr. Finn? So he doesn't. But her constant use of "blind man" reminds him, in a way that even his own blindness doesn't, that he can't fucking see.

There's an earthy loam to her scent. She works in the dirt and doesn't wash much. She smells of pioneer womanhood.

"What are you doing here?" he asks. "Why'd you run away before?"

"Didn't run so much as walked out the front door. I said my piece and thought you might take heed."

"Your piece didn't make any sense to me. I still don't know what you're—"

"But you didn't listen to me. And now here I am trying again, even though I feel foolish wasting so much of my breath in a single day." Her voice softens. "I've never been inside the Hotel before. It's . . . pretty."

She just doesn't believe he has no idea what she's talking about. They keep chasing each other around in dwindling circles.

He says, "You should've come in before to get your head looked at."

"It doesn't ache any."

"Still, we should get you checked out."

"Said I'm fine, didn't I?"

"You were bleeding. You might have a concussion."

Harley lets out a little hiss to hush him. She steps closer, then steps away. "I don't like them."

"Who?"

"These girls who attend here. They make fun of me. They come into town and they get hold of some holler boys, get drunk on our whiskey, and then they chitter and whisper and point. They point at me and other folk like me. They point at my younger sisters and my baby brother. They're so surefire smart, they're always smiling and showing their back teeth."

"They make fun of everybody."

"So much the worse, then."

"I simply mean, Harley, that it's nothing personal."

"It is for me."

"That's just the way it is with most spoiled teenage girls."

"You think that makes it all right? That isn't class, the way they slink about and spit like kittens."

"You're right."

Finn thinks about Lea Grant and Caitlin Jones, and realizes that they do spit a little like angry kittens.

Harley makes a similar sound, a young girl's sound full of indignant energy. "Just as good a chance they're gonna be crying soon. The whole lot left."

This girl likes making threats, and she certainly thinks she has a righteous reason for them, but she refuses to share an explanation. She blames him for something, but what the hell could it be?

"Why are they going to cry?" he asks.

"Never you mind about that. So long as you know it's true."

"You'd better start answering my questions, Harley."

"Yeah, that right? Or what, now? Hey?"

He's got no follow-up to that. "Who thumped your head?"

"It'll be a concern of yours quick enough if you don't put things in order."

"What things?"

"Your people. You're still just hoping for the best, aren't you?"

Finn lets out a long even breath.

He pictures Harley in his class, her hand hesitantly raised, answering worn-out, boring questions in new and intriguing ways. He almost doesn't want to find out what she's talking about because he doesn't want her to stop speaking. Her voice carries him.

That Tennessee belle, that Apple Cider Queen he sees when he sees Harley, turns her blue eyes on him, staring with some dismay as if he was a stupid child. Her wild dirty blond hair is finger-brushed to frame her face in a riot of corkscrew curls.

"You aren't listening to me, man. You're turning a deaf ear now too. We aren't going to get out of it that way."

"I don't know what you're talking about."

"You can't lie your way free of this."

"Is that what you think I'm doing?"

"Isn't it?"

"Harley, just tell me whatever it is you're here to tell me. If you're here to tell me anything at all, that is."

"You're a curious one. You're a crafty one, you are, man."

He imagines her crinkling her freckled nose. The beauty spot at the corner of her eye draws his attention.

"Why'd you ask if I wanted to die?"

"'Cause you called down the grief on yourself, don't you know that? What'd you think was gonna happen? You that blind you can't see how this is all your fault? Isn't it so, by your own reckoning? I tried to help. I offered to give you a chance to make things right. That's more than most would. But you wouldn't take it. Your disarray is gonna cost you, and maybe me, and surely some of these plush girlies."

The way she talks to him, about him, it's like she's known him for years. "Listen, why don't you—"

"I told you they'd be coming sooner or later."

"But you never said who."

"I shouldn't have to. Why should I have to?"

"Harley, if you came here to help, then just tell me what this is about. Because I promise you, I don't know."

"And what's your promise worth?"

What the hell else is he supposed to say? "Everything."

"That isn't ever the case."

It's as if she can't respond plainly to him. It somehow goes against the grain of her understanding of life. He likens it to the neighborhood folks in Brooklyn never speaking out against anybody remotely connected to the mob. It's not so much fear as it is conditioning. Being tight-lipped becomes a part of their very nature. He understands that Harley Moon's making a tremendous effort, fighting against her instinct just by being here.

She takes a step away and he does what he can to keep her from vanishing. His hand snaps out and he grabs ahold of some fabric. "Wait. You can't leave. The blizzard is getting worse."

"I live in snow."

Then she's gone again.

Leaving him holding only a scarf. His stomach tumbles with a panic he can't name. Where's Roz? His heart slams, wanting out. Where's Violet? Who's coming here?

AS HARLEY'S FOOTSTEPS ECHO FAINTLY, A sharp pull of paranoia hooks Finn deep under the heart. It's as if he's becoming less defined the farther she gets from him. She's got a barb inside him. It tugs and makes him wince. The feeling propels him forward. He holds on to the banister and in a rush sort of skips sideways down the steps like Astaire did it in fifty films.

Lea and Caitlin are still on the landing, continuing with their whispered discussion. If it's a discussion.

He hears "Yukon," "swindle," "erratic pulse." The phrases "fierce proponent for justice," and "the auspices of erections." He wonders if they heard him and decided to string together a series of disparate words to confuse him.

He moves toward them and says, "That girl who just went by—"

Lea looks at him with Carlyle's mistress's sleepy eyes, her smiling pink lips. "Nobody came this way, Mr. Finn."

"I thought she came this way."

"It's only us. You've been running. There's a flush to your cheeks, Mr. Finn. It's like a fetching afterglow."

With her pale features forming an expression that

says she wants to get back to Oklahoma, the stink of the
Port Authority still on her, chickenhawk at her door,
Caitlin tells him, "A girl on the stairs who was never
here. Is this an undertaking toward parable? A blind man
searching for a girl who's not there."

"A deaf man listening to the radio . . ."

". . . with the plug out. Perhaps there are others trailing about that we're not aware of," Lea says. "Blind men,
I mean, and not necessarily in the allegorical sense."

"Hordes in the attic. They breed like mad."

"We should set traps."

"With what lure, do you suppose?"

Lea pauses. "Fresh meat."

Finn thinks, It might be time to leave this place.
The noose is already tightening.

Lea really does need a good smack in the teeth. It's
feeling more and more true. He flexes his fist around the
cane. It takes a moment for the rage to ease through and
calm him.

"Are you still digressing, Mr. Finn?"

"Like you wouldn't believe," he says.

"Note the shoulders constricting," Caitlin says.

"Noted." Lea nods forcefully enough that it stirs a
slight breeze.

"He had no fun at the fake *fete* either."

"We told him as much."

"My guess is that Violet wasn't in attendance."

"Ladies," he says, "I want you to go stay with the
others."

"What's this, Mr. Finn?"

"Why is this, Mr. Finn?"

He's not sure how to answer. He already appears

foolish enough to these two, and maybe to the other girls as well. His authority has never been fully asserted. His voice wavers. His stance wavers. His character wavers.

Carlyle's mistress, grinning in court, sitting in front of Carlyle's sons and connecting with Carlyle across the room while witness after witness is brought in to point the finger and say what a piece of shit Carlyle is. The sister of a murdered vice cop weeps to the left. Carlyle's sons are well moussed and smell of talcum. The older is already in the syndicate and the younger looks like he should be playing video games. The mistress opens a compact and powders her chin. On one occasion she catches Finn's eyes and her chubby cheeks quiver as she smiles. Lea says, "He looks ready to strike someone."

"Who are you going to strike, Mr. Finn? Are you going to slap us?"

"We deserve a good slapping."

"Well, you do," Caitlin says.

"You too. It's not his fault, not really, that his life has taken on the edifice of a male fantasy."

"With so much slappable nubile flesh about."

"All of us virgins waiting to be deflowered by an older man."

"One we look up to and trust?"

"And force him to bear witness to our blossoming sexuality. Our lesbian fumblings. Sort of bearing witness."

"Well, you fumbled."

"A bit at first."

Jesus Christ. They both laugh almost savagely. Finn's heard that sort of malice many times before. Even

Murph picked up on it. *They live off in another room*. Perhaps they're just too damn smart.

"Go to the lounge and stay with the others."

"Why, Mr. Finn?"

"Just do what I tell you, Lea."

"You sound scared."

Finn moves forward and finds them both hunched against the wall, beneath the windows. The ice pelts the glass like angry insects. He imagines the bugs smashing through like an Old Testament plague.

One of the girls, he thinks it's Caitlin, brushes his fingers with her lips. He sees the jailbait honey down at the station thanking him for sending her back to Muskogee.

He grips each girl by the elbow, forces them to their feet, and prods them toward the stairs. "Go."

"Why are you scared?"

"You've been drinking too much, ladies. Go on."

"That's not it," Lea says.

"What's going to happen?" Caitlin asks. "You're upset. You wouldn't hurt us, now would you, Mr. Finn?"

"No, of course not. Listen to me—"

"The Lord requires celebration," Caitlin says. "All that dancing, the wine, the wafers, the candles, and like that—"

"Sacrificing foreskins, slaughter of lambs, Isaac on the altar—"

Wind buffets the glass. The roof creaks and moans. The storm is hammering even harder. The vibrations working through the walls are causing the piano down in the lobby to strike another violent chord.

He slips loose from the girls and urges them toward

the party. The music is turned way up again. Lea and Caitlin mention "buyer remorse," "field hands," "necrotic," and "the extremity to which I have come."

They wander away hesitantly. Finn turns. The windows clatter, calling to him as if they have some secret to spill.

It's normal, perfectly natural, in this situation, under these circumstances, to personify things.

Good, because he feels like talking.

He says, "I'm here, I'm here. Relax. We'll settle this now."

FINN SPENDS FIVE MINUTES MOVING AMONG the corridors of the Gate House calling for Harley. He's not satisfied she's not here, but what the hell else is he supposed to do? He heads out the front doors, the piano barking angrily as he leaves. The battering wind is like a punch in the face.

It's freezing. His breath catches in his throat. The valley is swollen with snow. The ice helps to clear his mind. He knows with a perfect understanding that there's someone at the school who shouldn't be here.

He heads back toward his office. He tries to feel if he's stepping into someone else's footsteps, but there's no way to tell. The walk is completely covered over again but he's still got his bearings, hears the knotted chimes clanging, knows exactly where he is. That's something anyway.

Despite the fact that his voice won't carry far he feels the need to shout her name out here too. "Harley! Harley!" It's still so foreign to his tongue that it's like screaming gibberish. Then, as if there's a better chance she might respond, he calls, "Moon! Moon!" He sounds like a fucking idiot. He yells, "Roz! Roz?"

He's got to move. The temperature is still dropping.

The blizzard's worse than he'd expected. And he doesn't even have one of his stupid hats on.

Three years upstate and he's still not used to how things work around here. Everybody burrows for days. The county takes its sweet-ass time digging them out. In Manhattan, you slow down for a breath and you'll get mowed down by the five hundred guys on your heels. If three feet of snow drops in three hours, the cabs will still smash it to slush. Pedestrian traffic never stops.

Up here, every spring thaw dredges bodies that have been frozen for three or four months, sometimes twenty yards from their own houses. Some holler folk says, Oh yah, that there's my brother Augie's boy Boomer, wondered where he'd got hisself to, we was waiting on the deer meat he promised.

Finn arrives at the Main House but has trouble getting the door open. Feels locked at first but he strains and the latch finally turns. Weather like this is when everyone bitches about the historical society preserving the original construction and design of St. Val's. There's more than a century's worth of wear nestled beneath the cosmetic renovations and necessary upgrades.

You can feel the hotel reasserting itself. You step inside and can almost feel Rutherford B. Hayes standing shoulder to shoulder with you.

He makes his way to the nurse's office and finds the door locked. The knob is frigid, no one's been this way for a while.

At the bottom of the stairway he stumbles on the goddamn slate. He stomps twice on the stone and can feel the need for action rising in him. He's this close to unleashing a flurry of blows against the wall. Wouldn't that be righteous, break his hands because he got mad at the paneling. He moves up the steps holding the banister, listening to the whispers in the wood.

A noise on the second floor quickens his stride. He thinks, Finally, here's Roz, here's Duchess, here's Harley, here's Violet. His world is a small one. He wonders how much further it can shrink.

Nearing his office, he hears a groan and thinks, Roz, did someone thump your head too? Are you wandering the halls now, your forehead bleeding, looking for me?

"Who is it?" he asks.

There's no response.

He asks again, steel and heat in his voice. "Who's there? Roz?"

A flat wet cough, almost shaped like a word, is the answer.

He takes a step toward it.

"Who is it?"

His name meets him.

"Finn."

It sounds like Vi.

"Violet?"

"Finn."

He steps forward into a thick blanket of mingling odors so strong that it snaps his head back. The scents of sperm and sweat and terror are so powerful that he gags and lets out a squawk.

And woven among them all is the stink of blood.

He raises the back of his hand to block his nostrils. "Ah . . ." Finn starts to drift and lets out a growl, clutching the cane tightly and forcing himself to stay in place. "Vi? What's?"

"No, Finn, go—"

"Christ," he hisses, and the midget halves are hacking at each other in his belly, the fury of Howie is overwhelming.

The end is here and you know it.

Vi whimpers, "Run. Run away, Finn."

She can't speak clearly. Her voice is contorted by pain. She's outside his door, on the floor, clutching herself. Finn kneels beside her. He touches her swollen face. Her lips are split and bruised. She's been slapped and punched, her nose gushing. The blood flows and tries to take him along. He sees her the way he's seen a hundred domestic disputes, her eyes practically spinning with fear.

"Shh, shhh, you're all right now, Violet."

"You have to get out. You have to—"

"What happened?" he asks, and he's not sure if he's speaking to her. Something inside is trying to warn him. He holds his hand out and she grabs it, holds on tightly. Two of her nails are broken.

"They want you," Vi tells him. "Run."

"Who did this?"

"—run away, you have to leave."

"No."

"Run. Go."

"Stop saying that."

"There's two of them, Finn." Her voice is tight and strained. A gurgle of blood comes up and splashes against her teeth. Her hand clenches and she draws him near. "They have knives. Holler men."

He snarls, *"Motherfuckers."*

"They've been waiting for you."

"They're going to die."

Violet's been raped. Violet is bleeding. He thinks, Jesus, she's just a little girl. The irony doesn't escape him. He can't control himself anymore as he flails and falls into the ocean of color that used to be his life. He's going to get to use his strong hands again. He knows he's smiling.

TEN SECONDS BEFORE THEY'RE ABOUT TO bust down the back door to a fish market where one of Carlyle's captains does most of his business, Ray decides to shake up the universe by telling Finn, "He wants me dead."

There's no point in asking who or why. Finn's half suspected that Ray's been moved up from a minor dirty-bankroll cop to major corruption over the past year. He's got a much nicer apartment, some extra flash in his clothes, and a new SUV that seats twelve. Like he's going to be driving the women's softball team around? All of that, but Ray's probably only on board because it's pretty dumb not to be.

But Carlyle's up on charges again and this time it looks like they might stick. The DA's wife was paralyzed by a shoddy car bomb six months earlier and it sent the guy nuclear. Finn has another subpoena but Ray doesn't, which was really fucking imprudent for the DA's office to do.

Ray keeps giving Finn the look. There's some serious strain on their partnership. The threatening notes are being slipped into Finn's locker again. He's examined the handwriting and wonders if any of it is Ray's.

At home, Danielle told him that some pervert has

been making phone calls. He explains the situation to her. She's got to be on guard for whatever might be coming down. She packs a .32 and they go to the gun range together. She's already a better shot than he is.

In the deep night Dani turns over in bed and asks, What'll happen when they finally ask you about Ray?

He doesn't know the answer. He's never perjured himself on the stand because he's never had information that could help put the big players away. But if IAD ever comes sniffing around, Finn will have to decide how far out on the ledge he's willing to go.

Now, with this one comment about Carlyle wanting him dead, Ray has confessed to all kinds of illegal activities, subterfuge, extortion, kickbacks, and chicanery. Finn rolls his eyes and pulls an aggrieved face, knowing why Ray has chosen this moment to confess.

It means Ray is going to pop Carlyle's captain in the back of the fish market. He's switching sides in the middle of the game. He's going to help hang Carlyle's ass out on the flagpole and he wants Finn to open fire and frag however many crew members might be inside stuffing their faces with calamari or counting up the day's receipts.

"You are such a motherless bitch prick asshole," Finn says.

It gets Ray grinning. "You love me anyway. Okay, now, follow my lead."

"Did you just fucking say 'follow my lead'?"

"Come on."

The door isn't even locked. These syndicate guys aren't worried about anybody or anything except a RICO case, and the feds take so long with those that by the time the court date is made all the mob players can pretend to have Alzheimer's by walking around town in their bathrobes and slippers.

Ray goes in first, Finn on his heels. Inside are the captain, two well-known shooters, and a couple of other notable wiseguys sitting around a table drinking white wine and having what looks like trout almondine.

Finn does the talking, by the book, reads off the Miranda shit, tells them to get up against the wall. The captain stands while everybody else keeps eating.

You've got to give them one thing, the crew is old school and very cool.

The cap pours himself more wine and asks Finn and Ray if they'd like a glass. Ray is still smiling, actually breaks off a chuckle, and puts one hand out like he's going for the bottle.

Ray says, "Sure, I could use a sip."

But what Ray's really doing, what Finn knows he's doing, is getting into firing position. Finn's got a half second to wonder what he should do next. His mind works fast. The world will never miss any of the syndicate soldiers in this room. This crew has committed more murders and Class-A felonies than any sixty mooks you might pull out of C-Block on any given day.

But he can't kid himself, he can't let Ray butcher anybody in cold blood. Finn fully realizes that Ray is at least halfway thinking about taking Finn out too, just to be on the safe side.

After twenty years of friendship, almost thirteen on the force, five with gold shields, he finally sees with a painful clarity that he's never really liked Ray much.

He does the thing he knows he shouldn't do, that

will not be good for him at all. That will cause strife and much anguish in the coming days, despite staying true to himself.

Finn reaches out and clamps his hand onto Ray's wrist. He squeezes and Ray lets out a grunt of pain, turns his eyes onto Finn, and tries to break the hold but can't.

The crew knows this isn't SOP but they're all smart enough not to immediately go for their guns. In a way, it's a show of faith in Finn. Look at that. Even while he wrestles with Ray he also struggles with the notion that these guys are on his side, wishing him well, hoping he'll win.

You can't go ten goddamn minutes in this life without some kind of confusing shit like this rearing its head.

The fraternal order of blue brotherhood wants you dead and the wiseguys are practically toasting you with Sauvignon Blanc.

How did the battle against evil go today?

Ray leans in close and says, "Knock it off, choirboy."

Finn keeps the crew covered. They're trying not to look interested. Two cops in the back room, clearly off the grid, doing bad things, and the wiseguys are still picking at their fish.

"We're not going down this road."

"We're already on it, and nearing the end of it. Just another half step or so and we're off it for good."

"You can never get off it, that's the point."

Ray hides his anger and disappointment behind the full-wattage charm. "Hey now, don't you know anything? After they bump me, how long do you think it'll be before you follow?"

"That's not—"

"And after you, Dani?"

The invocation of Dani's name is meant to freeze Finn. It works. His muscles lock so abruptly that his elbows crack like rifle shots. His fist tightens on Ray's wrist and the small bones grind and scrape until real agony squirms in Ray's eyes. At least he's not smiling anymore. Sometimes Finn thinks he'd pay anything, even his life, just to knock the edges off Ray's grin.

Ray sucks air through his teeth, makes a fist of his free hand, and goes in for a short jab to Finn's ribs. Finn parries, keeping his grip locked on Ray's wrist and continuing to squeeze harder. An almost orgasmic moan rushes from Ray's chest and one of the mob shooters inches toward a cabinet like he's about to jump for it.

His name is Franco or Marco or Loco, and he's supposed to be pretty good with a sawed-off twelve pump. Finn catches his gaze and lets him know without any words, but in no uncertain terms, that if he tries it, everyone in the room dies together. Ray kicks out for Finn's groin.

"Kicking is for sissies," Finn says. It's a comment fourteen years in the making. He thought he'd get more catharsis out of saying it. He should've waited longer.

A couple more syndicate guys stroll into the back room from the front market area, looking to get a plate of dinner. There's definitely too many to ace now. Finn releases Ray and the two of them make exactly the same gesture, motioning the new guys farther into the room by wagging their guns at them, C'mere, c'mere.

Now he and Ray are side by side, shoulder to shoulder, and the familiarity and comfort returns them to where they ought to be—partners trusting each other. Ray is back to being himself, the version that Finn knows perfectly well. None of this follow-my-lead shit.

Ray eases his way to the table and takes a long pull of wine directly from the bottle. Without warning, Finn rushes over and rabbit-punches Franco Marco Loco hard, knocking him to the floor.

Hey, they have to fully comprehend that they shouldn't even fucking think about pulling a move on you.

After his Adam's apple has been working steadily for fifteen seconds, Ray finishes off the Sauvignon Blanc, takes a breath, and lets loose with a loud belch. He throws the empty bottle on top of the fish and says, "You'd think with all this brain food around here, you pricks would've learned a little something by now."

Cap says, "I learned something about you today."

"Yeah? What might that be?" Ray is grinning again, in charge, indestructible. "What? Tell me. Let me hear it."

Cap is cool enough that he just stares with a touch of amusement in his face. Finn sees what's about to happen as plainly as any prophet. Ray gets the cuffs on Cap and knees him hard in the nuts. There it is.

While the cap is tossing his lunch Ray says, "I didn't quite catch that. Next time, speak up a little."

Leading the limping wiseguy out to the car parked down the block, Ray can't even keep his voice down to a whisper. He glares at Finn. His finger slips on and off the trigger. Finn watches the finger very closely.

"Do you have any idea what you've done?" Ray asks.

"Maybe not."

"I know too much. I have too much on them. They're going to ace me."

"I won't let that happen."

"You can't stop it, choirboy."

"Haven't you botched things up enough?" Finn thinks they should have it out once and for all, but on a city street in front of Carlyle's captain isn't the best time. Cap is moaning and starting to struggle some, so Finn chops him across the back of the neck. Cap hits the cement and lies there twitching. "You had to move up in line to be a big dog? You couldn't just take a little under the table? You had to jump all the way into bed?"

"You still don't know how it works. You're the dumbest son of a bitch on the force. Nobody else wants anything to do with you. Nobody else would partner up with you. Nobody trusts you, not since the very beginning. Not since the rooftop."

"It's your ass on the line now. If Carlyle's afraid of what you know, then so are the boys on the payroll."

"You don't know how often I've stopped a hit going out on you."

"Yeah?" Finn says. "Next time tell them to go for it. Do what you got to do. I will."

"Because it's your job to protect the innocent."

"It's yours too, you prick."

Finn had to admit to himself that at the time, he really didn't know what he'd done.

But all the following years of darkness gave him plenty of time to dwell on that moment, as his choices continue to sweep forward through time to find him again with each new puzzled breath.

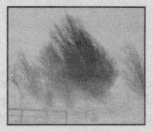

"FINN!"

Someone's always yelling at him.

"Motherfuckers."

"Finn!"

He's on his knees and Vi is on the floor, shouting in his ear.

"I'm here," he says.

"You need to run."

"I'm here. Where are they?"

"I don't know."

He shrugs out of his coat and wraps it around Vi's shoulders. She groans at his touch. "Did you hear them leave the building?"

"No." She coughs and it's a wet red sound. "But I think I might've—might've—"

"Passed out?"

"I think so. Maybe."

"You're bleeding. How badly hurt are you, Vi?"

"I don't know."

"I need to get you up and into my office."

"No! We'll be trapped then."

She's right. You can't barricade yourself in a room with only one exit. With a pebbled-glass door.

"You can hide."

"No, they'll find me again."

"Let's use the phone."

"I want to go home," she says, sounding about nine years old.

"Oh Christ," he begs, and tightens his hold on her.

Then he gathers her up, unlocks his office door, and leads her inside. She's terrified and starting to mewl. It's a sound he's heard a thousand times before and never heard before. It's a whimper that's lived inside him for five years, and perhaps longer. He shuts the door and locks it again.

He needs to call someone. Alert Judith and Murph to what's happening. They can prepare for trouble, keep an eye out. Call the cops, get their country-hick asses out here on their Sno-Cats. He tries the phone. Dead. He wonders if it's the storm or if the holler men have cut the hard line.

"Tell me what happened."

"There's two of them. They raped me. They held me down." He turns his head to face the window, thinking, My enemies have found me. Whichever ones they are. An ill will had been thinking on me. They will punish my loved ones. There's two of them, and I have to kill them.

"It was all so quiet," she continues, breathing shallowly. "One of them didn't talk, not the whole time. I'm not sure he can. He punched me. He kept hitting me. He has a knife." Her voice firms again with an unbelievable resolve. She tries hard to keep from cracking, but she's going to. They all do.

The sobbing starts and she forces her words out between gasps. "He put . . . his knife in me first. He stuck it in . . . before him . . . before he stuck himself in . . ."

"Shh, Vi, you're okay now." Finn listens to himself, thinking he sounds so much closer to the edge of hysteria than she does. Everyone is stronger than he is. She actually touches the side of his face with a bloody palm, trying to comfort him.

"I came back to see you. I'm sorry. I came back to your office . . . hoping you'd be there. I'm so dumb . . . I can't control myself . . ."

"None of us can." Jesus Christ, she's just a kid. "Don't worry about any of that. Did you see a gun? Any guns?"

"No."

Two of them, still nearby. But in the building? Could they have missed him out in the storm? Where he was yelling his head off, calling for Roz, for Harley, for Moon?

"He didn't make a sound," Vi says. She's stopped crying. She's trying to hand over information, something that might help. "The other, he's . . . retarded, I think. He *leered* the whole time. Or maybe he's just crazy. He put a piece of tape over my mouth. He was happy. He said he was my friend. While he was holding me down. I tried to fight, I swear I did."

"I know you did."

"I swear, I swear to God."

"It doesn't matter."

"It does, it does!"

Finn knows it's costing her a great deal, talking this way, open with him. She's making the effort to keep calm, to distance herself from the situation, and she's doing it for his sake.

His heart is slamming crossways inside him.

Roz. Did they get to Roz?

"His name is Pudge. He talks in the third person. He called me girlie. He told me 'Pudge likes you, girlie, Pudge is gonna take care of you.' And I could tell he meant it. He was careful when he held me. He's strong. Very strong. Insane strong, you know? He thought he was being nice. Sweet to me. The other, Pudge called him Rack. I think they're brothers. Rack, he's strong too, but he's bad, Finn, he's a bad one. I could feel it. I could feel it in him. He's dead inside. God. He . . . he only let me go because he knows we can't get away. How can we get away in the storm? Where could we go? He never made a sound."

Finn's got to get word to the sheriff's office, the state troopers, someone.

She can tell what he's thinking and says, "The storm's too intense. No one can see anything out there."

"I don't need to see."

"You can't do anything. No one's going to help us."

Finn presumes that Rack planned it this way. Backwoods boy, probably knows these hills and valleys better than anyone, has some hard-chugging four-wheel drive truck on campus that can grind through the drifts.

"Did the one who talked . . . Pudge . . . did he say why they were doing this?"

"No. He just said it was your fault."

She spares asking him why.

But Harley Moon, she knows the answer. She said

he would pay. Finn feels a sudden burning resentment
for the girl.

Violet goes into a coughing fit and spits blood. The
aroma of it soars into his head. Finn grits his teeth and
turns his face away, the past inside him wanting to take
over. He's suddenly partially aroused, his temples throbbing. The craving for light and vision is so strong it's almost impossible to resist. Especially because he doesn't
want to. He's an addict. He's a junkie for his lost sight.
His own history recedes like a red tide.

Violet moans and goes into a coughing fit. She could
have internal bleeding. It would be like Vi to say nothing, dying while she patted his hand. He should've
checked her more thoroughly but he's afraid to put his
hands on her. Worried about what he might find, what
he might become.

Every move he makes or thinks of making is wrong.
Finn reaches out and touches her belly, checking for
knife wounds. Moves his hands upward across her ribs,
feels the fractures. Then continues on to her throat.
Then her face. The nose needs to be packed. "Violet, we
have to go—"

"Please hold me. I'll be okay in a second, but ... I
need ... please ... just for a second ... I mean, like ... like
maybe how my father would? Like ..."

He hugs her to him and she lets loose with the beginning of a wail that she muffles against his chest. He
lets it go on for as long as he can. Then he hushes her, the
way a father might. They need to get the hell out of here.

"Can you walk?"

"I think so."

"Come on, let's go. We've got to get you over to the

Gate House. Everyone else is there. If we get separated, you go alone."

"Why would we—"

"If it's a whiteout, aim for the lights. You can make it. You tell them to lock everything. Call the sheriff's office, the state troopers. Someone's cell should work if they take it to the roof. You tell them to fight if they have to."

"I will. You and I, we both will." Her voice so cool, so in control. Preparing him as best she can for what's to come.

Finn only caught one school shooting while he was on the force. A substitute teacher who was dismissed for reasons that boiled down to him just acting too fuckin' weird. Guy came back six weeks after being let go, packed to party. He carried a pair of TEC-9s, a five-shot S&W .50-cal. Magnum, and a satchel filled with an assortment of pipe bombs, handcuffs, sex toys, and flavored lubricants. Fuckin' weird, yeah.

He popped a teacher and the principal on his way inside, then marched to his old schoolroom. He let all the male students go and most of the females as well.

During the siege he kept hidden behind seven girls, blocked the windows with taped-up newspapers, and went on to indulge himself for five and a half hours. He let one of the girls contact her parents explaining in detail what he was doing to them. What he was forcing them to do to each other.

It got extreme enough that one of the girls tried to toss a desk through the window and jump to safety. She broke her back and he lobbed a bomb down on top of her, killing her and Finn's sergeant, who'd made a move to help.

SWAT went in twice. Both efforts were massive fuckups. The first time they blew a wall and killed one of the kids but never got a clear shot at the perp. The second time they blew the door to find the perp hiding behind two of the girls. SWAT's sniper was good and fast but the perp wanted to die with his finger on the trigger. He shot one of the students in the back before he went down. The .50-cal. took out her entire torso.

When Finn made it into the room the body was still there and he got to see the girl's head sitting inside her own stomach cavity. The rest was on the walls.

He thinks of it all again as he tells Vi, "It's going to be all right."

He pulls his blade, knowing it won't be enough.

She leans on him as he opens the office door. "Come on, Vi, we have to leave."

She staggers along beside him down the hall. He tries to block out her noise and focus beyond it.

With one arm around her he pulls her along. Soon he realizes he's dragging her.

"Leave me here," she says, and crumples beside him.

"I'm not leaving you here. Come on."

"I can't."

"You can, Vi, you have to."

"Something inside is . . . scraping together."

"You've got a couple of broken ribs. You can make it. Now get up, Violet. I need you to move. Get the hell up, Miss Treato, do you hear me?"

"Yes, Finn. You need me."

"Yes, I need you. Get up."

Violet levers herself to her feet and shrugs into his arms. She sighs against his chest, clinging to him. Half-hanging there, half-embracing him like a lover. He tries to think of the best way to get out of here. He's got to keep the girl safe, needs to find Roz, has to get over to the dorm. Murph is there. Murph is tough. Murph's got balls. Murph's got notions. He'll put up a fight. A part of Finn wishes that Ray were here for backup.

He and Vi move down the corridor again.

Every few seconds she lets out a pained whimper and tries to squelch it. She's still trying to be the woman he wants—tough, independent, uncomplaining. A strange calm descends over him the instant he truly decides that no matter what happens from this point on, he's going to kill the men who did this to her.

They maneuver down the stairs together.

Her weight pressed against him, he allows his shoulder to slide along the wall. This stairway has killed a lot of people over the years. Its extravagance was made for dramatic suicides.

"I think I've figured out why my mother hates me," Vi says.

"She doesn't hate you, Violet. No one hates you."

"She does. She hates me because she knows I like older men. Maybe she thinks I'm going to steal my father from her."

It actually sounds pretty reasonable to Finn.

She pants her words. "Or her gynecologist... Dr. Calhoun. Can you imagine, having an affair... with your OB-GYN? Gross."

Vi's beginning to unravel a touch. He's got to hold her together until they get to the others. If they're attacked on their way across campus, Finn will fight, Vi will go it alone. Out in the storm, he'll have the edge, while they're blinded by snow and darkness.

On the ground floor they take five steps toward the front door and Vi stops short, one heel squeaking.

"Oh God," she whispers. "I can see them through the glass in the door. They're outside and coming in here."

NO TIME TO BE GENTLE. FINN dumps Vi on the floor and she cuts loose with a yelp. He makes an awkward leap, extends his cane, and snaps off the switch to three of the overhead lights. Even at night Murph keeps half of them on to deter prowlers.

Finn thinks, Okay, none of this "hey, I'm at home in the dark, I've got the advantage now" bullshit, but shadows will help.

He hears their footsteps approaching.

"Run," he tells her. "Use the west door."

"I can't."

"Get up and run, Vi."

"I can't."

He wonders if he's got enough time to rush over and hit the lock. It won't keep them out for very long, but a few seconds either way still counts.

But the chance is gone. A burst of freezing wind and ice crystals whips into the lobby. It sounds like someone's taking a bucket of sand and throwing it across the floor. Finn can feel the cold on his teeth. He's grinning again.

He breathes the fresh air in deeply. He's got the cane in his left hand, the open knife in his right. He holds the blade down against the side of his leg. The rage runs over him in a friendly, loving manner. It licks his earlobe, it tickles his balls.

"So what's this all about?" he asks the holler men in the hall.

No response. The front door slams shut.

Vi is doing an incredible job of controlling her panic, but a brief moan of terror drains from her.

Finn snaps his cane down and the echoes return. His facial vision shows him that there are two men in the lobby before him. They stand on either side of the corridor, about six feet apart. His bones tell him that the men are large. He can hear that they're creeping forward with an animal canniness. Sons of bitches. One snickers. It's a twisted, degenerate sound.

Finn lets out the same kind of chuckle, equally sick. One is retarded. The other doesn't speak.

Finn decides to ask the big question.

"What's this all about, Pudge?"

He's not expecting an answer, but Pudge mutters with an odd guttural bleating, "You done did bring this on yourself, blind man."

"And how'd I do that, Pudge?"

The grating titters again. "You owe us."

"What the hell do I owe you?"

"You know what you done. You know the way that led us here. You know the way of where we're going."

"What the fuck does that mean?"

Finn whips his cane down again, senses they've covered half the distance to him. The knife feels righteous in his fist. His shrink says this is asserting his independence, feeding his need for security, taking a hand in his own self-preservation, but Finn thinks that in some fashion he's been waiting for this moment. Hoping for this moment.

In response to his rage, Finn turns the knife point just enough so that it jabs into his leg. The sting refocuses him.

"Pudge, you hurt a little girl. You're the one who's got to pay."

"We don't want to hurt no one. That girlie, she gonna be all right. She all right. I like her. I only kissed her up some."

"You motherfucking bastard," Vi hisses. She's trying to clamber to her feet. Finn wants to lend a hand, but the situation is precarious, tremulous. A delicate tableau liable to shatter in an instant. He waves her back with his cane, hopes she'll run for it. Vi takes a step forward. "You rotten son of a fucking bitch."

Finn wishes she hadn't spoken. He needs these two to concentrate and stay focused on him. He needs to keep this argument going. People who are willing to talk have an inherent expectation to continue the conversation. He can keep Pudge busy.

But Rack. Who is Rack? What is Rack?

The gruff bleating is baffled. "You mad at me, girl? You shouldn't be mad at me none. We made you a woman. Made you a woman's what we done. That's a good thing. It's a good thing for you. You find you a husband soon. Soon enough, you find one."

When he imagines Pudge, Finn sees Stan Collins, a guy he went to the academy with. Two weeks in, during a self-defense class, Stan had an aneurysm that left him disabled. Since Stan wasn't technically a police officer yet, the brass weren't about to pay a lifetime of special-care bills. A long, very public legal battle ensued. Finn remembers seeing Stan in front of the microphones at press conferences, his overwrought wife and two little girls standing behind him on the courthouse steps, Stan speaking in a kind of strangled growl, lips perpetually tilted into a drooling smirk. With his thinning hair they couldn't hide Stan's surgery scars as easily as they'd done with Finn.

"Give us what you owe," Pudge says, "and we can get on our way."

Finn thinks, Maybe this is all just about money. Maybe this is the way these backwoods pricks pull a score. This is their version of a heist, a smash-and-grab. "So how much do we owe you, Pudge?"

"You mean you don't know? You don't know what you owe, man?"

"I've forgotten."

"You shame yourself. You shame my family. We deserve to be paid for our product. We cooked our load. You carried it on. You carried it on and we deserve to be paid. We need a new truck. It's time for a new truck."

Aha.

Product.

Cooked product.

They're crystal-meth makers acting like Finn's fucked them on a deal.

Do they have him mixed up with Murph? Does Murph still have notions? Was he trying to rise above his station? Did he throw in with these two to rob a bank?

Or is it one of the girls? Claiming he's the chief in

charge while they rip off backwoods bathtub meth-heads?

He's hoping there's still a chance to defuse the situation, but the rage flows up his throat like venom and he feels the need to spit.

"You shouldn't have touched the girl."

"She all right, man. She all right, she is."

"Did you beat on Harley Moon too?"

"Harley? You seen Harley?"

"I have. You thumped her head."

"She's our sister," Pudge says.

Fin thinks, Ah, the Moon brothers. He smacks his cane. Rack is stone solid still.

"Isn't for you to question us about her," Pudge continues. "Isn't for you. We take care of our own. That's right. You're the one. You're the one not looking out for your house."

It's true. Finn hasn't looked out for his own house. No matter who's responsible for this, he's the man in charge. Harley came to warn him. She was persistent. She tried twice. He was thick. He was dense.

"You like hurting little girls, Pudge, you and your brother."

"That isn't any of your say. None of your say at all. None of it is."

Finn snaps the cane down again. The sound fills his face. They've both moved up another couple of steps. "I'll protect my house."

"Give us our money. We need our money. The truck, it don't work so well no more."

Vi's managed to stand. Finn hears what sounds like a kitchen faucet with a slow drip. They cut deep inside of her, and she's bleeding much worse than he'd thought. She's not attempting to run. Finn shifts on the balls of his feet, trying to keep himself in front of her.

He addresses the silent one. The really bad one.

"You got anything to add, Rack?"

Rack says nothing.

"You let this idiot do all your talking for you?"

Rack says nothing. Pudge gives a grunt of exasperation. He says, "I'm smart enough, blind man. My brother, he run the show. He run the show but I talk. I do the talking, I do. He less for words than me."

So if they want cash, he's got to play them along and buy himself some time. "I don't have your money here."

"You gonna get it."

"I've got it, just not here. But I'll pay you."

"You remember how much it is?"

"Yes."

"How much more time? What time you gonna need?"

"One more day."

"That all? All the time?"

"Yes."

Pudge rubs his chin, which is thickly stubbled. The leisurely scrape of knuckles against the bristles is in sync with Vi's blood spattering the tile.

When he imagines Rack standing there in the hall before him, Finn sees his own shadow thrown against a wall. It's perfectly recognizable as his shadow, standing at an angle with the outline of the shades discernible, the cane in his left hand, the knife in his right.

"My brother don't believe you, man. Where you

gonna get the money tomorrow if you don't have it today?"

"I can get it."

"Where? Where you gonna get it?"

"What difference does it make?"

"We don't believe you. It's not a believing thing, what you say."

"Who else do you hurt, Pudge?"

"Isn't none of your affair. If you had paid when you was supposed to, if you'd done what you were supposed to, when you were supposed to do it, then—"

"Did you hurt anyone else?"

"We got our ways, man."

It's like talking to a goddamn cinder block. "I know you've got your ways. Have you hurt anyone else?"

They move in closer.

"We got us a nurse, case anybody bleeds a little."

So they've got Roz. Finn takes a step forward. Maybe they've harmed her. Perhaps raped her. Perhaps left her for dead down some lonely hall, stashed in a room, or maybe murdered out in the snow. Finn can cut at least one of their throats.

They move in closer.

"So what are you going to do, Pudge?"

"That's the question there. The question that we got an answer for. We gonna hurt your house some more. We gonna teach you the lesson that needs to be taught. She didn't learn none either, your lady. Your girlies. A little more blood's what you need for the lesson to hold."

Finn's shadow elongates and moves across the wall, taking two steps forward. Finn goes to meet it.

He chokes up on his cane and swings it in a short arc. It slaps Rack across the face but the holler man doesn't make any sound. All Finn can tell is that Rack has a strong jaw.

This is going to take time. Rack is going to draw his arm back and throw a vicious punch aimed for Finn's chin. Finn reacts as if he can see it all happening, twisting aside to let the fist pass his ear by inches, then snapping his elbow back hard into Pudge's belly.

It's an enormous belly. Finn wonders what he was expecting considering the guy's name is Pudge. He sees Stan Collins's thinning hair waft, his gaping, drooling mouth tugged to one side, black bags under his eyes. Finn stays in close, it's the only way he can fight. He doesn't need to have his hands on these guys all the time, but he wants to be near enough that contact is inevitable. He's got to keep these two off balance.

He brings the knife up and stabs at an angle. He strikes nothing. Finn turns on his heel and slashes outward. He misses again.

He moves in another half step, swings the blade around, and this time catches some thick clothing. It's a coat covered in fur. It's made of tanned animal skins. No good. Vi is shouting. Vi is screaming. Finn whips the cane around but can't find Rack. Only four seconds in and already he's fucked.

But the knife worries Pudge enough to make him back off. He says, "Blind man, you want to know who else I hurt? I'm going to hurt you now. Now I'm going to hurt you."

Only those outside the darkness think they can hurt

him. They're all mistaken. He's met his death already. The worst has already happened.

But he's got to protect Vi.

She's moved to his right, close enough behind him now that he feels her breath on the back of his neck. The slow tap-tap of dripping continues. At this rate she'll be dead in ninety minutes. He angles his head to the side and says over his shoulder, "Where?"

"Rack's to your left, ten feet away. Pudge is five feet straight ahead."

"You just don't learn, girlie," Pudge whines. "You don't learn and you don't live right. It's a sad state. You sadden me."

Vi hisses in response. Finn hears a knife leave its sheath. It takes two full seconds to draw. Maybe an eight-inch blade. Rack's not dicking around. But anybody who wears a sheath on his belt probably isn't. He likes to jab little girls.

The rage is humming inside Finn, washing on and on like a river. His mind skitters. He waits, listening for footsteps. There aren't any. Then there are. Rack is sort of galloping around. Pudge is moving. Vi touches Finn on the small of his back, where he likes women to touch him. She wants him to move away, to retreat with her. He moves backward and steps into her blood.

"You aren't no good with that sticker. My brother, now, he's good. He's real good."

Finn snaps his cane down and the echo washes over the holler boys. The sound waves return and touch Finn everywhere.

He turns and faces his shadow. It moves the way he

does, it holds the weapons he does, it is ugly in the sun, like he is.

He's got no choice. He has to lure them away from Vi. He's got the knife. His hands are strong. He cannot survive against two armed men, but he can wound them, maybe badly. He's not afraid to die, not even for something as stupid as this, whatever this is. All that matters is his duty. It's all that remains of his being a cop and being a man. It's his job to protect the innocent. It wasn't a lie. It wasn't a foolish comment after all.

He thinks, I am a stone in the night. I will not break.

I dream of murder.

Violet says, "I love you."

Her voice courses through him. She fastens to his side, leaning on him for a moment before standing on her own. He hears her knuckles crack. She's balling her fists. Vi is fighting alongside him. She's fighting for him. She actually rushes forward. He drops the cane and reaches out to stop her.

But he's too slow.

There's a sound like the sound of the incident.

His skull is fragmenting.

A breath eases from Violet's lips and rattles on and on until it stops forever.

Within him, in the place where he's weakest, Finn shrieks. His scream moves up through him, gaining momentum and force until it erupts through the bottom of his brain. He lunges and gets his right arm around Pudge's throat and smashes his left elbow into Rack's cheek. It's pure luck.

The three of them move together like a trio that has

practiced this dance many times before. They fall
against the door and glass shatters and wood splinters as
they crash through. Finn tries to slash at Pudge's carotid
but his neck is protected with a thick scarf. The storm
inside Finn meets the storm outside.

He slips, goes down in the snow, and tries to wheel
to his feet. The wind is fierce and tears at Finn's face.
Rack is beneath him and Finn hammers wildly. He slams
down with the meat of his palm, hoping to crush Rack's
throat. He scrambles as quickly as he can through the
knee-deep snow. He hopes he's headed across the lawn
and into the woods bordering the academy. He'll draw
them after him.

It's a good plan except he trips and slams into something that tears his shirt practically off his back. The
wind deafens and disorients him. He does an awkward
somersault in midair and lands in a two-foot-high bank.
He's gone over the hedges bordering the front walk of
the Carriage House.

Pudge is on top of him in a second, huffing loudly.
Finn drives the blade deep into Pudge's face and twists.
Feels like he's gone up through the roof of his mouth
and into the cranial cavity. Finn's hands are suddenly hot
and a burst of steam blasts against his chin. A crazed
dying squeal escapes Pudge's lips and he hacks up blood
into Finn's face. Finn spits it back.

It tastes of sunshine. The killing blizzard grows brilliant with Finn's life.

PART III
OPTIC NERVE

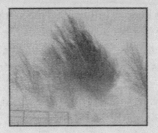

THE CAR BOMB THAT GOT RAY takes off the last two toes of his left foot, sends some shrapnel into his ass, and burns away his eyebrows and most of his hair.

It happens the morning he's supposed to be deposed for Carlyle's trial. The DA goes on without him. Finn's called up and spends his time on the stand coming to the conclusion that Ray had planted the bomb himself. Ray's done such a good job of it, totaling the car but barely being hurt, that Finn wonders if Ray wired the DA's wife's car too.

As with any bad marriage, there are still appearances to be kept up. Finn shows up at the hospital later that afternoon with flowers and a handful of books. Dani's already at Ray's bedside, talking animatedly about North Carolina. She thinks Ray wants to retire now and live off his disability.

Finn walks in and she says, "You've got to find the people who did this. You've got to find them and kill them."

Finn says, "Sure."

He puts the flowers on Ray's chest and Ray sniffs them once then holds them out to Dani, who is starting to cry as she heads off to find a vase.

She wants Finn to kill the bad guys. It's not to get revenge for Ray, but because she knows the trouble is hitting closer to home. She's giving him the green light to do what he has to do to protect their home, to make certain they'll be safe.

A lot of wives, they'd tell their husbands to buckle down. Take the cash. Lie on the stand. Lose the evidence. But Dani knows that for Finn, the lesser of two evils is to pull the trigger.

"How'd it go?" Ray asks.

"About what you'd expect. Shouldn't you be on your stomach letting your ass get some air?"

"They've got me so numbed up I wouldn't feel it if they drove a Lionel train set up my wazoo. I'm supposed to be turned on my side but I worry that in mixed company my johnny might come up to take a peek."

"Anyone who might be interested in that will be turned off by your blistered noggin."

"You'd be surprised."

"I probably would."

Ray's got a .38 only half-slid under his right leg, ready to pull it if an unfriendly face shows up.

"They took their run at me. You'll be next."

There's no reason for Carlyle or anybody else to come after Finn unless Ray's been telling lies. He's probably getting paid twice as much as the rest of the blues on the take, pretending Finn's been in on every underhanded deal. It's a joke that actually makes Finn chuckle. The cops think he's too clean and the mob figures he's dirty up to his neck. No wonder Ray wanted to pop the whole crew. In his own way, maybe he was protecting Finn. When he wasn't thinking about icing him.

The nurse shows up to give Ray his meds. There's six little cups of pills. She says something quietly to Ray that sends him into his *if I laugh loudly enough I might get laid* laugh. He swallows the medication and sips the water she offers him like it's champagne. She rubs some salve on the bald eyebrow ridges.

As she passes Finn he notes that her eyes are dilated. Her shoulders are a bit slumped. He thinks downers, but nowadays some heavy antidepressant or even Ritalin will do the same trick.

She tells Finn, "I'm Rose but everyone calls me Roz."

"Why?" he asks.

"Why what?"

"Why do they call you Roz if it's not your name?"

She considers it a second. "I suppose because I let them."

He gets the feeling that she's telling him some kind of a secret but he can't imagine what the hell it could be.

"Are you the cop who's going to catch the bad guys who did this?" she asks.

"Catch them and kill them," Finn says.

Over his next few visits he notices that Roz comes around to see Ray about twice as much as she hits the other patients' rooms. She even gets in on a couple of the photo ops. Reporters quiz Ray about what happened and how it ties in with the Carlyle case. Ray never takes the "no comment" route—he talks a lot but doesn't say much. Roz poses provocatively lying next to him in his hospital bed. One, sometimes two extra buttons on her uniform are undone. She's got nice cleavage. The media guys eat it up. Ray eats it up. The hospital administration doesn't.

She takes a lot of heat. She's already got a strike against her because she's had some trouble with meds on the job, but nowadays they don't fire you outright for that sort of thing. They send you to rehab. She flirts hard with Ray and to a lesser extent with Finn, cocking her hips and flashing little fuck-me grins. Danielle notices and rolls her eyes.

At home she tells him, "That one, I know the type. She's going to cause some serious troubles. Mark these words."

"Consider them marked," Finn says.

Roz is twenty-seven and has never been married. She came close once but the guy ran out at the last minute to do a drug deal in Mexico, where he was shot-gunned out of his boots by *federales*. Finn learns all of this over the course of an afternoon while having coffee with her in the hospital cafeteria during her break. She's eager to talk. He likes her voice, the oddball way she sees things, even the shit she gets into. It's an aggressively forged, kooky kind of path.

A couple of infections have set into Ray's foot and it gets a little dicey as to whether he'll lose it or not. Ray shows no fear through any of it. He's pretty mellowed out, says the drugs are good and Finn should try them.

Finn's been getting a fair amount of pressure from all corners during the Carlyle trial. Nobody believes he knows as little about the inner workings of the organization as he does. He thinks, Maybe a half a stick of dynamite affixed to the undercarriage of my car, a little shrapnel in the ass, it wouldn't be such a bad idea.

IAD comes around to ask questions. They know the precinct is deep in Carlyle's pockets and they're on a scouting mission to see who's taking what. Ray stone-walls, pretending to be too loaded on pain meds to give a coherent response. They turn their attention to Finn.

One midnight, maybe five minutes after Finn and Dani have finished making love, his cell goes off. They're both still breathing heavily and she's holding him close, licking his neck the way he likes, her wet thighs cooling his hot skin, and she tells him, "Don't even think of getting that."

But he has to, and she knows it. He presses his lips to her brow and leaves them there, tasting her warm salt caught in the crease of her frown. She shoves him off with both hands and goes to the bathroom. He snatches the phone and barks his name into it.

It's Roz. She's crying, sounds high, and he hears the serious strain in her voice. She's at a breaking point over something, and if she's calling Finn then it's got to be over something that has to do with Ray.

She wants him to meet her at an all-night diner six blocks from the hospital.

When he gets there, she's got a cup of coffee in front of her. She's been having trouble sipping it because of a split upper lip. She's been smacked around pretty good.

Even in bed with his leg turning yellow from infection, three IVs in his arm, and a catheter up his crank, Ray can do a nice job of quickly slapping the fuck out of somebody. Finn knows the work well.

Sliding in across from her, he says nothing. It's strange, but for the first time he realizes she's very attractive, even with the swollen nose, bruises, and welts. Or maybe it's because of them. He perks in his seat a little. He's got plenty of issues and maybe this is one of them. It's been a long time since Ray has worked a woman over, and Finn feels the old outrage rising in him.

"I have no idea how much you know about the situation," she says.

"Nothing," he admits.

"How can that be? You're partners."

"That's a good question."

"I thought partners knew everything about each other."

"I know what he's capable of, I just don't know what he's been up to lately."

"If you had to guess."

"I'd guess that you're stealing and running drugs for him."

"Not too hard to figure out, is it?"

"No."

The waitress asks if Finn wants anything and he's a bit surprised to find that he's hungry. Being out of the house after sex with Dani has revved him up, broken the usual pattern of reading for an hour and falling asleep in her arms. Then having deep, vivid, sometimes amazing and horrifying dreams.

He orders a large breakfast platter, pancakes, sausages, home fries. The waitress says they don't serve breakfast until six, even though it's right there on the menu. He gives her a cold eye and she tells him, "Hold on, I'll ask the cook if he'll accommodate you." Finn has no doubt that the cook will.

Roz explains how she's been stealing meds for Ray, who has a lot of contacts on the street and on the force.

She mentions a couple of names that Finn knows are informants, a few others he recognizes. He's a little shocked to hear that one cop he always thought was clean is actually involved.

Ray is making a bundle and so is Roz, but it's all going to blow up soon if she doesn't slow down. The other staffers are getting suspicious. They've got to put the operation on hold until the heat is off. She mentioned it to Ray earlier tonight after giving him head. He grabbed a fistful of her hair and punched her silly.

"We had to take another toe," Roz tells him. "There's a possibility he'll lose the leg up to the knee as well."

She speaks with great sympathy and heart. She's at least a little in love with Ray even if he did smack her around. Like so many beaten women Finn has met on duty, Roz has her wires crossed where love and abuse are concerned.

Finn tries to stick to the topic of drugs. "How much are you pushing?" She tells him quantities of pills, some meds he's familiar with, a lot that he isn't. More and more tranqs are popping up every day.

He adds, "Cash-wise?"

"Not much, really. A couple grand a week profit."

Doesn't sound like much until you add it up. A hundred g's in their pockets means a quarter mill of pharmacology flying out the window annually. The hospital is going to come down hard on her when they figure it all out, unless she cuts some kind of deal.

"What do you want from me?" Finn asks.

"I don't know. I just wanted to talk to someone. I'm afraid all the time now."

It's the first smart thing she's said. She's either going to get thrown in prison or have to turn on Ray when he's wounded and already under fire, backed to the wall, amped up, ready to explode.

Finn tells her, "You should be."

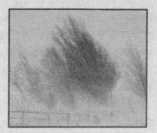

LOST IN THE STORM AT NIGHT, Finn takes account. He has shoes, pants, a torn long-sleeved shirt that offers almost no protection. His cane is gone. The knife is gone. He took off his coat to wrap around Vi. He has no lighter, no phone. He's fit and strong. Vi is dead. He's bleeding. The temperature is below zero. With wind chill, maybe thirty below by now. It's still snowing. There's no point in calling for help. No one's within earshot. Who knows if they'd listen anyway. Rack and Pudge might be local heroes, for all he knows. He can't trust any holler folk. He can't hear any chimes. He has no idea where he is. Most likely within a half mile of the school, trudging through one of the fields bordering St. Val's.

Dressed as he is, with no protection, no way to build a fire, he gives himself a very generous thirty minutes before he passes out and freezes to death. He's already soaked and icing up. Only his blood is warm and it steams as it leaks from his scratches and cuts, rising into his face, sending painful reams of colors and images into his mind that he has to fight through to stay in the cold and the dark.

It doesn't take long before he's caked with snow. His

wounds are already numb and he stuffs his hands into his armpits to try to keep some feeling in them. The snow he's tramping through comes up to nearly his thigh. He thinks that there must be some way for him to figure out where he is, how to walk in a basic grid pattern that will eventually lead him back to the school.

He tries the echo trick to see what he can do with his facial vision. He calls out loudly, "Hup!" Like shouting for a dog to heel.

His voice is immediately swallowed. There's no echo. What sound the wind doesn't snatch away, the blanketing snow drives down to the ground.

At first the fear is rampant inside him. His world is consumed by blackness, as always, even though he knows he's moving through the center of an endless blinding white. It's an odd contradiction that wants to force itself into his mind. Except that, like the fear, his thoughts have begun to freeze.

SLEEP WANTS HIS ASS ALREADY.

It's a kind whisper, a sweet lover making promises.

Despite everything, Finn's a little shaken to find that he doesn't want to die. Who knew?

A growing sense of understanding asserts itself.

He's certain that Danielle is here beside him in the snow.

She's been following him all this time and has finally seen her chance to impress herself upon him again.

Low booms sound in the distance. They sound like shotgun blasts, but it's actually ice shifting on the river. It's the only noise he can hear besides the wind and his own breathing.

He wanders and climbs and crawls through the snow. It takes a while but words begin to drift toward him. A voice makes itself known. It's his. He's starting to hallucinate. It's probably not such a bad thing.

He's talking about Dani in her wedding dress, how stunned he was to see her so lovely walking down the church aisle. Ray stood shoulder to shoulder with him and said, "You finally did it, you prick, you've made me jealous of you."

"At last," Finn said.

"It'll never happen again."

Ray had been right.

Maybe the echo trick will work in Finn's mind. He has to shout something down the long corridors of his memory and see what bounces back to him.

She's beside him in the white and in the black, his dead wife.

He puts his hand out.

Their fingertips brush.

He falls and gets up again. He calls out in his mind. It's a name. It's Dani. It's a series of names. It's Roz. It's Violet.

He falls and gets up again.

There's no echo. There's no response. Now there's no feeling in his face or anywhere else.

He says something else. Perhaps it's another name, maybe it's a word that holds so much meaning for him that he can't keep it confined to himself. He's not sure what it is.

He falls to his knees and Dani urges him to stand. He takes a few more hobbled steps, goes down again. He tries to break his fall with his hands but they're stuck in his armpits. Christ, he's living out Jack London's *To Build a Fire*.

Some nameless mountain man tumbles into a creek and tries to keep a fire lit while he slowly feeds it bits of kindling. Failing that, he dreams of murdering his dog and dipping his frozen hands inside its hot carcass. But the panic in his voice scares the dog off, and by the time he gets his arms around it, his hands are too numb to hold a knife. The guy runs around for a while but eventually realizes it's all for nothing. With a growing sense of calm, he gives it all up and dies. The dog scampers off.

At least there's that. At least the dog made it out okay.

If he lives, Finn will fucking scrap the story from his next semester's syllabus.

Dani brushes his hair out of his eyes.

He drops on his face.

With tremors racking him, he rocks to his feet. His teeth chatter so violently that he's lost a couple of back fillings. He tries to draw his mind more tightly to him, to wear it like a blanket.

Move, he thinks.

Stop moving and you die.

But, seriously, shouldn't you dig like a dog, get under the snow, make, like, I don't know . . . an igloo? He thinks he saw that in a movie once.

He needs to get some insulation.

Finn walks into a tree and smacks his forehead hard. He goes to one knee, impressed he has the strength to resist going all the way to the ground. He manages to lever himself to his feet again. The pain is as sluggish as he is, moving through his skull almost as if it's limping. He tries to feel the bark and smell the tree, but his nostrils are full of ice and the crisp wind burns away all odor. His hands are too numb to describe to him the tree's texture. He still can't pinpoint his whereabouts.

Nausea overtakes him and he vomits.

He holds his hands out to catch it. The idea disgusts him but he thinks this is the kind of thing a mountain man might take advantage of. Jack would know. Jack would give him the thumbs-up on this, he's certain. His bile will be warm.

It doesn't matter either way because he misses his hands. They aren't working properly anymore.

He hears Ray say, Aw shit, my shoes! You know how much these cost me? They're Italian. You goddamn prick!

This is your fault, Finn says.

How the fuck is it my fault?

I'm here because of you. I'm in the dark because of you.

Don't blame that shit on me. Christ, you even hit my socks . . . motherless motherfucker . . .

Finn tries to bring his arms up to his chest but can't feel them there. He wants to sleep. But he knows the dreams there will be just as bad as the dreams here, so what's the point? He thought he had at least thirty minutes, but it hasn't even been that long. He lets out a brief chuckle, thinking, Weak, how weak.

Ray says, It's not so bad, right?

No, not really.

Trust me, it's better than prison.

No doubt.

Dani tells him, Don't listen. Focus on me. Look at me.

Finn tries to open his eyes but the lids feel frozen shut.

You'd think it wouldn't matter, but it really gets to him. He rubs at his face. Well, he tries to rub at his face anyway. He thinks one of his hands is probably there. Yeah, his palm is mashing his nose. There's a strange sound of cracking. Has he broken his nose? Has it come off? Maybe he's finally, after all this time, falling to pieces, like fragmenting ice. No open casket for him.

Vi, lovely in her coffin, her mother at last loving her. The boy, Mark Reynolds, back from Greece, will have to have his parents search out a new prospect for him. He's got his kids' names picked out already. Eleanor and Kenneth. He's got to find a new girl to give him Eleanor and Kenneth because Vi is dead.

Finn relaxes in the snow. He sighs contentedly.

A beautiful ache moves through him.

Danielle says, Stand up, lover.

SHE DRAPES HERSELF AROUND HIM AND draws him close. Finn nuzzles her cold throat and feels that she has no pulse. The muscles are taut, though, the neck smooth, it's where she likes him to lick. It's where he likes to lick.

She's in his arms again where she belongs. And he's here again, where he never should have left.

Okay, so he's dead.

Thank Christ.

She says to him, I forgive you. It's done and it doesn't matter anymore, we'll never bring it up again.

No, it's over. It's over now.

My man, my lovely man. My sweet boy, let me hold you. I've been waiting so long to have you again.

My girl, you've always been my girl, will always be my girl.

Of course.

He asks, What do we do now? Tell me what to do. Where do we go?

Now you come with me.

Where, Dani?

Follow me, my sweet man. I can lead you back to where you need to be.

Back?

Where you need to be.

There's nowhere I need to be.

Yes, there is. You think you have someone to kill. You're going to do it soon.

I have to.

You're not a killer.

I am. I can be. I just stuck a knife through a man's head.

Because you were forced to. It's not the same thing, love.

Blood on your hands is blood on your hands.

It's all right. You're confused. You'll understand soon. You'll accept who you are.

Who I was doesn't matter. I've been remade. I am reborn. The darkness feeds me, Dani. It becomes me.

It wasn't your choice.

I was chosen for it.

You're so right, my man. Do you want me to leave?

God no.

Yes, you do. That's why you're still trying. It's why you're still struggling.

I am?

You are. You want to live. You aren't finished yet. You still have too much to do.

Am I alive?

You're dreaming.

I know, and it's a terrible dream. I dream of murder.

We all do. Now wake up.

I am awake. You're dead.

That's right.

And I'm alive.

Yes.

I'm not finished yet.

Stand up, lover. And ask yourself, How did the battle against evil go today?

Finn stirs. He manages to bring his wrist up to his viciously chattering teeth. He bites into himself, enjoying the taste.

RAY IS GOING TO GO DOWN hard. Carlyle is cutting him loose and so is the force. Everybody wants his ass.

Finn knows that he's the main reason why. He didn't cover and didn't go to bat for his partner, so Ray got caught out in the open with nobody to help divert the heat. A lot of guys would've lied under oath and perjured themselves, stolen evidence, and intimidated witnesses. Some would've gone even further for their partners, maybe aced one or two key people before they gave their depositions. Finn doesn't feel a fucking bit guilty, not even when Ray gives him the death glare.

Visiting hours are over by the time Finn gets to the hospital but nobody bothers him as he heads up to Ray's room. Ray had surgery today and was out of it when Finn called this afternoon.

"They took the foot," Ray tells him. He throws the covers back and shows off the bandaged stump.

"I heard."

"Roz told you?"

Finn doesn't respond. Roz is now under investigation by the hospital mucky-mucks and is about to get shitcanned and probably arrested. Finn wants to say something encouraging or at least sympathetic, but he's had a slow burn going since he saw some fresh bruises under Roz's makeup.

He says, "Don't touch her again."

"She's my girl."

"Cut her loose."

The charming grin eases across Ray's face. "You like her."

"No. I just don't want to see any harm come to her. Any more than's already been dumped in her lap."

"Nothing was dumped on her, she volunteered. She masterminded, truth be known. Me, I'm just a gimp who couldn't stop a train that she started down the tracks."

Ray acts like he really believes it. He's talking with his hands, sorta bouncing in the bed like an excited little kid. The stump wags around.

Finn says, "Just let her go."

"Because she's an innocent and it's your job to pro—"

"Enough of that. You ran your own game. I've done all I can for you."

Instead of arguing, Ray just nods his head in a yeah yeah yeah kind of way. The stump is aimed at Finn. It's not the same as having somebody point an accusing finger at you, but it's pretty damn close.

"There's still a way out for me," Ray says.

Finn knows there is. Ray's talking about laying waste to Carlyle. With Carlyle dead, things fall back into place the way they used to be. The DA won't go on the warpath anymore, and the force will be too embarrassed to hang one of their own if there's not some mobster big fish on hand to take the brunt of the headlines. Ray will still take a rap, but he'll only get a nickel jolt, tops.

"You want me to pop the head of the local syndicate?" Finn asks.

"As soon as my prosthetic comes in, we'll go together. How about that?"

Finn looks deep into Ray's eyes. He's trying to see if Ray is thinking about the final scenes of *The Wild Bunch* and *Butch Cassidy and the Sundance Kid*. It's easy to want to be dead when you're being left out to dry by everybody you ever trusted. The idea is even more appealing if you don't have to go alone.

But that's not what's in Ray's eyes. Finn sees something else entirely, but can't figure out what it is.

He checks his watch. He's meeting Roz at the diner in ten minutes.

For some reason, it seems important to Finn that he manages to save Roz. If he can find a way for her to get out from under, if she can redeem herself, maybe it proves that Finn is able to put the brakes on Ray's action. Maybe it proves that Finn is a righteous cop.

He knows he's a good one. He knows he's a clean one. But he's not sure he's a righteous one.

When he gets to the diner, she's already eating a salad and drinking a beer.

"You've got troubles on your mind," she says between bites. "What's he done to you this time?"

Finn ventures a lie, never the smartest move. "Nothing."

"Don't give me that. You're the worst liar I ever met. How in the hell could you be an effective cop when you don't have a poker face?"

"Simple. I rarely lie."

Roz tsks. "No wonder he runs roughshod over you."

"Nobody runs roughshod over me."

"Everybody runs over you. Even me."

He sits and she moves in on him too fast. She's climbed halfway across the table to get into his face.

"I've only known him for a few weeks and I know him better than you," she says.

"Nobody knows Ray."

"That's exactly what I mean. Don't you see, Finn?"

"See what?"

"You're the *only* one who doesn't know him. Everyone else, they're on to him, they've always been on to him."

"What are you talking about?"

"Forget it."

He likes staring at her. She's attractive enough, brunette with a short boyish haircut feathered across her forehead. Her smile is knowing and slightly coy, very much like Ray's. Those eyes, even when she's stoned, are large and expressive. She seems to use a lot of balm to make her lips glossy. In a lot of ways he thinks she'd be perfect for Ray. If only Ray wasn't such an asshole and about to take a fall. If only Ray didn't make her run drugs and smack her around so much.

"Is there time enough to make it right for you?" he asks.

"Probably not. I more or less confessed to the hospital and claimed drug addiction. It'll give me enough time to figure out my next move and maybe they'll leave me with my RN status, if I really do join a rehabilitation program. The narco cops have been putting pressure on

me but compared to what they usually deal with, Ray
says they'll probably give me a pass."

"Do you do the shit?"

"No."

"What are you on?"

"Nothing."

And she says he's a bad liar. "What are you on, Roz?"

"Sometimes I take downers."

"And?"

"Uppers. And Oxycontin. Vicodin."

Under the table, Roz puts her hand on his leg and
her fingers slide toward his inner thigh. She brushes his
groin and Finn shifts away, his face expressionless.

"Knock it off."

"I'm done with him. But he won't let me go."

"He's going to be sent up."

"Not forever, and not for a while."

"He'll cut you loose."

"How do you know?"

"I told him to."

"You don't tell him anything, Finn."

"Shut up, Roz."

"Rose. I want you to call me Rose."

He tries it out. "All right, Rose."

"Don't you see what's happening? What he's doing?"

Finn stares at her. He can tell she's a jealous and to-
tally irresponsible woman. Jealous of him, jealous of Ray,
always feeling like the raw deals she gets are somebody
else's fault. She puts her hands on him because she's territorial. In some strange way, she thinks she owns Finn
because he's trying to help. The hook is in.

She leans in and kisses him with a mouthful of beer, which she allows to run down her face and throat.

He doesn't return the kiss. When she draws away, he looks down at his wet shirt and says, "God damn it."

She gives a throaty chuckle. "Sorry." She studies him. "You have such beautiful eyes."

"Come on, let's go."

"I'm serious."

When they get back to the hospital, Roz walks in like she expects someone to fly out of a dark corner and snap the cuffs on her. She leaves him without a word. He's got no idea where she's going.

It's late but he decides to check in on Ray again.

Finn steps into Ray's room in time to see one of Carlyle's men, dressed like an intern but wearing cowboy boots, trying to smother Ray with a pillow.

All these people, they think it's easy suffocating someone with a pillow. They don't think the person will resist like a fucking wildcat. The guy's already got a bloody nose because Ray's managed to clock him a couple of times in the face. The leg is kicking. The stump is waving around.

Finn draws his piece and says, "Heya, enough of that, all right?"

Carlyle's boy quits trying to smother Ray. He turns and looks at Finn standing in the open doorway like he's going to try to run right through him. He's crazed with fear. He seems faintly familiar.

Carlyle's crew is stretched so thin that they're using all kinds of third-raters now. The mook throws the pillow on the floor and Ray wags his stump some more, going "You rotten prick, Donald! All the times I let you slip on those vice raps!"

He's not even out of breath, that's how good a job the mook did with the pillow.

The guy rushes Finn and Finn cracks him across the nose with the barrel of the gun, knocks him back into some machinery that beeps angrily. One of Dani's flower vases smashes. The mook picks up a jagged piece of pottery and holds it out in front of him like a knife.

Finn says, "Hey now—"

Donald rushes forward, slashing wildly with the shard of vase. Finn pops him once in the leg, hoping just to put him down, but hits an artery. Arterial spray starts painting the ceiling. Finn shouts for help and tries to get a tourniquet on the mook, but it's already way too late.

In ninety seconds a couple of doctors show up, but the guy's already mostly bled out. Finn's covered in red. Ray is grinning.

DANIELLE HAS HIM BY THE HAND and his hand is freezing. His blood has stopped running. Finn staggers beside her, half-carried by her, barely more than deadweight. The long, ice-encrusted hair of his dead wife whips into his face.

He rouses in her arms. "D...d...ani?"

"You're a strong one. You're gonna be all right."

The voice. He can't see Danielle. Instead he's struggling to walk beside that Tennessee Apple Cider or was it fucking Blueberry Parade Queen. It doesn't matter. Or maybe it does. Blue-eyed with a spatter of freckles across her cheeks, a darker beauty mark at the corner of her eye. He recognizes her. Or does he?

His mind whirls and goes, Wha'?

He stumbles and falls in the snow. The banks are so high now that it's not much of a forward flop. He's surrounded by cushioning. She grunts and goes, "None'a that. You gotta get up. We're almost there." She tugs at him and he thinks he might be moving. "You aren't afraid of a little snow, are you? There's plenty worse to fear."

Harley Moon.

He's amazed that this hundred-pound teenage girl is

practically carrying him. He tries to ease his weight off her but nearly drops again.

Moon, he thinks. Like on the tombstones.

He stumbles and this time hits something solid. At first he thinks a tree. He can't quite prop himself up with his numb arms and he collapses against it, one cheek on its icy surface. It's flat. It's smooth. A wall. Brick? No. He hears Harley grunting, fighting something, putting in effort. Beneath the wind there's maybe a creaking. He can't be sure. He doesn't give a shit.

She grabs him by the shoulders and tries to turn him aside. Then she shoves him and he goes barreling forward. He hits the ground hard.

Not the ground, a floor. He's out of the blizzard. She closes a door behind them and comes forward to slap the snow off him.

Her gloved hands are tiny but strong. She pounds the hell out of him, trying to get his blood pumping again. Hypothermia. Jesus, he feels like he's crystalized and is delicate as glass. She takes off her gloves and rubs her hands together to warm them, then places them on his frozen chest. There's barely any feeling at all. He wants her warmth. He thinks of Roz. He thinks of Vi. He thinks of Dani and he groans in sorrow and anger. She was with him out there. His girl forgave him.

Sleep tries to drag him off.

Harley admonishes him like a child. "No. None'a that. You stay awake now."

He tries, but the black currents that are always pulling at him are dragging him down once more.

"Stay right there, blind man. Don't you crawl around none. You listenin'?"

She puts a blanket over him. No, it's a coat. She helps him to put his useless arms through the sleeves. It's too small for him, but he manages to wrap himself inside it. The hell is going on? He was almost dead.

He wanted to be dead. But he's got something to do. He can't remember what it is.

On the floor he shudders violently. Harley strips his clothes off him, holds him, massages his head, strokes his face, the rest of his body, especially his fingers and toes. He hears metal ringing around him in time with his fierce tremors.

He figures it out. They're in one of the sheds outside the west door of the Main House, at the back of St. Val's.

His brain's starting to warm up. He thinks, Vi is dead. I killed that fucker Pudge. He thinks, I have to get into the school. Rack is on the move. Christ knows what he's doing. Duchess, Murph, and Judith are strong, they'll fight. But that knife. The things that prick does with his knife.

Why didn't Harley get me into the school? She's afraid of her own brother. Does she know Pudge is dead? Does she know I killed Pudge?

He tries to speak but he's shaking too badly. The noises coming from him, like an engine that won't turn over.

She reaches down and puts her hands to his chest again and rubs over his heart. She massages him until the pins and needles of feeling start to stab the shit out of him. It hurts like hell and Finn tightens up into a fetal position, moaning. Harley doesn't loosen her hold. She kneads him even harder.

"I tried to help, but you called down the wrath."

He wants to tell her to stop goddamn saying that, but he can't form words yet.

"Not them girls' fault though. Not even the ones I hate, the ones who make fun of us in the holler. I told you to pay it fast. I told you. But you didn't listen."

He owes, he realizes. He owes plenty. He's going to pay back, oh yes.

"They saw my ears twitching and now I'm out here with the dead too."

Finn spasms at that. He manages to turn his head. He pulls his trick and stares. He's looking directly into Harley Moon's eyes.

He tries to speak, but nothing but a hissing stammer escapes. He tries again.

Out here with the dead.

He reaches in one direction. He reaches in another.

"Don't do that, blind man. I told you. Just settle yourself."

He crawls and she fights to hold him in place. She's a strong little girl. He huffs and growls, disgusted with his own animal noises.

"What'd I say? Stay right there. Aren't you ever gonna listen to me?"

His nostrils have thawed. A faint but caustic group of odors reaches him. Gasoline. Oil. Finn puts out a hand and feels the bottom of a weed whacker. He strains and touches a gas can. He turns over and moves like a slug on his naked belly.

Finn reaches again. He smells semen and blood. He touches a shoe.

He crawls. He finds a cold ankle, and from there

continues on, the nerve endings in his hands on fire with feeling.

A knee. A thigh. The jeans have been tugged down. He discovers a cold hand with something trailing from the wrist. It's a rope.

Finn clambers to his knees and continues to inspect the body.

Roz is dead.

She's been tied up, hands in front of her, the knots fairly intricate. But the rope is now cut. Not bitten through. Harley sliced the bonds on Roz's corpse so she could pull the coat off her and cover Finn with it.

He reaches for her face. An oily old rag has been shoved into Roz's mouth. She vomited and choked to death on it.

We don't want to hurt no one.

Harley says, "They done it. They aren't all bad, really. Pudge, he gets excitable sometimes. It's just his way. They just got their mind set on something and there isn't nothing can turn them away from that. They're on a path."

She didn't learn none either, your lady.

Finn pieces some of it together.

Roz never forgot anything back at the shop. She'd been dealing meth this whole time, and Finn hadn't known. He should've realized, but he just hadn't seen it.

When he mentioned Harley's name to her this afternoon, Roz knew something was wrong, that something bad might be going down. Had she cheated them out of some cash? Stolen product? Was she fronting for Murph? For some of the girls? Fuck. She didn't go back to town, she went to find the Moon brothers. But they must've found her first, raped her, and stuffed her in here, let her die gagging.

He touches her face and her eyes are still open. He closes them.

"Why'd your people rob us?" Harley asks. "My lot, it's with them. Should be with them. But I liked this nurse lady. Met her a few times at the house. She was sweet. She told me I could go to school here someday. Educate myself so I could go down to the city, get a decent job. I believed her. She had a way about her. She talked nice. She loved you, I could tell."

When he sees Roz dead before him he sees his own shadow before him, there on the floor. It knows it's being watched.

Finn's shadow faces him without eyes.

It's another few minutes before he can speak.

"Wh-wh...ere's..." He gulps heated air. His shudders are slowing. "...your b-b-brother?" His mouth burns with the name. *"Rack."*

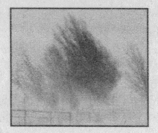

FINN MANAGES TO DRESS HIMSELF AGAIN in his cold, wet clothes. Harley Moon shouts at him to stop, but Finn opens the shed door and heads back into the storm. She yells that she can't follow him, she screams that he's a lunatic. He understands.

It's all right, he knows where he is now. No way he can miss the Carriage House.

Ice and wind attack once more as he staggers through the drifts. He buries his hands inside Roz's pockets. The coat is too small to zip closed, and the snow stings his chest and throat. It doesn't hurt much this time and can't slow him down at all. He plods and inches along, practically stuck in place.

The wind chimes in front of the dining hall can barely be heard above the howling wind, but they're there at the edge of his hearing. He's trained to hear them. He isn't going to fall down this time. He won't fail again.

An easy thirty-second walk takes him five hard-fought minutes. He's beginning to freeze once more as he blunders against the Carriage House doors. They're stuck and he has to throw himself against them and pound with his fists before he can yank them free. Finn takes two steps inside and flops on his face.

"Jaysus!" Murphy shouts. He squats and tries to help Finn get to his feet, but it's not happening. "You're a bloody mess! Has everyone gone mad? I come in for a wee dram of Jay and another bite of lamb and find the two of you on the floor?"

Two?

Here they are up in the sticks and no one has a gun.

"G-get knives," Finn tells him.

"What? You need help. You're hardly more than a block of ice, man! We need Roz. Where is she, I'll find her."

"Get—"

"Stop your bickering! You need blankets. Are there blankets here?" Murph's hands are on Finn, panicked and moving over him, trying to help but without knowing how. "For fook's sake, what's all this shite, now? You've been cut near to ribbons. And Duchess has a cracked jaw, found her on the floor as well. And here it's me who's supposed to act like the idjit child."

"Is she . . . ?"

"I'm fine," Duchess says. "I'm right here."

"Knives. D-d-do it."

Murph's breath stinks of Jameson. He's been pouring back a lot tonight. "Why in Christ's holy name would I want to do that?"

Duchess says, "Finn, what's happened to you? Where's Roz?"

Finn stands and stumbles. She puts an arm out to help. The smell of blood is so strong that it fills his belly. Even so, there's not much of a tug in his mind. A swirl of color, mostly red. Duchess has been beaten. She's strong, she fought like he knew she would, but she's gotten off easy. He falls into her embrace and she says, "You need help. You've got hypothermia. There's coffee. Hold on."

He hisses, "Two holler men…are on campus. W-watch the girls."

"Couple motherfuckers broke in here. One of them chipped my crown."

The kitchen door opens and closes. Finn almost hits the floor again but Murph grabs him.

"Enough of this tossing," Murphy says. "What goes on here? Some bloke decked Duchess? I thought one of the young wans might've gone daft after too much eggnog."

Neither of them has been to the Main House, Finn realizes. They haven't seen Vi dead in the hall. "We need to get over there," Finn says.

"Over where?"

"Gate House. The g-girls, we have to—"

"The dorm? Why the hell didn't you say that, then? You can't go anywhere, man, you've gone six shades of blue. How long were you out there? Who's the bollix who put this coat on you? Here, wear mine." Murph's voice is getting squeaky with frustration as he strips Roz's coat off Finn and manages to fit his own on him. It's large and warm and soft as a comforter. Finn floats for an instant and nearly passes out.

He rouses when Duchess presses a cup of hot coffee to his lips. "Here, drink this."

A steaming mouthful goes down but at first it only increases his chills. The tremors are so bad that it feels like a seizure. Murph lets out a sound like a terrified cat. Duchess grabs Finn by the shoulder and tries to quiet him. The fit passes quickly but it pulls the opening volley of a bellow from him.

Murph's scared and confused and his neck cricks as he turns from Finn to Duchess and back again, waiting for answers and getting nothing. "You were on your way double-jig time to meet the Holy Mother, Finn. You're still bleeding. Your wrist, Jaysus, is that a bite mark? I have to stop the—"

"Phone?" Finn asks.

"Land line is out from the storm," Duchess tells him. "Tried calling my Ruby a while ago. And I don't have a cell."

"Neither do I. Who the fook am I going to call? Me sainted ma, may she roast eternally?"

Something's wrong here but Finn can't get it together enough to figure out what it is.

He decides to lay it out flat for them. "Listen. There's one or two hard cases loose in the school. Holler men, drug dealers." His lips squirm. He can't say that Roz is dead in the shed, that Vi fought and died for him.

"That's who you two have been clashing with?" Murph asks. "What are these fooks here for?"

"They say I owe them money."

"And do you, now?"

"No."

Duchess dabs a cloth against her mouth. Spit and blood bubble across her chin. She takes a breath that sounds like air is being forced sideways down her throat. It's a noise he's heard a thousand times before. It's the fear and worry making way for a confession.

He turns and looks at her. She's still smiling in the kitchen, wooden spoons in each hand, banging the shit out of her pots.

She whispers, "I have to tell you something."

He is stone. He won't break. He dreams of death. He has someone to kill. Her disheartened tone has given him a last needed clue. He pulls the story together before she can relate anything more.

"Yes, you do," Finn says.

Finally his voice is back. His true voice. He tries to get to his feet but can't do it alone. She takes his hand. They're both trembling. He thinks of Roz touching the side of his face like she wanted to explain something. Like she was silently asking his forgiveness. It makes sense now. While they were making love she mentioned that Duchess's granddaughter didn't get into St. Val's. Roz was trying to explain.

He thinks, That's what it meant.

"Tell me, Duchess," Finn says. "Tell me why my house isn't in order. Tell me how you and Roz have been running meth with these assholes. Tell me why you didn't pay them. And while we're at it, tell me where you've been delivering it. No, let me guess. Up to Sing Sing for Ray?"

THE THREE OF THEM MOVE WELL now, as a unit, Finn propped between Duchess and Murphy, picking up speed through the dining hall.

Murphy coughs Judith's name. Murph might bitch about her, but Finn now realizes that the Irishman truly does care for Judith. He should've guessed. Anyone who complains that much about a woman must be doing so in order to hide from his own heart.

The windows rattle like they're about to shatter. "It's pounding away like the end times. Shite, the lights are flickering. We may lose them yet."

Duchess is trying to find the words to explain herself, but she hasn't got them yet and probably never will.

He hears the metal blades clanging. She's got butcher knives. Murph asks, "The hell's that?"

"Keep an eye out," Finn says. "That bastard might be outside."

"Och, only one?"

"I think I killed the other."

"Jaysus! You're a hard man even now."

They get through the door, and the storm slashes at them. Murph's coat can only do so much. The ice instantly gets back inside Finn. His core temperature is way down, the furnace practically out. The rage fans the fire and keeps him alive. Sometimes being a touch nuts helps out in the strangest ways.

They move quickly through the blizzard, with Finn staggering and Murph pulling him along. Finn slows even more, and his legs nearly fold beneath him. They get to the Gate House and the three of them hit the doors as one. Finn's limbs are dead and he goes sprawling.

The butcher knives strike a ringing series of notes that lift Finn's chin and try to carry him away.

The blades are here to help. They tell him, We're with you, buddy, we're on your side. We fit your hand, we await your firm touch. We won't fail, we'll lay open, we'll rend. We wish to slip in, debone, flay. He imagines them peering over the rim of Duchess's pocket and looking at him, grinning like wicked children. He wants to say, Thanks for giving me a hand.

"I'll run ahead and check on the girls," Murph says.

"No," Duchess orders. "Help me with him."

"You two will be fine. But Judith, and the wans—"

"If we split up now, who knows what'll happen. You're going to stay right here. Help me. He might die."

"I won't die," Finn says.

Duchess warms him with her huge meaty hands. Murph, unsure of what to do, tries to follow her lead. Finn can barely move but feeling is starting to return. He's got to go through the agony again. His thoughts are clear for the first time in who the fuck knows how long.

"I needed the money," Duchess admits. "For my babies."

"The money," he repeats. After all this, he wants to laugh. Nothing is funny and everything is funny. The fury of Howie wants out like vomit. It begins as a sick little snicker, the kind lunatics covered in blood make when you catch them in the basement, rubber gloves on, finishing up with a wife or boyfriend or the cat or the kid.

Murph goes, "For fook's sake, man—"

Sure, for fook's sake.

Finn clamps his mouth shut and the need to laugh is instantly gone. He snakes his hand out and grips Duchess's throat. He draws her close until their noses touch.

"How long?" he asks.

"About three months."

Since the beginning of the semester, when the trouble first started with Vi. Maybe Roz thought she was helping herself out, building a nest egg in case he got booted from the academy in disgrace. She was covering her bases should he decide to run away with the girl.

"Am I right about Ray?"

Duchess is motherly love incarnate. She is soothing him, warming him, keeping him alive. Her words are clipped and rushed. They land on him with real weight. "Yes."

That prick. That motherless motherfucker prick. "That prick."

"Roz suggested we work with him. He had connections in prison and on the street. He had a couple of guards on his payroll. No fuss or anything. She'd go for a visit and just hand it over, and Ray would sell on the inside and give her our pay."

Most cops, they were terrified of the joint. But a dirty cop, he was king of the castle. He'd still have his street connections, his CIs, the skels and mooks on the corner, a list of the other dirty cops on the force. He'd have nothing to fear.

"Who cares about any of this shite now?" Murph says. "The two of you shut the fook up."

They get Finn on his feet. The three of them start into the corridor, heading for the stairway. The Christmas tunes are blasting.

"Nothing out of place here," Murph says. "The ear-bleeding music, it's still playing above."

"The deal," Finn says. "Tell me about your deal."

"She came to me after I told her about my Ruby. She needed someone to cover for her at times."

Finn grins. It's Ray's grin, he knows. "All that talk . . . about working the rehab—"

"Don't you judge me, Finn. Don't you do that."

"Take the girl out of the street but never the street out of the girl."

"Shut your goddamn mouth."

The piano hums its harmful intent. The low C fills the lobby, fills Finn's chest, makes him ache even worse. The piano is asking for the truth. The music demands that he speak.

"Roz is dead," he says. "Vi too, she's dead."

"Oh my sweet Jesus—"

"Shite this," says Murphy. "Shite this all. Come on."

They begin to rush up the stairwell together. Finn feels like he's in the lead, but Duchess drags him along by the left hand and Murph holds him up on the right.

He says, "You went into business with two lunatics."

"You think you're gonna find some trustworthy hustlers to hook up with?" Duchess's voice is full of tears. "They're all crazy. No different here than in the Bronx.

Not like you could choose honest folks to go into crime with."

"What happened?"

"She visited Ray and he put out the word, somehow connected with them Moon boys."

Ray's got an even wider circuit than Finn suspected.

"Why do they think I'm involved?" he asks.

"I don't know. Maybe it's just the way of their minds, those two fools. They probably figured women could only be working for a man."

Finn doesn't buy it. It doesn't make sense, not even for two mental backwoods meth cookers.

He thinks, Ray told the Moon boys. Ray got me involved. Ray set this up. He'll be out of Sing Sing in a few weeks and he knows I'll be coming for him.

"Keep going," he says.

"Who fookin' cares, you two!"

They round the landing and continue up the stairs. Duchess says, "The last load, Ray didn't pay Roz. He ripped her."

Finn feels stronger. The knives continue easing up out of Duchess's pocket, wiggling their shiny asses at him, his face bright in the glowing stainless steel. The sight of his own features disgusts him.

"How much cash?"

"I don't want to tell you."

"I don't give a fuck what you want, Duchess."

"Nine thousand."

Of course Ray would rip them off the last batch. Ray gets out of prison soon. There's no reason to pay. He was done with the deal and grabbed everything he could. What was anybody going to do? Arrest him?

With his disability checks, the sale of the house, and what he's saved up over the years living in the cottage, Finn's got close to two hundred grand in the bank. What's he going to spend it on? No kids to put through college. Blindness cuts down on your book buying and movie-ticket purchases. No need for a plasma TV or high definition DVD player. Not being able to see cuts down on your choice of hobbies. Even this New Year's visit to the city was only for Roz. What the fuck's he care about the Plaza?

"Why didn't you just ask me for the goddamn money?"

"She wouldn't. And she wouldn't let me. She didn't want you knowing—"

Knowing that she was doing the same stupid shit that got her hooked up with Ray in the first place. It was definitely escape-strategy cash. She figured Finn would get iced if he really did plan to go through with facing down Ray when he was released from prison.

Or maybe she just wanted to be Ray's girl again. Maybe she'd always been Ray's girl at heart.

On the third floor, Murphy breaks loose and starts down the hallway at a clip. His voice is weak as he calls, "Judith." It finds assertion. "Judith!"

Finn feels the sorrow struggling up from his depths. A couple of grunts slip past his lips before he clamps down on the crazy urge to howl.

He says, "Knife."

Duchess hands him one, handle first.

It's got a sweet balance to it, a nice cutting blade maybe five inches long. It'll do.

They move along after Murph, toward the girls. His

heart is hammering, his body hot, and the icy sweat pours off him.

He shrugs free from her and says, "What else did she tell you about Ray?"

"That you've been waiting five years to kill him."

THE ROCK AND ROLL CHRISTMAS CLASSICS are still playing, much louder than before. Finn imagines blood everywhere, sees himself moving among the dead. He rushes along on his own. Duchess is behind him, telling him to slow down, but he hears Murph ahead. Saying what, what the hell is he saying?

Finn calls, "Murphy!" He stumbles into the communal suite and kicks a cushion in his path. He holds the knife out before him, low so he can slash upwards and disembowel Rack. He wishes Pudge were here too. He wants a chance to kill Pudge all over again.

Moving deeper into the room, he concentrates beyond the music and can hear one of the girls. Who is it? He's never felt quite so helpless.

He shouts, "Who's here! Murphy! Rack!"

"Hey, Mr. Finn," Suzy Smyth says, and the girl with the soft-ice-cream cone and the sunscreen smudged on her forehead steps close to him, colorful sprinkles on her lips. "What's up with the butcher knife? You drunk? Where's your glasses? You're a mess. What the hell happened to you? This what single malt does? I'm glad we didn't let you get the liquor."

"And your cane. Where's your cane?" Sally Smyth,

also carrying a cone, also smudged with sunscreen, her copper ponytail swinging back and forth, sounds spooked. "That's a knife. What's with the knife?"

"And you're bleeding!"

"Mr. Finn, you all right? You been slugging it out with somebody? Why you holding a knife? What's going on?"

"Where is everybody?" he asks, putting the knife away in his pocket. "I need a phone."

Lea Grant says, "We told you." Carlyle's mistress, her mouth gleaming with a hint of lipstick, sleepy-eyed, protected. "We told you he was acting off."

"It's because the Lord requires sacrifice," Caitlin tells the rest of them. He's turning, turning, trying to get a bead on each girl as she addresses him. The room is full of body heat and making him drowsy. "Even in the face of celebration. Why wouldn't he be frightened? He should be. We all should be."

"You two freaks have cooked your brains," Sally says.

He hears the snap of a cell phone. Suzy presses buttons. "Nothing, as usual."

Sally tries hers. "One bar. No good. We need to go up to the roof. Sometimes it's better. Who are we calling? It's damn cold up there."

"Stay off the roof, the weather's too vicious."

Murphy slips in from some corner. He's found the beer stash and he's sucking at a bottle. He knocks it back in a couple of loud pulls. He's not sure what he should say in front of the girls. He grabs Finn's arm and yanks him aside. It's the sort of thing he knows better than to do, but he can't help himself.

Murph leans in to Finn's ear, lowers his voice.

"Judith isn't here. Neither is that other child, the one who's all elbows and knees."

"Jesse."

The music dies. After a few seconds, it starts up again.

"Electric's hobbling along."

Duchess moves in from behind, a guard watching their backs. Her gravity and girth are comforting in a way words never are. "Shhh, shhhh." She's a hell of a shusher and dampens the tension in the room, quiets them all. She orders the music to be turned down. It is. Finn can almost think again.

Duchess says, "Girls, listen to me now, and you listen good. Where's Mrs. Perry? And Jesse?"

"Mrs. Perry went to look for you all," Sally says. "She was worried because everybody just split. Where the heck did you all go? Jesse hung around for a little while, but, let's face it, she's a sweet kid, but she's just not happening, you know? She's got no cool. All she wants to talk about are books. Who wants to talk books on vacation? Or even when you're not on vacation. So she bored us and she left too. I think she went to find Vi. And look, Mr. Finn—" She moves in close to him as well. "— Caitlin and Lea...Mr. Finn, gotta tell you the truth here. Those two, we never liked them. They're a drag on our good time, you know?"

And Suzy joining in, to nail the point home. "We made a promise and stuck to it." She pauses. "Mr. Finn, seriously, Nurse Martell should give you a look-see. Really. You're one messy cat."

"You're fucked-up, Mr. Finn, you need some help. Daddy-o, what—"

"When did they leave?"

"I don't know."

"Think! When?"

"Who knows?"

Lea pipes up, her voice cutting through the room as well as Finn's head. "Odd that no one's asked about Vi."

"Or indeed Nurse Martell," Caitlin notes. "And yet they're not here among us. Where might they be?"

"On an altar, stretched out?"

"In the woodland, surrounded by priests of blood?"

"Why else would anyone be carrying knives?"

Finn really wants to smack them in the teeth. Duchess and Murphy huddle around and draw him into the other room. Suzy tries to follow and Duchess shouts, "Get back in there!"

"Whoa, what'd I do?"

"Go on, girl!"

Suzy leaves. Murph asks, "The hell do we do now? Where are they? Not the Carriage House. The Main House?"

"Yes," Finn says. "Judith went to find you, and Jesse went to look for Violet."

"Jaysus. I feel like I might shite myself."

Duchess's voice is laden with guilt. "This is all my fault. Mine and Roz's. I'm going to have to pay for this."

"She's already paid."

He wants to grab her. He wants to throttle her doughy neck, get a nice Indian burn going as flesh tightens against flesh. The rage feeds on his love, all of his lost loves and half loves. Finn's muscles dance. It forgets that this is all his fault too.

"In the movies the heroes are supposed to be more

clever and outwit the bad lads," Murph says. "But I'm not clever, I'm a fookin' idjit in most things. Tell me what to do. The only time I ever fight is in pubs, and I always lose. I'm a happy drunk no matter what bollix is after me. It always ends with me on my back in an alley offering to buy a round. These pricks . . . what they've done . . . lovely Violet, and Roz, God's mercy. Judith. She'll mouth off to them. She'll mouth off and give them a good lashing. She'll call the wrath down."

"Any chance you have a gun?" Finn asks.

"No."

"What kind of a bank robber doesn't keep a gun around?"

"You believed that load of shite I was passing off? You think if I knew how to rob a bank I'd be mowing lawns and shoveling parking lots for a living in this rotted burg?"

"I'm going to go cut somebody," Duchess says.

Finn's hands snake out and each one grabs a wrist, Duchess's left and Murphy's right. They gasp. It's an easy trick, the way they always gesticulate, waving, talking with their hands. He needs contact.

He needs for them to realize this is another significant moment in a chain of crucial events that started long before today.

"You two are going to stay here," he says.

"What's this?" Murph asks.

"Like fuck," Duchess says.

"Watch over the girls."

"And the hell are you going to do? Och, in case you've forgotten, man, you're not a cop anymore, and you're beaten, frozen, and fookin' blind."

"I haven't forgotten. It's my fight."

"What can you do alone, you damn fool?" Duchess asks, and the girls, who've all been listening in at the doorway, are instilled with that silence and stillness of real fear. "I'm going over there and I'm gonna cut those motherfuckers."

"No. Both of you stay here. Rack is waiting for me."

"How do you know? You could be wrong, you gob-shite pisser."

"That's why you need to stay here and stand ready. Especially if the lights go out."

"Madman."

Finn keeps one hand on the wall, leading himself out into the corridor, where he moves quickly and efficiently up to Roz's apartment. He's kicked in plenty of doors in his time. This one goes easy. Finn slips inside.

He has an extra cane folded under the bed. He has his own little drawer of effects. The closet is full of his clothes and coats. It's not until after he strips off his torn shirt that he wonders why, after all this time, he doesn't have a key to Roz's apartment. It proves, perhaps, that they've never fully trusted each other.

His life is full of proof without substance. Answers without acknowledgment. He gets into dry clothes, puts on another pair of shoes. He finds one of the stupid hats with the ball on top. He tears the ball off and puts on the wool cap. He snaps his cane open. He readies the knife in his belt for a quick draw.

This is all just the warm-up to a different showdown. Ray will be out in three weeks.

THE SCREAMING TENSION INSIDE IS DAMPENED by his own history. He could never talk the father off the roof, never take the shot that might save the kid. It was Ray who got the job done, and Finn who got the meaningless medal. He realizes that, in spite of everything, he owes Ray a great deal.

Sweeping his cane in front of him, Finn moves quickly and confidently down the hall to the staircase, rushing down the steps to the lobby. The pounding wind brings up a low C, and now it's almost a monkish chant. It tells him more blood is coming, but he shouldn't be afraid. Its voice is as clear as the shouts of his lieutenant, the smarmy voice of the mayor. He's no more a harbinger of murder than anyone else. Finn knows it's true.

He moves out the door into the storm. Its rage meets his own. He moves in the direction to the Carriage House at a nice clip through the drifts. He stumbles along the snow-choked walkway but keeps his heading. If he's wrong, he'll overshoot and be lost in the blizzard. He listens for the chimes and can't hear shit. That doesn't matter. He hopes it doesn't matter. He can do this. He has to do this.

He blunders to the hedges outside the dining hall.

He's somewhere near where Pudge's body should be, if Rack hasn't moved him. Finn fights his way past and gets inside. He heads for the east door.

Outside again, he staunchly marches toward the Main House and is almost carried there by the driving wind. It's hard going through the snow, but he's inured, protected this time. He's got his fucking hat on.

His breathing turns heavy, and with each breath is a growl that forms the opening "J" sound of their names. Everyone needs a mantra to keep them going. He's had many over the last few years. Now he has two more. The names take shape in his mouth. He begins to spit them into the storm. He says, Jesse. He says, Judith. With each step he's brought closer to them and his own future.

Harley Moon, Finn's own personal ghost child, is dancing nearby. Maybe out on a frozen river or tangled in the white treetops. Up high on the snowbanks, twirling, her hair wild. He hears her saying, You're walking forward to your own doom, blind man.

Finn struggles along faster.

He can imagine what Judith thinks when she finds Vi's body in the corridor. He can imagine it but chooses not to. He thinks of what kind of scars Jesse is going to be left with after tonight. Whether Rack is on top of her right now, whether he plans on it soon. Is he one of those bastards who can have sex ten times a day and still burn with lust? Finn remembers Rack's coat, made of animal skins, and thinks of him rutting like a barnyard beast. He wonders whether either of the women is still alive.

Reaching the west door, Finn pushes his way inside.

He doesn't shake the snow from himself. He grabs the knife and swings his cane, knowing that Rack is somewhere deeper in the building.

But he has to inch along anyway, he has to be sure.

The door slams behind him. It doesn't matter. Noise is his friend. He slaps the cane down. He sees nothing with his facial vision.

His mind continues drifting, trying to drag his body along. He shouts Judith's name and then Jesse's name. He calls for Rack. He's practically screaming. His voice is the voice of a lot of crazy bastards he's had to put down in the past.

"Jesse! Judith!"

He refuses to think of Violet's body at the other end of the hall. He forces his thoughts away from her saying how much she loves him. He presses past the day they almost made love, when he ran his hands over her. The effort makes him grunt.

Finn moves to the stairs, taking them two at a time.

The "J" names want out. His lips part, but instead of shouting now, he speaks softly, as if in conversation. "Jesse. Judith."

He holds the banister tightly as he rounds the landing. Smacking his cane against the wall, he gets a reading of what's ahead. No one's in the corridor. He can hear nothing, smell nothing. He tries Judith's office first.

The door is locked. Forcing it open is easy, he doesn't even need to use all his weight. His strength has been waiting for him to accept it. The door bows inward and the lock snaps. He asks, "Judith?"

He sweeps the floor with his cane. He puts his back to each corner, hoping Rack is hiding and will jump the easy target. Finn's breathing begins to hitch and he takes a second to calm himself once more. He slips the carving knife back into his belt, under his coat.

He's impressed by the scope and magnitude of the design that has brought them to this moment. The secrets, the storm, the easy choice of victims. Vi just sitting there outside his office, waiting for him.

Then he hears his name, murmured.

He doesn't know if it's Judith or Jesse who speaks it.

Or if it's Dani or Vi or Roz, reaching back through the veil to find him.

Or if it's Rack, wearing his shadow.

Out in the hall, he immediately knows he's not alone.

He slaps his cane and senses two people in the corridor, about twenty-five feet in front of him.

"Miss-ster Fi-inn," Jesse says, her voice broken by a panicked tremolo. The sound of his own name is every nightmare he's ever had.

"Jesse, are you all right?"

"I think so," she says and breaks down sobbing. "There's a man. He's...he's holding me. He's got...he's got this knife...the really big sharp knife...oh God, he's licking me, *he's licking my ear—*"

Finn hears her trying to control herself and stifle the tears, but she's fourteen, for Christ's sake.

"Where's Mrs. Perry?"

"In your office. He punched her in the face and kicked her. He kept kicking her. He kicked her in the mouth. Her teeth. Some of them, they broke." She stops and sucks air like she's been underwater for minutes. She goes into a coughing fit. *"He's chewing my earlobe."*

Jesse squeals in pain. Rack is hurting her.

Finn takes a step and Jesse shrieks.

And Rack saying nothing, doing nothing, wanting his nine grand.

Finn waits. There's nothing else for him to do.

He keeps his eyes on Rack. His shadow keeps its eyes on him. They are swaying together, moving to the rhythm of their shared pulse. They converse in a language made of darkness, beyond comprehension.

It's instinctual, genetic. It's found in the structure of blood going back ten thousand generations to when man first looked out at the night and sought refuge behind a rock. He and Rack are brothers closer than Rack was to Pudge, closer than Finn's ever been to Ray.

This second is so brightly lit and clear that Finn actually turns his head aside as if to shield his eyes from the sun.

"He bit me, Mr. Finn! He bit my cheek. He bit my ear. He's biting my ear, Mr. Finn! He's got a knife. He's nicked my throat. He's doing it right now. Oh God, *I'm bleeding*!"

Finn knows. He can smell it.

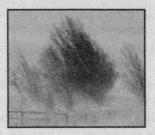

IN HIS HOSPITAL ROOM, WHITTLED FOOT hiked in the air on pulleys, blood smears on the bed, Ray's grinning because he knows Finn has made a serious mistake shooting Carlyle's boy.

Turns out it really is Carlyle's boy. Finn thought he recognized him. Donald Carlyle, twenty-five, had a taste for back-alley preop transsexual prostitutes, chicks with dicks who let their hormone injections slip so they still had a touch of five o'clock shadow. Donnie had taken over the job of punching Ray's ticket, trying to show his father he could handle whacking somebody. These mob kids, they're always insecure as hell and have so much to prove to their mob boss daddies.

Ray's grinning because now Finn's in the soup right alongside him. No way that Carlyle can let something like this go. It doesn't matter that Finn has nothing to say on the stand and can't sink anybody's boat. Carlyle's going to move on him. And if Finn's got any sense at all, he's got to step on Carlyle first. It's what Ray's been hoping for.

Cops come in and out of the hospital room, every one of them giving Finn a look. Some seem proud of him, and some have eyes that seem to say, You've screwed the pooch bad, son.

After the body is carried off and Finn is taken down to the station to give his report, IAD comes after him again. They want him to testify to a whole load of shit that isn't true and a lot that is. He wonders why they need his testimony for anything, they've already got wiretaps, street sources, digital video feeds, and tax evasion documents. Nothing he says will help their case in the slightest.

It doesn't matter. They think they've got him by the nuts. He wants to call Dani but they tell him no. They tell him they can get him into witness protection, move him out to Tempe, Arizona.

Finn thinks, Arizona, you can't play a round of golf anywhere in the whole damn state without sharing the green with a mob enforcer turned rat or some syndicate accountant who took too big a slice of pie.

He's cut loose at four in the morning. He owns the roads heading home beneath a vault of night littered with blazing stars. He tries the house again and gets voice mail. His thoughts are a riot of impossibilities and dead ends. He and Danielle are headed for North Carolina, not the fucking desert.

When Finn is a half mile from home Ray phones and says, "You'll find Carlyle in the usual place. The fish market. Do it soon, he's going to move fast on you."

Finn's too tired to think about it anymore. And it's his anniversary tomorrow. He wonders if he should broach the subject of moving to Tempe before or after he gives Dani the diamond pendant he's bought her.

She's asleep, of course, when he slips into bed.

Spooning her, he's amazed, once again, that she's still here, that she's always here for him. He drapes his hand over her thigh. With only a slight stirring, she grabs his wrist and draws him closer.

Morning arrives without warning. Finn doesn't even remember shutting his eyes. He's immediately alert as Dani exits the master bathroom, nude and with a smear of baby powder across her right breast. She glides into the hall and down the stairs.

He needs a shower. Under the hot jets he feels a little sharper and more optimistic. He allowed Ray and the IAD to rattle him. Carlyle isn't a fool. He's a middling crime lord and a businessman. Pricks like that don't put their own kids above cold cash and common sense.

Downstairs, Dani is mixing eggs in a bowl. She's naked at the stove. His heart does a little stutter and begins to ache. She's that beautiful.

She glances back over her freckled shoulder and asks, "Pancakes or French toast?" Still moist from his shower Finn leans into her, nuzzling her throat, nipping at the throbbing blue pulse there, and then draws her down to the kitchen floor. He likes the feeling of the cool Italian tile under his back.

They make love fast and with a crazed kind of intensity. It's angry sex except he's not angry. She's miffed that he left the way he did last night and still hasn't explained where the hell he was. He feels like he hasn't been inside her in years.

On top of him, his cock slipping from her wetness as he continues to pant on the floor, Dani levers herself up but doesn't completely stand. She reaches for the junk drawer behind her, slides it open, grabs something, and then sits back down on him. It's a hell of a way to fuck a man. The motion tickles him, begins to arouse him again. He hardens enough to ease back inside her. He palms sweat from his eyes.

Even when she sticks the S&W .38 in his face, glaring at him, on the verge of tears, he's thinking about how lucky he is that she's stayed with him for twelve years.

She says nothing. Neither does Finn.

He planned to take her out tonight to their favorite restaurant down in SoHo. Ritzy but not too ritzy, with a violinist who travels table to table and knows how to break your heart with Bach and Haydn. Danielle touches his brow with the barrel of the gun, taps him twice. She draws breath in through her teeth.

"Are you fucking that bimbo nurse?" she asks.

He's more stunned by the question than by the fact that she's drawing down on him in his own kitchen. She knew he was going to make love to her on the tiles so she had the gun planted right there in the drawer. She knows him that well but hasn't figured out yet that he'd never cheat on her?

"No," he says.

"You lie to me and I'll kill you."

"I've never lied to you, Dani."

"Don't feed me that, lover."

"It's the truth and you know it is."

He's been spending too much time with Roz and visiting Ray, rushing off when he gets calls at midnight. But as a cop he's inured to the usual drama most couples go through. All that sobbing, screaming, throwing shit around the room, he's dealt with a thousand domestic quarrels like that, and Dani knows it. She's going for the

grand statement here, trying to get through his hard
shell.

He's had plenty of guns pointed in his face too, but
never by his wife after making love on their anniversary,
so her ploy works. It does perk him up, even if it doesn't
scare him the way it's meant to. It kills him that she
doesn't have complete faith in him, but he can't really
blame her. It's almost impossible to have faith in anyone
or anything nowadays.

"I'm not screwing around."

"I told you once what would happen if you did."

"I know you did."

"Do you remember?"

"I remember, Danielle."

And he does. At the tail end of some bullshit romantic comedy about cheating couples, he leaned over
to her and said, "You pull any of that shit on me and I
might have to put a contract out on you."

She responded, "You do it to me and I won't farm
out the hit, I'll put one right between your eyes."

It was a good comeback. Now he thinks maybe it
wasn't just witty repartee. "Dani, that's enough. I
haven't done anything."

"I have doubts."

"You shouldn't."

"I have significant doubts."

"Then you don't know shit about your husband."

"That's what worries me."

She pulls the trigger.

The hammer falls on an empty chamber.

The click is as loud as if the gun had actually fired.
They both jump a little. The tile floor is no longer cold

under Finn's back. It's like white-hot steel against his flesh. He's lathered in icy sweat like he's been trudging through waist-high drifts of snow.

"You never pull the trigger on a gun," he tells her, "not even an empty one, not even if you've checked it twenty times. You never do it. Not unless you want to kill somebody."

Tears flow down her cheeks, pool around the edges of her mouth, and then run off the end of her chin. They strike his forehead like Chinese water torture.

Danielle drops onto him and he wraps his arms around her. He figures his cock would've shriveled up into the center of his fucking chest, but no, he's still hard and still inside her. She starts to ride him. It's over in seconds.

She says, "You stupid goddamn prick, you're the love of my life."

JESSE WHIMPERS AND HER BLOOD DRIPS down her neck, pattering onto her blouse. Finn shrugs out of his coat and lets it fall from his shoulders. He draws the carving knife from his belt.

The situation doesn't call for a blade. It was dumb to bring it. He realizes that now. With a snarl of disgust he flips it aside and listens to it hit the wall and then clang on the floor.

He's still not sure who or what Rack is. A mental deficient like his brother? A sociopath? Full-throttle psycho? A working stiff who's cooked crank for so long that his brain is misfiring? Can he really have caused all of this for money?

Jesse blurts, "Ow! Ow! He's cutting me. He doesn't want you coming near him. I think he wants you to get rid of your cane too."

"Is that right, Rack? You don't want me near? I thought that was the whole point. How else am I going to pay you?"

Finn steps forward. He pulls out his wallet and opens it. He's got about $150 in cash. The bills fall from his hands. Whatever else he is, Rack is a punk drug dealer stiffed out of a payoff.

"You still want your money, Rack? Or are we beyond that now? It's yours if you want it. I swear. I'll bump it up some too. Fifteen grand. You'll have it after the holiday, as soon as the banks open. Will that do it? Will you leave now?"

There aren't any choices left, and Finn's glad for it. He's used up his options long ago. There's something liberating about being taken away by the ocean. He stops fighting and allows himself the luxury of simply traveling where the world wants to take him.

Jesse screams, "He's grabbing my breast, Mr. Finn! He's squeezing! He's hurting me!"

Finn's shadow is squeezing Jesse's breast, its mouth open against the sun.

Finn hisses, "Stop it."

He raps his cane and can feel in his bones where Rack stands. He allows himself a moment to process the information.

Then he hauls his arm back and hurls his cane.

He imagines that the stick turns over twice in the air and strikes Rack in the face. Even as he's charging forward, Finn shouts, "Jesse, move!"

It's all very proactive. No need to go to your death lying down. He figures there's no out for him, and he's not looking for one. The blade will enter his belly, probably low, nearer to the groin, and if he doesn't die on the spot, and despite the doctors' best efforts, he'll croak of sepsis before a month goes by. That doesn't bother him. Just so long as he gets his three weeks and the chance to meet with Ray again.

Blundering ahead, Finn lowers his shoulders and goes in for the tackle. The fury of Howie has always been with him, waiting almost twenty years to be released this very second. Finn hears Jesse tumble to the floor as he grapples with Rack.

His mind, as usual, feels fragmented and seems to hover outside of his body. It's like he can still experience life through the bone, blood, and brain matter that flew out of his head the moment of the incident.

He hopes Jesse's all right, imagines Violet's body downstairs spasming toward rigor. He sees Roz without her coat, vomit-strewn and wearing an expression of awful acceptance. Duchess tonguing her busted crown, Judith with her mouth mangled. Words and phrases assail him in the dark. He hears "fear," "erratic pulse," "dissuade," "fierce proponent for justice," and "haunting lyricism of the damned."

Finn strikes and connects with Rack's shoulder. He tries again and hits nothing. Then there's slashing pain across his belly. Rack is aiming higher than expected. The point of the blade enters a good inch and Finn sucks in his stomach and contorts away. He brings his forearm around and down, trying to catch Rack's elbow. He misses and kicks out, definitely strikes Rack's knee.

But the guy doesn't make any sound. It's difficult to home in. Finn feels breath against his ear, turns, and strikes for the ribs. There's nothing but a huff of air. Rack leaps on him and Finn twists before falling. He's on top of the holler madman, on the floor. The two of them flop around and scramble for purchase. The knife scrapes the back of his neck, draws blood but nothing bad. Finn brings his elbow back, hoping to hit bone. He hammers Rack's knee, doing more damage.

The blade must be coming for him again.

Finn snakes aside and a thick trail of agony opens across his ribs. He gauges where Rack's face must be and throws an uppercut. It's a beautiful move, everything working right, sweet Jesus let it hit. He hears Rack's jaws slam together. It's an exquisite sound, a sharp contrast to his own rasping.

He pictures his shadow wheeling now, climbing to its knees, hoping to stab down with the knife. He's time-traveling, one second ahead. Finn blocks the blow with his left arm, gets to his own knees, throws two upper-cuts that shave Rack's chin. He tries again with a third and connects once more, hears teeth crack.

Rack tries to slash but only manages to scrape Finn's back. Finn sees this is just some bizarre show-and-tell being performed in front of his class. The girls take co-pious notes. Caitlin Jones calls his performance "spuri-ous." There's modest applause. He viciously chops at where he hopes Rack's wrist is. The connection is pure and solid. The blade goes skittering. Finn whips his arm back and tries to snap it across Rack's nose. There's no real way to shove shards of cartilage into somebody's brain, but the thought propels him. It's a wasted effort, and he misses wildly. The motion causes him to hyper-extend and he feels his shoulder blade pop, his rotor cuff on the point of tearing.

This isn't a time of knives.

The two of them tumble over each other and fall to the floor again.

Rack grabs Finn by the throat. It's all right. This is a good thing. Finn faces him, manages to lock his hands on Rack's throat too.

The moment lengthens. Rack tightens his hold. It's excruciating but Finn lets out a choked gurgle of laughter. His grip is strong. His fists close. Blood slurps across the floor.

Shadow meets flesh.

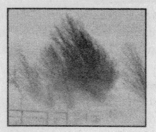

AS DANIELLE SHIFTS ON TOP OF him, pulling away so that her breasts draw against his chest and his semen drips from her onto his legs, Finn sees a boy standing behind her in the kitchen holding a popgun .22.

He recognizes the kid from the courtroom. It's Carlyle's even younger son, Freddy. Freddy's got more tears in his eyes than Dani does. Jesus Christ, all three of them having a good old-fashioned crying jag together.

The boy's what, seventeen maybe. His hands are shaking badly. It doesn't look like he's ever held a gun before. Freddy's not in this to make his bones. Clearly he's been driven out of his head by grief. He wants revenge for Donny's death. His chin is as smooth and perfect as a woman's. A razor's never even touched his face.

Danielle gasps and looks at the boy, flings an arm up to cover her tits. The kid growls something about his brother. He trips over his tongue and repeats himself, the same unintelligible snarl of pain. It's an honest and human sound, something you don't hear much from someone with a gun in his hand.

Dani is still gripping the empty .38 and Finn snatches it from her and holds it on Freddy, hoping it'll be enough of a bluff. Freddy doesn't seem to notice. He doesn't seem to notice anything.

Finn doesn't waste time trying to talk Freddy down. Instead he flips Dani off of his lap, rolls to his feet, and cracks Freddy across the temple with the barrel of the .38.

It should be enough to put him down but it's not. The kid's so heartbroken that he barely registers being smacked in the head. Blood pours down the side of his face and Freddy suddenly snaps to and remembers why he's here in the first place. His wet eyes focus.

Finn's eyes are a little dewy too, and he hates having to brawl with his crank hanging out, but he chops Freddy again, missing his head and slashing him along the neck with the .38's sight. Behind him, Dani is looking for something on the counter to fight with. She throws aside the spatula, the broken eggshells, and knocks over the maple syrup.

He wants to say, Honey, listen, I got this. Go put something on, will you?

She goes for the knife drawer.

Finn's in control. He's got Freddy by forty pounds of muscle and he knows how to fight. But the kid is fucking insane and won't give up the gun. Finn can't break his grip. That's it, enough of this. Finn shifts his feet, getting ready to hook Freddy under the heart.

You've got to give the kid some credit, he does the unexpected and shrieks like a teenage girl having her ass squeezed.

The sound of it sort of spooks Finn and he takes a step back, his fist no longer moving forward at all.

Freddy snaps up the pistol. It's pointed directly at Finn's belly button.

The kid's got delicate fingers, Finn notices, as he watches Freddy's index begin to squeeze the trigger.

None of this should be happening. Finn has the overwhelming sense that he's standing at the crossroads and has just made a wrong turn. He grabs Freddy's wrist and tightens his hold, feels the small bones grinding together. He has the feeling that he's done this before and will do it again.

The kid screams and Finn yanks hard, turning the barrel away from himself.

He thinks, No, wait, I shouldn't, Dani—

The popgun goes off.

It's one of those magic bullet shots. Finn watches as a small wound appears in Danielle's left side, immediately followed by another tiny spurt of blood as the slug exits her collarbone. The stink of burnt flesh makes him draw his head back.

Finn wrenches the .22 free from Freddy and brutally backhands him into the refrigerator. The kid lets out a contented sigh and slides to the floor, leaving a smear the whole ride down.

Dani is still on her feet.

She takes two steps toward Finn and drops into his arms.

She throws up a wad of blood and her eyes roll and then focus again. Her gaze is warm and everlasting, in its own way, even as it hardens and her body goes slack. He sees his future laid out before him in absolute clarity. The loneliness, the darkness, the hot and eternal nights of guilt and madness. Finn's rage is thoroughly honed and precisely directed. He's alive and his wife is dead in his embrace. It's his fault. Finn hasn't looked out for his own house. He draws her more tightly to him. His silence fills his mind, and the room, and their home, and retreats across the surface of the earth. He is perhaps more calm now than he's ever been. He angles the .22 to face him. A breeze stirs the yellow curtains. The morning light is immense. He'll never remember pulling the trigger.

WITH THE PATIENCE OF THE AGES, Finn sets about killing and dying. Rack is wiry and powerful the way men who've spent their lives in the steps of their ancestors are. Finn knows this is a man who chops his own firewood, catches his own dinner, poaches animals in the wilderness in order to make his own clothing. This isn't a guy who's learned from the classroom or even the street. They're raised differently in the deep woods. What was Rack before Three Rivers began to die? The same?

Finn's hands go deeper into the meat of Rack's throat, searching for an answer. Rack's hands fasten on his windpipe just as securely.

This is a different kind of dying from the others he's tried before. Just as soothing in its own way. Finn's thoughts turn red, then blue.

He screams without sound. In his silence, Rack is probably screaming too. Why the fuck not.

Jesse sobs off to Finn's right, where she's shrunk against the wall. He thinks, They don't run away, they never run away. He tells them to go and they stay. If only they had more teenage girls on the force none of this mess ever would've happened. Her wails fill the entire building. It proves Rack didn't do any serious damage to her anyway.

Finn hisses at her to run but there's not enough breath for him to form words. He lashes out with his leg in her direction, trying to motion her to get going, but it doesn't help. She's here until the end of this thing.

Adrift, he's in many places and he's many people. It's not exactly his whole life flashing before his eyes, but he's getting a good number of the highlights. He takes stock. It's been an all-right run. He also remains here on the floor, throttling and being strangled, his arms locked. He and Rack are face-to-face, nose to nose, lips to lips. They could kiss or bite each other's tongues off. Maybe they will yet.

He's a good cop, maybe too good in some ways, and not nearly good enough in others. He's someone not to be trusted. He's on the roof and can't take the shot, and he should've been let go on the spot. He's a lecher who's put his hands on a teenage student, and he should've been arrested on the spot. He's a husband who couldn't protect the woman he loved, and he should've died on the spot. When you get down to it, he's a carnival freak on the midway, luring the rubes in to see the show.

He's eternal vigilance, dedicated and steadfast. He doesn't do enough, he's never done enough, but at least he's always had an honest purpose. Right now, it's to kill. You can't get any more honest than that. His shoulder cracks again, and the pain rides up into his blue thoughts, turning them a sweet shade of indigo. The steel plate in his skull is covered with engravings in languages unspoken for ten thousand years.

There's a sound of animal fear. It comes from one of

them, perhaps both of them. He wonders which of them wants to live more, and for what reason. Finn tries to create a list but he is stumped by the time he reaches number two.

He wonders if Rack Moon, this knife-wielding rapist, has tender dreams for his family. If he has any true loves. If his regrets are any more heartfelt. If somewhere in the hills he has a wife and children worried about him, waiting at the window. He sees a boy and a girl, six or seven years old, a fire burning behind them but the firewood getting low. One of them will have to hike out to the shed and get more.

Finn thinks, This prick likes hiding bodies in the shed. What are his kids going to find? Who else has gone missing? Who else hasn't paid?

There's a sound of human fear. It has a subtext that is almost musical.

Rack's hold loosens and Finn's tightens further. Even shadows want to survive between the moments when clouds pass overhead.

I am stone in the night, Finn thinks. I will not break.

Rack's hands withdraw. Finn gasps and chokes but doesn't let go. Rack tries to yank Finn's fingers from his own neck, but it's too late, he's too weak to do anything about it now.

Finn sees his silhouette, flat against brick, performing a burlesque of panic.

A few seconds more and Rack's actions slow, then stop, and then he's nothing but deadweight on top of Finn. They lie there cheek to cheek, sucking air. Finn doesn't have enough strength to shove his shadow aside.

The two of them remain like that, Finn breathing deeply, Rack's breaths coming slow and shallow.

Moments shift to minutes and eventually Finn is able to crawl out from under Rack Moon. He tries to call for Jesse but he's got no voice. She's not crying anymore, he doesn't know where she is. Maybe she's run away at last.

He reaches with his good arm, but he's got no idea in which direction he's stretching.

Then there's a knife at his throat.

"YOU STILL OWE," HARLEY WHISPERS IN his ear. She holds her brother's enormous blade steadily, with confidence. He guesses that she's greatly skilled with it. She's probably the one who skinned the animals and sewed the hides together to make her brothers' clothing. "I didn't want none of this, but I need that money."

"I promise...you'll get it...next...business... day..." he rasps in a voice he's never heard before. Blood pools at his nostrils so he has to turn his chin or drown, as he falls into a blackness that's still not nearly so deep or endless as blindness.

DANIELLE'S BEEN IN THE GROUND FOR three weeks by the time Finn finally comes around in the hospital.

The doctors ask him what his name is and who's the president. He says, I'm not a goddamn idiot.

He asks about Dani and everyone ignores him. He keeps asking. They give him motor-skills tests, have him try to pass a ball back and forth between hands. They're impressed as hell that he can hold a conversation. They want to know what the last thing he remembers is.

Finn asks about Dani again and when they continue to ignore him Finn reaches out wildly and grabs the nearest asshole and begins to throttle him. Security is called. Three muscular jerk-offs start wrestling with him right there in the hospital bed, a guy who just woke up from a coma, punching him in the stomach and face. It's not for another fifteen or twenty minutes that Finn realizes there aren't any bandages over his eyes. He's blind.

The investigating team asks Finn a lot of questions too. They take it in rotation, asking about Dani, Ray, Carlyle, Carlyle's captain, Carlyle's sons, and some other shit. Finn says little because they want him to say little. They've rewritten the facts to suit their needs. They've got enough bad news on their plate without admitting that a cop accidentally killed his wife and then tried to blow out his brains. And fucked that up too.

Freddy's gun was a drop. The kid at least cleaned up after himself before he ran out of Finn's house. Or somebody wiped it down anyway. No fingerprints, no blood, it was like the kid was never there.

The team's already written it up that Dani shot Finn in a fit of jealousy and that he killed her in self-defense. Forensics must be laughing their asses off at that one. How a guy with his brains blasted against a kitchen wall could shoot anybody in self-defense is another question they're not asking. Bad as it looks, it looks better than the truth, and it saves his rep. Makes the force look better. Everybody's ass is covered and the force escapes a full-scale investigation into corruption.

Finn plays like he has amnesia. It makes everyone feel better.

IAD shows up afterward and asks him all the same questions about all the same people and events. They don't want to know the answers either. Not on this one.

Roz has been let go from the hospital but the administration doesn't follow up with charges and she retains her status as an RN. She shows up twice a day to bring Finn flowers, air freshener, potpourri. She reads the newspapers to him.

He finds out that Freddy Carlyle has been sent to a private hospital in Tempe, Arizona. Freddy was so attached to his older brother that when they buried Donald, Freddy jumped in after him and made a big scene in front of all the wiseguys and the feds taking photos. A few days later, Freddy tried to hang himself with his shoelaces and pulled down the ceiling fan in the rec room.

Finn's rage is aimed elsewhere. He's got nothing but sympathy and a complex kind of understanding for the kid.

He goes under the knife again for more touch-up surgery.

Despite everything, Carlyle manages to snake his way out of an indictment when one of his boys finally manages to blow up the DA. It's the sort of thing that went down all the time in the early seventies, when the mob was icing opposition in the streets with no subtlety at all. Carlyle shows up on the news a lot, giving interviews on morning shows. He's articulate and sharp and has learned the fine art of sounding like one of the downtrodden masses who is nothing but a pawn of much greater forces.

In his hospital bed, Finn listens intently.

As he suspected, Ray goes down but only gets a nickel jolt in Sing Sing. So do a couple of other cops and a few members of Carlyle's crew. It's a cakewalk. They'll buddy up in the joint and take over the place within a week.

Ray phones from prison and says, "I told you they were going to move fast."

"You didn't tell me that Freddy Carlyle worshipped his older brother. For him, it was personal."

"Yeah, that kid, he had some weird wiring. I didn't think he'd have the heart to take a poke at you."

"He didn't, really," Finn admits. "I wonder, though. How'd he get my home address so quick?"

"It's the syndicate. They've got thicker files than the FBI."

Ray pauses and Finn hears a lot of distant noise, laughter, singing on the other end. "What's going on?"

"The pussy boys of C-Block are putting on a talent show. Some of them are pretty good dancers, and they all do Barbra Streisand to a fuckin' T."

"Cher too?"

"And Bette Midler. If I gotta hear that 'Wind Beneath My Wings' shit one more time, I may have to shank somebody. It's not the song so much as how it gets everybody crying. Even the bulls."

"You gave Freddy my address, didn't you? You told him it was me who wasted his brother."

Ray, in his expert arrogance, doesn't deny it. His voice takes on a nuanced tone, one that wouldn't register with almost anyone else. Discreetly concealed anger and resentment seep into his words. "I knew he wouldn't pull the trigger. He didn't have the heart. You fucked it up. You fucked it all up. You should've just iced Carlyle, it would've made everything right again." Ray actually tsks. "What are you going to do now?"

"I'm handling it," Finn says.

He gently hooks the phone back into its cradle. He climbs from the bed and crawls on the floor, his mind so starved for information that it draws on his memories at odd times and confuses him. For a moment he thinks he's back at his house, on the kitchen tiles with Dani.

Then he hammers the floor with his fists. The pain defines and gives shape to his hands. The shape of his fractured hands gives his arms substance. The arms help to delineate the torso. The neck grows from it. He feels the definition of his face and head again. And residing within his skull is his brain, and within that his mind, and within that himself.

He's still here, despite the everlasting darkness.

The evening nurse discovers him under the bed two hours later. He's got his fractured fingers up his nose. He's been trying to snort the blood from his torn knuckles, the smell keeping him in the past where he can relive his life in excruciating detail. It's his wedding day. It's his first day on the job. The fury of Howie has found him again.

It takes twenty stitches to close the gashes. When they put his broken hands in casts, he cries.

Over the next two weeks they up his medication and call in four psychiatrists to talk at length with him. At first he's honest, hoping someone can explain this phenomenon to him.

But the shrinks all act with varying degrees of condescension. They think he's either crazy or out for attention. Finn starts telling them what they want to hear and learns to hide his cutting. Even with the casts he can just manage to hold on to a safety razor and run it a little too deeply against his chin.

One night, Roz tries to make love to him in the hospital bed and he elbows her onto the floor.

A few nights later she tries again. He doesn't fuck her but he doesn't kick her out either.

A couple mornings after, he's awoken by two quarreling voices. Some bitchy couple arguing whether they should eat in the commissary or hold out for the diner a few blocks down. The woman says her blood pressure is dangerously low.

The man says, Jesus Christ, I'm still waiting for a time when you're not being held in the fucking thrall of hypoglycemia.

Finn recognizes the voices. Besides, only one person he knows would ever say "thrall."

There's a pressure on the edge of the bed, tilting the mattress at a sharp angle. Finn can see the woman sitting there, those sleepy eyes with a swirl of poison in them, the thick ringlets slipping down over both shoulders. She's digging around the gifts that people have sent him, looking for something to munch on.

He tells her, "There's some chocolate in the drawer."

"Why would I want any of your candy bars?" Carlyle's mistress says.

Finn often can't tell if his eyes are open or closed. It disturbs his visitors but he hasn't gotten used to wearing shades all the time yet. He knows that Carlyle is a man used to staring into the eyes of his enemies and reading whatever might be hidden there. Finn enjoys the fact that, in such a small fashion, he's at an advantage.

"Do you know why I'm letting you live?" Carlyle asks.

"Yes," Finn says.

"You do?"

"Sure."

Carlyle pauses. "Tell me."

"Four reasons."

"You count four?"

"Yeah."

"Let me hear them, please."

"All right. One, I'm no threat to you. Two, you know

I had no choice where Donnie was concerned. You should ace whoever gave him the green light."

"No one did."

"Then whoever was looking out for him didn't do a good job."

"Go on."

"Three, you owe me for what your boy Freddy did."

"He did nothing to you."

"Of course he did, he was the catalyst for my wife's fatality and my own . . . self-destruction."

"You speak like an English professor. By definition no one else can be held responsible for another's self-destruction."

"I see it differently," Finn says, and smiles.

"Go on."

"And four, you can always point me out in the crowd and say, 'See there, that's what happens to people who go up against me.'"

"That doesn't sound like me at all."

"No, it doesn't."

Carlyle's mistress is hunting around for candy bars again, doing it slowly, trying to be silent.

"Your partner set much of this in motion," Carlyle says.

"You set it in motion, he just went along. That's what he does. He always takes the easy money, the easy shot, the easy way out."

"And you never do."

"It's an ineradicable flaw in my character."

"I could eradicate it."

"I strongly doubt that."

Finn waits. He thinks, It wouldn't be so tough to

dive on him right now, smash the casts into his throat until I crush his larynx. I could pound on him for however long it takes. I can snuff him.

He leans forward. Carlyle springs to his feet and backs away.

Finn grins and asks, "How's Freddy?"

"On suicide watch."

"So am I."

BY THE TIME JESSE GETS BACK with Murph and Duchess, Rack is gone and Judith is wandering the halls with a dislocated jaw and several of her teeth kicked out.

Harley must've gotten her brother out of the building, who knows how. Maybe he was only hurt, maybe dying, maybe dead, but she managed to drag him off. Finn will never underestimate the holler folk again.

Using the plow on the front of his truck, Murphy manages to beat through the snowbanks to get to Three Rivers. It takes him more than an hour to dig his way five miles to town. It takes them twenty minutes to get back in the county's Sno-Cats, six folks packed into the two confined front cabins. The sheriff, three deputies, Murph, and a small-town doctor like they don't make anymore, replete with black bag. Say what you want, they know how to rally.

The authorities check out Finn's story.

There is no one in Three Rivers by the name of Rack Moon. There is no one called Pudge Moon. There was no body found out in the snow where Finn says Pudge's corpse should be. There's no Harley Moon who takes care of five younger siblings.

Finn nods and lets it go.

There is no county coroner. The doc will do the job when he gets Vi and Roz back to town. Right now he's got the bodies wrapped and packed out in the snow.

Duchess wants to confess to her role in the meth dealing even though there's no evidence against her either. Finn tells her to shut the fuck up. He's not sure why.

The doc tapes up Finn's wounded shoulder and gives him some oily liquid that should help his damaged throat. The sheriff asks more questions but Finn's voice is gone.

A week goes by, full of police reports and some media coverage and funerals. Finn's got his arm in a sling. His voice is raspy as all hell, the thick fingerprint bruises so bad that the makeup folks ask him to wear an ascot. It makes him laugh, which causes him to choke. They ask him what's so funny. It's a good question.

He is lauded as a hero by certain parents. There are no photo ops with the Three Rivers Sheriff's Department. Vi's father shows up for the body. Her mother never visits. Finn takes nine g's out of his savings and has Duchess drive him out to the Moon house. He leaves the money on the front porch to a shack that smells like nobody's lived there in years.

"This the place?" he asks.

"Yeah," Duchess tells him, "but there's no footprints in the snow, except for ours. Nobody's been here for a week or more."

"Doesn't matter."

He's paid up and fulfilled his promises. Maybe it'll be enough.

Judith's son Billy or Bobby or Billy-Bob is forced out

of his bomb-shelter basement apartment and compelled to take his mother to the dentist. Finn goes along because Judith, for no reason she names, wants him to. The son is in a constant state of frustration, wanting to get back to his *World of Warcraft* with the Senegalians and Polynesians. Finn sits in the dentist's waiting room listening to them setting up Judith with a temporary bridge. The whining of her kid and the whining of the drill both give him a migraine.

When Judith gets out, she says, "Jesus, I should've just gotten dentures."

Her jaw's still a little misaligned and she has trouble forming certain words. While her son speeds them back to St. Val's, knocking ninety the whole way, Judith admits to Finn that she's getting another divorce and Murphy is moving in.

"*Slainte,*" Finn says.

The authorities don't seem eager to drag Ray's name back into the press. There's no proof against him or anybody else at Sing Sing. The cops know Finn is hiding something, and they're suspicious as hell.

But Finn figures there's no reason to mention Roz's part in it all. What the fuck's the point?

Vi's parents have the juice to chase this thing into the headlines for months, but they don't bother.

The fallout will certainly close the academy. Judith tells him she's already started shutting the place down and sending out résumés. He thinks the school would be better off left abandoned for five or ten years, and then turned back into a hotel. By then Three Rivers will be properly dead and ready for some developer to come in and open up a couple of factories and bring the people back down out of the hills and make them mingle with a new work force sent up from the city.

Back in Manhattan, Finn lucks out and finds a furnished studio apartment in the Village around the corner from NYU. He lands a job within a couple of days. He suspects he's the token handicapped teacher on campus and that's why the wheels are so greased, but he doesn't give a damn. He doesn't have to start until the fall semester.

He sits in his shrink's office.

She asks him, So how have you been?

She's got the disinterested air of a prom date you run into twenty years later at the supermarket checkout.

When she shifts her earrings jingle and her necklace clicks. Maybe pearls. He has no doubt that they look beautiful, but they rattle falsely. He can hear her pulling up her stockings, snapping them around her thighs. She smooths her hands along the meat of her legs, either admiring or critiquing.

She has a rendezvous after this, must be a second date, someone she's really trying to impress. Leaving right after their session, she can barely control her excitement. Or maybe she's just trying to show off for her next patient. She's got a crush on some sex maniac describing his most detailed acrobatics. Tells her how he likes to punch them in the back of the head while he's digging in from behind. It disgusts her and makes her moist.

She coughs into her hand, put off by Finn's silence. Without a chance to gauge him by his eyes, he must appear inscrutable to her. She's not in control. She's never been in control but she only realizes this when Finn's in the room with her.

The tingling earrings sound almost plaintive. They make him want to reach for them, draw them gently from her ears, and pet them, tell them, It's all right, it's going to be all right now.

He wonders if she'd still tell him that this is a natural reaction, treating the sounds of inanimate objects as if they were people. If it would still be normal for him in his situation, under these circumstances, to want to comfort things, especially if they're hers and he took hold and didn't let go. If he held her up on her date with the next patient who's wanting to touch her thing. If he made her late in grabbing his thing.

Finn thinks of crooking his finger, trying to get her to come closer, so he might whisper in her ear that she was right. It certainly was important for him to assert his independence. To feed his need for security, take a hand in his own self-preservation.

Of course, if he'd had nothing more than pepper spray, he'd be dead right now. He's already bought another blade and keeps it in his pocket.

He begins to speak but he can't recognize what he's saying. The voice is small and sounds like it's coming from a neighbor's apartment down the hall. He strains to hear the words but fails. The voice is animate, angry.

He's chewed his cheek open. Right now he's remembering being down at One Police Plaza, waiting on line for his uniform and his issued piece. Ray's beside him, oddly quiet. Maybe another fifty guys ahead of them. There's a fair amount of nervous laughter. They've graduated the academy but they're not officially cops until they're sworn in. A couple of the guys are talking about how they're glad they've landed in the shittiest precincts in the city. More action so they'll make more busts. Better chance for promotion. They're already talking about gold shields, making detective first grade before they're thirty.

The shrink is saying, I think we need to explore that.

He has no idea why he's here. He should be able to handle what's coming down the line for him. The rage has only increased. He tries to burn it off in the gym. Except for a nagging in his shoulder he's in the best shape of his life. When he finishes his reps he runs twenty on the treadmill. In his exhaustion he doesn't often think of Dani or Roz, he thinks of Vi. He still thinks of her every day, trapped somewhere between being his daughter and his lover. The guy down the hall is still talking, still chuckling, the fucking nut. The earrings jangle. The blood covers his teeth. The shrink says, Time's up, and Finn thinks, Right, I have to kill Ray now.

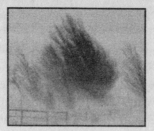

THE MORNING TRAIN UP TO OSSINING is filled with attorneys, guards, frantic parents, and angry wives with weeping kids who've never even been touched by their jailbird daddies. The mood is savage hopelessness, which appeals to him.

Finn moves his concentration around the car, seat by seat, listening in on different conversations. The bits he catches are by turns poignant, scathing, and boring. One seething woman snarls, *"I told him not to do it. I told him!"* Maybe she's talking to herself, or a friend, or to anyone who might listen. She spits and pounds the seat beside her. A child runs up the aisle, takes a header, and skins a knee. His braying is as loud as a siren wailing down Sixth Avenue.

The Metro-North commuter rail line slices right through the prison, past the umbrella-roofed gun towers and the abandoned death house. Finn's only been to Sing Sing once before, checking a lead that went nowhere during a murder investigation.

The front entrance is at the end of a tree-shaded residential street. Beyond that are over two thousand men pacing under twenty-four-hour regimented surveillance on fifty acres of cement and steel in hangar-sized cell blocks.

Finn disembarks with the other passengers. No one offers to lend a hand. He follows along with the crowd until he hears them getting to the checkpoint, everybody pulling their IDs. If memory serves, there's a bench around here someplace. He swings his cane, walks around for a minute, finds it, and sits.

The chill air is bracing but he doesn't think he's capable of ever feeling cold again.

An hour passes and the wind rises. Finn doesn't move. His thoughts are full of gentle warmth lifting through him.

The front gates open and he hears an odd shuffling walk. Ray's limp has gotten much more prominent. The prosthetic's seen some wear after five years and Ray's in need of a new fitting. He's practically dragging the leg now.

Then laughter. It's a familiar sound that, despite himself, makes Finn smile. He stands and waits for Ray to step up.

When Finn sees Ray he sees Ray. And he sees himself. And sees his shadow. His head is full of vision. He has to suppress the mad notion that he is no longer blind.

Everybody's got a right to be as much of an outlaw as they want to be, so long as they don't cry foul if they get nabbed for it.

"Hey there," Ray says. "Goddamn, it's cold. Figured you'd meet me."

"Yeah?" Finn asks. "Why?"

"It's the way you are."

"I guess it is."

"So, you here to kill me?"

Laying it out like that, still so full of cool.

"Would it surprise you if I was?"

"No," Ray says. "You packing?"

"I've got a pocketknife."

"So you're not planning to shoot me in the head."

There is one question that's been bugging him. "How much have you got stashed? Just wondering what the number is, considering how much it cost." Finn figures it's got to be half a mil at least that Ray's socked away.

"Let's not bother with that. I have enough."

"So why'd you burn Roz for the nine g's?"

"You going to ask a lot of stupid questions?"

Finn figures no. "You were surprised that Carlyle never iced me, weren't you." It's not a question.

"Actually, I thought maybe you'd do him instead."

"I thought about it."

"You think about a lot of things, but you never do shit."

It's the truth. Even when he had eyes he was blind, always letting Ray lead. "You should think about what you owe."

"What I owe?"

"That's right."

"What do you mean?"

Finn says, "Your house isn't in order."

"My house?"

"You've had an ill will thinking on you. My ill will."

"What the hell are you talking about now?"

It's not enough. It will never be enough. Finn will

never be able to explain that moment when Dani lay down in his arms and the world came to its sudden end.

Finn waits for some reaction from his shadow, watching for it to break into a run or throw a fist. He waits for Ray to admit his betrayal, show some real heart, fear, or anger of his own. But he won't, that's the way Ray's built. It's why he's always been in charge.

"Well, we could always walk up the street a ways and just unload on each other," Ray says. "You know, beat the crap out of each other like the two feistiest little kids on the block. Sometimes, after that, they're friends for life."

"We've never fought."

"No, we haven't. You can pull that Bruce Lee shit. I've learned a few dirty moves in the joint that I didn't already know, if you can believe it. We can find a quiet place, a nice park. Maybe it'll get the poison out of our systems. Maybe afterward, we'll be able to talk. And do some business. All we need is a good slugfest. You want to?"

Ray's voice is full of the same staggering weariness that Finn feels. Each year and mile of their lost friendship is in his timbre, as well as all the offenses he's endured over the five years in prison.

They walk together. This is the culmination of more than two decades of friendship, partnership, deception, blood, agony, heartbreak, darkness, and betrayal, and Finn just doesn't feel all that much. Another man would look for answers. Another man would want to know his own reasons for partnering up with a guy like this. But Finn knows there aren't any. They were meant to be partners from the start, no more or less than he and

Dani were. Than he and Rack were meant to meet each other in the hall.

Finn's withdrawn beyond hope and even hate. Standing beside him are his many ghosts, all his mistakes and lost loves, the dead and the nearly dead and the missing. Maybe Ray can feel the same weight on his back as he hobbles along. Finn tilts his chin into the wind. When Ray lets out another little laugh, childish and sincere, Finn knows the next move is coming. In the darkness he's aware. His hands are trembling so badly with the need to do something that they nearly hum. Ray slows and then stops to lean over. He puts a hand to Finn's shoulder to help him balance while he checks his fake leg. Finn thinks, There it is. There's Ray's new dirty move. Jailhouse guards aren't going to check a man's prosthetic four times a day. That's where he's got whatever he needs hidden. His drug money and his shank. He's going for the blade. He's going to raise it up and stick it in.

Finn thinks, His hand will tighten on my shoulder and haul me down to meet the honed point, entering low and going deep, the pain devastating but not unbearable. Not until he starts to drag upwards. Whatever else it will be, it will be a beautiful and perfectly timed maneuver. Perhaps Finn will block the move and make his own. You want to? He can have his pocketknife out in an instant. Fighting with Rack was a time of hands. This will be the time of knives. He can take the lead. He's ready to kill or die in the middle of the street. There's a faint flicker of promise. It's his job to protect the innocent. You want to? Dani's eyes are wet, Vi's are full of need, Roz's are flat with a kind of dreariness. Ray's hand tightens on Finn's bad shoulder. This is how the battle against evil has gone today. Over here, over here. Your time is up.

"Let's," Finn says, and waits for the world to grow hot with heaving light, love, and color.

ABOUT THE AUTHOR

TOM PICCIRILLI lives in Colorado, where, besides writing, he spends an inordinate amount of time watching trash cult films and reading Gold Medal classic noir and hard-boiled novels. He's a fan of Asian cinema, especially horror movies, bullet ballet, pinky violence, and samurai flicks. He also likes walking his dogs around the neighborhood. Are you starting to get the hint that he doesn't have a particularly active social life? Well, to heck with you, buddy, yours isn't much better. Give him any static and he'll smack you in the mush, dig? Tom also enjoys making new friends. He's the author of more than twenty novels, including *The Coldest Mile, The Cold Spot, The Midnight Road, The Dead Letters, Headstone City, November Mourns,* and *A Choir of Ill Children.* He's a recipient of the International Thriller Writers Award and a four-time winner of the Bram Stoker Award. He's also been nominated for an Edgar Award, a Macavity Award, the World Fantasy Award, and Le Grand Prix de L'Imaginaire. To learn more, check out his official website, Epitaphs, at www.tompiccirilli.com.

Don't miss
Tom Piccirilli's
next novel

THE
UNDERNEATH

COMING IN 2010